**IN THE ROUGH-AND-TUMBLE
MINING TOWN OF JOHNS BEND,
IT'S HARD TO TELL AN ENEMY
FROM A FRIEND ...**

BEN CARTWRIGHT—With three healthy sons and the most prosperous outfit in Nevada, Ben Cartwright knows he's a lucky man. But his luck is about to be tested to its limits when he gets involved in a shifty deal with three unscrupulous businessmen ... the kind who traffic in ruin, deceit—and even death.

JOE CARTWRIGHT—At nineteen, Ben's youngest son is all grown up and eager to prove it, so when things heat up in Johns Bend, he follows his own instincts ... to the mines where Les Shannon lost his life, and where the key to this whole deadly business lies a thousand perilous feet below the ground....

CHLOE SHANNON—Ben Cartwright was one of her husband's best friends. Now, the grieving widow only wants to lean on Ben's shoulder—and to understand what drew Les Shannon down into that mine that fateful night.

NEAL HUBBARD—Ruthless and genteel, this distinguished man was Les Shannon's business partner. But even when it appears that their corporation is a fast-dying proposition, Hubbard isn't eager to have Ben join his little enterprise ... until he sees the color of the Cartwright money.

CRAIG ALBRITTON—Les's lawyer and business associate, Craig Albritton would never break a client's confidentiality ... but how far will he go to help a client who's already dead?

LUCAS DADLEY—The crude manager of the Madrid mining property, and Les's second partner, he's damned if he'll let a man like Ben Cartwright destroy everything he's worked for. And if women, bribes, and intimidation won't keep Cartwright out of his way, he'll just have to find a more permanent solution.

THE HIGH-STEEL HAZARD

STEPHEN CALDER

BANTAM BOOKS
NEW YORK • TORONTO • LONDON • SYDNEY • AUCKLAND

THE HIGH-STEEL HAZARD

A Bantam Domain Book / February 1993

ISBN 0-553-29043-6

Published simultaneously in the United States and Canada

Bantam Books are published by Bantam Books, a division of Bantam
Doubleday Dell Publishing Group, Inc. Its trademark, consisting of the
words "Bantam Books" and the portrayal of a rooster, is Registered in
U.S. Patent and Trademark Office and in other countries. Marca Reg-
istrada. Bantam Books, 666 Fifth Avenue, New York, New York 10103.

PRINTED IN THE UNITED STATES OF AMERICA

RAD   0 9 8 7 6 5 4 3 2 1

THE
HIGH-STEEL
HAZARD

CHAPTER 1

A sound brought him out of his sleep. A soft sound, muffled and surreptitious. Ben Cartwright's eyes came open instantly and he sat upright on the edge of his bed.

He tried to blink the sleep out of his eyes as he rubbed at the whiskers on his jaw and attempted to recall what had woken him. There was a faint sound from below, that of boot steps on hard earth, and then he knew.

Ben smiled. He had heard the door downstairs. He remembered that now. That would have been Adam on his way out to start the morning chores. Ben didn't have to look outside to know it was Adam. The first one up and out was always Adam, every morning without fail.

Now Ben could hear the much louder and more solid sound of footsteps inside the house and, a moment later, the very loud slam of the front door. Ben's smile widened. Hoss. Hoss never had learned to go in or out of that door without slamming it.

Chuckling, Ben stood. There was no sense in sitting there waiting to hear Joseph go out to join his brothers. There was no telling when that might be, within seconds or ten minutes from now, depending. Depending on exactly *what*, well, that was another question. Joseph was considerably less predictable than either of his brothers.

1

Ben yawned and cocked his head. He could hear, barely, the whisper of Hop Sing's slippers in the upstairs hallway. Right on time. Hop Sing poured Ben's coffee as soon as Adam left, and began preparing breakfast once Hoss was outside. None of them ever bothered trying to reconcile their activities with Joseph's.

The diminutive Chinese cook came into the bedroom without knocking, bearing a single cup of wake-up coffee.

"Good morning, Hop Sing. Thank you."

Hop Sing grinned and bobbed his head, his pigtail bouncing at the nape of his scrawny neck. "Nice day, yes."

"Is Joseph awake yet, Hop Sing?" If Joseph was too far behind the others, they invariably gave him a hard time about it—teasingly, to be sure, but a hard time nonetheless, and bickering was not the best way to start a day.

"I go see now." Hop Sing rubbed his hands together. "Take pan cold water with me. He be 'wake 'fore long. You see."

"Gently, Hop Sing, gently," Ben cautioned, not for a moment believing that the recommendation would be taken. If Joseph was still abed, well, he wouldn't be for much longer.

Hop Sing left, and Ben carried his steaming mug over to the French doors that led onto the balcony fronting the second floor of the big house. He pulled the doors open, unmindful that his feet were bare and that he was still in his nightshirt. There was not a woman within twenty-five miles to be offended by the sight.

He stepped out into the crisp, invigorating chill of the predawn and tipped his head back, drawing breath deep into his lungs and savoring the flavor and the feel of the clean mountain air. There was the bright aroma of pine lending its hint of spice, and from afar, the brittle, nearly metallic scent of snow. The smell of snow was carried on the breezes from the ragged Sierra Nevada peaks to the west, all the way across on the far side of Lake Tahoe, where it covered the higher peaks even at this mild and gentle time of year.

In the opposite direction, out across the pale and lovely high desert, the night sky had already taken on a salmon-colored glow that was steadily creeping nearer as sunrise approached and the darkness began to fade from black to charcoal and now to a luminescent gray.

Beautiful, Ben thought. If only . . . He closed his mind to that train of thought with no need for conscious effort. There was no place in his life for dreary dwellings on what might have been. He was much too blessed to allow any of that.

He took a step forward, the boards cold underfoot, and leaned against the balcony rail. Right out there was proof of how fortunate a man he was; right out there in the shadows where Adam and Hoss were busy with the morning chores, Adam in the loft above forking hay down for Hoss to distribute to the feed bunks in the nearby corrals.

Ben took a swallow of his coffee, savoring its heat at this moment almost as much as its flavor. He laughed out loud, barely avoiding spraying his own nightshirt, when from the other end of the upstairs hallway he heard a yelp and Joseph's voice crying, "I'm up, Hop Sing, no, don't, I'm up, I promise, *yeow!*"

There was a brief sound not unlike that of thunder, first in the hall and then on the stairs. A moment later the front door burst open and Joseph appeared in the yard below Ben, the youngster hopping on one foot while he tried to pull a boot onto the other. He was wearing trousers and suspenders but no shirt. The light was too poor to be sure, but Ben had the impression that Joseph's hair was plastered flat to his head with some sort of moisture. Now how would such a thing have happened? And at such an hour. Ben chuckled and watched Joseph scurry off to join his brothers in the barn. By the time he got there, though, Joseph was entirely back to being Joseph, swaggering just a little, and no doubt wondering how he was going to get back at someone—not Hop Sing, of course, and not his father, which left rather few candidates for his attention— before the day was out.

Shaking his head, happy, quite thoroughly at peace with the world, Ben Cartwright went back indoors so he could dress and be downstairs by the time the boys finished the chores and came in for breakfast.

"Pass me those . . ." too late, Ben saw. The last of the flapjacks bounced with magical speed from the platter onto Hoss's plate. ". . . biscuits," he concluded. At least there were a few of those remaining.

Joseph picked up the basket and started to pass it, then paused. "You don't want all of these, do you, Pa?"

"No."

"Good." Joseph's smile flashed, and he quickly grabbed two of the three biscuits nested in the basket, passing the last one on to his father. Hoss looked somewhat disappointed.

Ben ignored his middle son's wounded expression and plucked the last light and tender biscuit off the napkin. At meals around here it was Devil take the hindmost. "What was that you were asking, Adam?"

"About the timber in Packsaddle Hollow," Adam said over the rim of his coffee cup.

"Oh, yes." The deep, narrow little canyon lay on the south fringes of the sprawling Ponderosa ranch. Adam and Hoss had named it—it seemed a very long time ago—after a battered and weather-worn pack-saddle frame they found there one summer when they were children. Probably the origin of that mystery had to do with nothing more exciting than some prospector discarding a worn-out piece of equipment, but the boys' imaginations had given rise to one wild fabrication after another for months and months afterward. Ben doubted either of them would remember that incident, but the name had taken root and was now firmly fixed. To the Cartwrights that canyon was and always would be Packsaddle Hollow. "You say Ab is coming to cruise it?"

"Yes, sir. I told him one of us would meet him there and go along to mark the trees."

Ben nodded. Ab Tobin had contracted to buy standing timber from the Ponderosa's plentiful forests. Common practice among most landholders was to sell off all the lumber available and count on the denuded hills to replace that growth with grass for grazing. Ben believed instead in selling only selected mature trees, thinning the forests instead of replacing them. The sale of timber had become a major source of income ever since the Virginia City mines opened, with their insatiable demand for timbers to shore the deep shafts and unstable underground drifts, but there was no amount of income that would prompt him to do anything he honestly believed would harm the Ponderosa. In this case Adam would go along with the buyer and make sure there was not too much timber taken out of any one stand in the thickly forested canyon.

"You'll be gone, what, three or four days?"

"Something like that. Less if Ab comes himself. He knows what he's doing. We can trust him to get it right. Could take longer if he sends someone else. I'll just have to wait and see how it goes."

"Make sure you pack extra, then, just in case. And you'd best prepare for some cold weather too. You never know."

"Pa . . ."

"I know, I know, I worry too much. But take a buffalo robe with you anyway. It will make me feel better."

Adam's normally serious expression softened just a little. "All right, Pa. For you."

"Thank you, son." He turned to Joseph. "No wheedling to go along? I'm surprised."

Joseph made a face and shook his head. Which meant he was sparking some girl who lived in a direction other than to the south. Otherwise he surely would have been clamoring to join Adam in the timbering venture.

"Not me, Pa. I have to get those twos started."

"Yes, of course." Joseph was the horseman of the family. And he did have to get the two-year-old colts started under saddle. He only had another four or five months to accomplish it too. Ben smiled a little. Joseph was so *intent*. His passions were short-lived, but were no less intense for all their brevity.

"And what are you up to today, Hoss?" Ben asked.

"If it's all right with you, Pa, I thought I'd go down t' town and see if Mr. Brickell has those fancy new spurs I ordered out of his catalog."

"The gal legs?" Joseph put in, feigning innocence. "I thought you weren't gonna tell Pa about those."

"Dang you, Joe," Hoss complained, his broad face blushing a hot and brilliant shade of purple.

"Gal legs? What are those?" Ben asked.

Joseph laughed, and Hoss's color deepened all the more. Even Adam grabbed for his napkin and pretended to cough into it so as to hide his amusement.

"Well?" Ben asked.

"N-Nothing, Pa. Just a new style o' spur, that's all."

"If you say so," Ben said innocently, managing somehow to keep his grins inside. Gal leg spurs—as he knew quite well—were made so that the iron "legs" holding the rowels were fashioned in the precise and nicely curved shape of a lady's bestockinged leg. They were decidedly risqué. And madly popular as well. It was a wonder Joseph hadn't come home with a pair yet. Assuming, that is, that Joseph didn't own some. Yet.

"You'll like these spurs I ordered, Pa," Hoss said, changing the subject away from the gal legs. "They're real purty."

"You say they should have arrived by now?"

"Near as I can figure it, yes, sir."

"Then you really should go down and get them, I suppose."

"Pa, what about . . . ?"

"You can go too, Joseph."

His youngest son grinned and tossed his napkin onto the table. Joseph was ready to go to town. Right now.

"Don't be in such an all-fired hurry now, Little Joe," Hoss cautioned. "I ain't finished my breakfast yet." He reached for the sausage platter, tilting it over his plate so that everything that was left slid from platter to plate. "No more biscuits? Darn."

Joseph looked mildly frustrated. But only mildly. After all, he did have a trip into town to look forward to today.

Adam pushed his chair back. "May I be excused, Pa? I should get on my way soon."

"Of course, Adam. You will be—"

"I'll be careful, Pa. I promise."

Ben nodded. It was difficult not to say any more, difficult not to treat his sons like little boys. They were men grown now. Well, except for Joseph, that is. And he was a man grown, to hear him tell it.

Adam, though, fine and solid and dependable Adam, was thirty-four years old now. That seemed quite incredible, but it was true. Adam had his mother's dark hair, and her keen intelligence too. He was taller than his father, and, certainly in Ben's opinion, was much more handsome. Adam was a son a man could be proud of.

Then there was Hoss. Ben smiled whenever he thought of Hoss. Hoss was simply . . . Hoss. Big and physically powerful, but innocent at the same time. The word sweet came to mind, but of course could not be uttered aloud. Still, it was true. Hoss was open and honest and decent. With his broad, moonlike face and that wide gap in his front teeth, in many ways he seemed an outsized little boy. People who did not know him tended to mistake Hoss's shyness and sensitivity for slow-wittedness, although he was neither dull nor slow. Fortunately for those who did not understand him, Hoss was good-natured and tolerant. Most of the time. Hoss was twenty-eight now. Ben found that quite incredible too. How—When—had his sons grown so suddenly to manhood?

Finally there was Joseph. Mercurial, impish, ever-grinning, curly-haired Joseph. Bright and handsome Joseph. A charmer, a dandy . . . and a joy. Joseph would soon be twenty. Was that possible? Surely not. But it was true nonetheless.

Good Lord, how the time flew.

It seemed only the day before yesterday that Ben took up the land that was the Ponderosa. At that time he and Adam and Hoss—Joseph hadn't even been born then—were virtually the only white family living on this side of the mountains.

In the Truckee Meadows where Ben and his sons conducted business with passing wagon trains, there was now a railroad—who would have believed that to be possible?—and a town called Reno.

Now there was another town to the south, Carson City, where before there had been nothing but prairie dogs and jackrabbits.

And between them on the far side of the mountain they now called Sun there now was Virginia City. Neither Virginia City nor the great Comstock Lode had been dreamt of back in those days.

Ben smiled a little to himself. What was it someone asked him just last week or so? He'd been in the Glass Guinea having a brandy with some friends, and some pale peckerwood with a few shares of mining stock in his pocket and too much whiskey in his belly started acting the high and mighty smart aleck. The fellow—Ben didn't know the man's name and didn't want to—got to playing the blowhard and asking him if he wasn't sick, just simply sick, because he'd stopped those few miles short of owning the whole of the Comstock when he took up his land all those years past.

Humph! As if the treasures of the Comstock Lode could compare with these treasures he already had, Ben thought; Adam and Hoss and Joseph. Fine sons were the truest treasures any man could hope for, he believed. And no man had sons finer than he.

Ben Cartwright envied no man and never would. He believed that with all his heart.

"Are you done, Hoss?"

"Yes, Pa," Hoss mumbled around a last mouthful being stuffed into his face.

"Joseph?"

"Yes, Pa."

"Then let's all get on with the day." Ben stood. "That was fine, Hop Sing, thank you."

Ben's chest filled near to overflowing as he watched his sons troop away from the table.

Ben carefully folded his napkin and laid it aside. He sighed. Suppers were lonely, annoying darn things when the boys were away. Adam by now should have reached Packsaddle Hollow and wouldn't be back for days. Hoss and Joseph hadn't yet returned from their trip to town. Even Hop Sing was out of the house; Ben had heard the back door squeak on its hinges shortly after Hop Sing served dinner for one. The house felt large and empty with only himself in it. That was a foretaste, he supposed, of what it would be like when someday the boys married and wanted tables of their own to sit at come evening. It was a feeling Ben did not much care for, and one he would not relish having to live with as a regular thing. If that was selfish of him, well, so be it.

He poured himself a final cup of coffee and carried it into the small office where he kept the Ponderosa's account books. Bookkeeping was a most unpleasant chore for him. Probably because he disliked it so much, it was one of the things that he was not very good at. He tended to put it off much too often and for much too long. And that, of course, simply made the task all the worse whenever he finally did sit down to the unpleasant necessity. Tonight, however, the prospect of a stint at the ledgers seemed preferable to him than sitting in the parlor of a still and silent house. He lighted a whale oil lamp, rolled the top of his desk open, and fussily arranged everything close to hand. Coffee cup here, pipe and humidor placed just so, lamp wick adjusted precisely thus, the lamp itself positioned to throw its light exactly there. Eventually he ran out of acceptable excuses for delay. At that point he opened the current account book and pulled an untidy stack of papers near, plucking the topmost sheet from the pile and peering at it.

"Pa."

Ben was smiling. But then, he had been ever since the front door slammed, the noise of it a signature that identified Hoss just as surely as his voice did a moment later.

"In here, Hoss."

"Do you want to see something mighty purty, Pa?"

"You got them?"

"Just you take a look an' see if you don't think they're purty. Just you take a look, Pa." Hoss came into the office, his shoulders filling the doorway, but his grin capable of filling the entire room. "See?" He pointed proudly toward the floor.

"Indeed I do see," Ben said admiringly. The new spurs were shining bright with nickel plating, and there were bands of polished brass inlaid on the legs—not gal legs, thank goodness—while the rowels were large and had many sharp-tipped points. Rowels like that looked quite wicked but in fact were gentle on a horse. It was the more innocent-appearing, star-shaped rowel with only a few points that actually were capable of inflicting pain on an animal.

"Do you like 'em, Pa?"

"Very much."

"Joe ordered a pair just like 'em. But he's paying extra to get him some brass jinglers."

"Jinglers?"

"You know. Little bells, like. They hang off this here doodad." Hoss lifted his boot and pointed to a small protrusion on the nickel and iron spur leg. "Jinglers, well, they jingle. You know?"

"I see," Ben said indulgently. He couldn't much imagine why anyone would *want* to jingle and chime when he walked. But then, he was not of Hoss's and Joseph's generation.

"I take it you had a nice time in town, then?"

"Sure did, Pa. Real nice. We had dinner at the hotel. Chicken and dumplings." Hoss rolled his eyes and smacked his lips. Chicken was one of his favorite items—in truth, most foods were among his favorite items, but chicken was high on the list anyway—and they were rarely able to have it at home. Hop Sing tried to raise chickens for the table and get hens to set eggs, but it was a constant battle between him and the numerous coyotes, bobcats, hawks, and eagles that enjoyed chicken for dinner even more, and more often, than Hoss did.

"There's plenty left over from supper, if you're still hungry," Ben suggested.

"Good. It's a long ride home, you know. Reckon I worked up something of an appetite on the way." He turned to head off toward the kitchen.

Ben closed his account book—Hoss's return was a more than adequate excuse to put the work aside for the evening—and asked, "Where's Joseph? Putting the horses up?"

"Oh, Joe ain't here yet. He said to tell you he'll be along directly, Pa. Said I shouldn't wait on him neither. That's all right, ain't it, Pa? I mean, he's old enough to look out for himself and everything. It ain't like he's off somewhere strange or anything. It's only Virginia City. You, uh, aren't mad at me, are you?"

"No, son, I'm not mad at you."

"You look worried, Pa. You want I should go back an' keep an eye on Joe?"

"No, Hoss, I wouldn't want you to do that. You, um, don't think Joseph is getting into any trouble, do you?"

"Oh, he ain't drinking or gambling or nothing like that, Pa. He's just sparking some girl."

"Some girl," Ben repeated.

"I don't think you'd know her, Pa."

"No?" Virginia City had become quite the town in recent years, and it was perfectly true that Ben could no longer be personally acquainted with everyone there. But he certainly knew everyone who had been there for any appreciable length of time. "So who is this beauty, Hoss?"

"Her name's Samantha, but she calls herself Sam. Her pa is a, um, salesman, you might say."

Ben thought he could detect a certain amount of ... what? Not dishonesty, certainly. Ben was not at all sure Hoss would be capable of lying even if he had to. But if not actual dishonesty, then perhaps a lack of full disclosure. An omission of certain small but essential facts? There was something in Hoss's voice and, more, in his expression that hinted of truths that were not being fully elucidated.

"Sam," Ben said thoughtfully. "Now what sort of young lady is it who would call herself Sam?"

Hoss examined his new spurs, choosing to take the question as having been a rhetorical one that required no answer.

"What did you say the young lady's father does?"

"He sells things, Pa." That one couldn't be deemed rhetorical and pretty much had to be answered outright.

"What sort of things does the gentleman sell?"

"Well, um, medicines, Pa."

"Medicines? He's a doctor, then?"

"Not ... exactly."

"A pharmacist."

"I wouldn't know about that, Pa."

"A snake oil salesman? Is that what you are trying to not tell me, Eric Haas Cartwright?"

When his father referred him by his full and true name, Hoss knew some seriousness was called for. "Yes, sir. He's a wagon show operator, Pa. Indian Jim Whittacker."

"And this Sam. Is she ... ?"

"Yes, sir. She's part o' the show, Pa. She ... well, you might say she, um, dances. Sort of."

"Sort of," Ben repeated.

"Yes, sir. Sort of."

"When she's doing this dancing, Hoss, what is it that she wears?"

"Veils, Pa. She wears a lot of veils."

"I take it you've seen this dance, otherwise you wouldn't be able to describe it to me?"

Hoss dropped his eyes and blushed.

"May I assume that this dance takes place somewhere other than in public?" It wasn't like Indian Jim Whittacker's business was entirely unknown. In fact it was common. Sordid, perhaps, but common.

Hoss blushed some more. "There's this tent. Behind the wagon . . . ?"

"And Sam dances a little on the wagon platform, but if you want to see more you have to pay and go back to the tent?"

"Yes, sir."

"And of course you don't really see everything you expected to. But you do see more than you did outside. Is that about it, Hoss?"

"Somethin' like that. Yes, sir."

"And Joseph . . . ?"

"He thinks this Miss Samantha is awful purty, Pa. An' she is too. She has great big eyes. An' dimples."

"I'm sure she is very attractive indeed."

"You want I should go back to town an' find Little Joe, Pa?"

"No, Hoss, I think Miss Whittacker will prove entirely capable of defending herself from Joseph's charms. He, um, wasn't carrying a large sum of money on him, was he, son?"

"No, sir. After buying my spurs an' Joe getting himself a new silk bandanna an' paying for supper an' everything, we was both pretty well broke."

"That's nice."

"Sir?"

"I was just saying that this should be a relatively inexpensive lesson, then. But I think perhaps I've allowed

Joseph's education to delay overlong. I only wish I knew what I could do to take care of that oversight."

"Yes, sir. If you say so." It was fairly obvious that Hoss didn't have a clue as to what his father meant by all that. But at the moment he didn't seem to think it wise to be expanding their discussion. He turned once more toward the kitchen and Hop Sing's leftovers. Before he was halfway through the foyer he stopped and came back.

"Yes, son?"

"I almost forgot." Hoss reached inside his shirt and pulled out a slim packet of envelopes. "We picked up the mail while we was there."

"Thank you, Hoss."

"It's 'most all for Adam. Like always." Hoss grinned, and Ben knew Adam would be in for the usual round of teasing from his younger brothers just as soon as he returned home from his timber cruising tasks. For the better part of a year now Adam had been receiving letters—floral-scented letters—with a woman's spidery handwriting on the outside. No one but Adam knew what was said within those envelopes, though, and Adam wasn't telling. He hadn't even volunteered any information to his father, and that was most unusual. Unlike Joseph, though, Ben knew he did not need to worry about Adam's judgment. He was content to wait until Adam had something to say before that subject would be raised. Joseph and Hoss, on the other hand, felt no such reluctance to probe, pry, peer, and pester.

"Is there anything for the rest of us?" Ben asked.

"Something from Tobin Shoring and Timber." That would be a check, Ben knew. "The usual envelope from Mr. DeShong." Alton DeShong was Ben's long-time business factor—and friend—in San Francisco. He sent a statement of account along every month without fail. "And . . . let's see . . . this here from somebody I don't know. Lester Shannon? The return address is someplace called Johns Bend. I never heard of that neither."

Ben smiled. "Les is a friend from the old days. He

and Chloe did business with us when we ran the old store down at the Truckee Meadows. In fact, if I remember correctly, Les whittled a sword for you when you were little, and Chloe took the time to mend your britches."

"A sword?"

"I believe you were a pirate at the time. Les thought a proper pirate should have a sword."

Hoss beamed. "I remember that, kinda. This fella, he's tall and real thin?"

Ben laughed. "Les is thin, all right, but he isn't very tall. Of course he would have been to you at the time. You probably didn't come up higher than his belt."

"Ain't that been a long while back, then?"

"Yes, it has. And we've been friends with the Shannons for all that time. Not that we've seen them often, but I certainly haven't ever stopped liking them, or wishing that I could see them more."

"You grubstaked them?" Hoss asked. It was a reasonable enough question. And its answer was almost a certainty. Ben had befriended and staked a good many of the 'forty-niners who passed along the Truckee River on their way to the gold camps of California back then. Many of these people had succeeded afterward, and either repaid the Cartwrights in cash or assigned percentages of their California ventures to Ben and his sons. The Cartwrights still drew income from an astounding variety of businesses as a result of that long ago policy that no one should be allowed to pass by in hunger.

"Mm, yes, as a matter of fact."

"You mean you own something in this Johns Bend place?"

"I suppose we probably do," Ben said.

Hoss shook his head. "I don't know how you keep track of it all, Pa."

Ben laughed. "Actually, I don't, son. The truth is that I'm a terrible businessman. The only thing that saves us is the fact that we have wonderfully loyal friends. They are much more faithful about paying attention to who owns what than I will ever be."

Hoss handed the mail to his father and said, "If you don't mind, Pa, you can pay attention to this here stuff. Me, I got to go see what Hop Sing has in the pie safe. I'm powerful hungry after that ride from town."

Ben set Adam's letters aside on a low table and took the rest of the mail to his desk. He could feel virtuous about working at the desk while he was opening the mail, and yet not have to think about those miserable account books while he was doing it. That didn't seem a bad combination at all.

CHAPTER 2

B en looked up with a smile. Adam was home. It had
been six days Adam was away. Ben had missed
him. He got up and gave his eldest a hug to welcome him back. "How did everything go down south?"

"Fine, Pa. We marked all the timber they need to fill
this contract. You won't hardly notice what they take out."

Ben nodded.

"There's a lot of good forest down there, Pa."

Ben lifted an eyebrow. Knowing Adam, he felt fairly
sure there was more to this than idle chatter.

"While we were cruising timber for Mr. Tobin, Pa, I
got to thinking. There's no reason why we shouldn't start
a little milling operation of our own down that way. One
small steam donkey engine and a few teams of heavy
horses for skidding the logs, some hand tools and a couple
wagons for delivering lumber down to the rail siding,
that's all we'd need. Call it a crew of six on the engine
and saw, and sixteen, maybe eighteen men cutting trees
and hauling timber. Those and a few more men to haul the
milled lumber. I think we could make a nice profit and still
not harm the forest. In fact, it needs thinning. What we
would take out would only let in more light and help the
younger growth. And, Pa, there's quite a market for lumber. Quite a market."

"Have you thought your idea through yet?"

Adam shook his head. "Not yet. I didn't want to do that until I mentioned it to you first, Pa."

"You know I'll trust your judgment," Ben said. And that was the simple truth. Adam had a fine head for business. More so in many ways than his father. Except for his one basic rule of demanding decency and fairness in all trade, Ben tended to let business affairs run their own course. But then Adam, being young, was still intent on trying his wings. If Adam had his way about things, the Cartwright family would diversify their interests to the point that none of them would be able to remember all the ventures they were into. It was hard enough as things were, with Ben and his sons owning bits of this and snippets of that from old investments and—much more often—old involvements with the businesses of friends. From his earliest years in this country, Ben's policy had been to help his friends whenever and however they needed. He often was repaid with small percentages of his friends' affairs, so that now he owned fractional interests in, quite literally, more ventures than he could keep straight in his mind. He didn't want the family affairs to become that fragmented too. But on the other hand, he truly did trust Adam's judgment in most matters. Hoss's inclinations might be swayed by sentiment, or Joseph's by emotion, but Adam's thinking nearly always was cool and precise and carefully reasoned. "Give it a good looking over and make your estimates, then we'll talk again," Ben said.

Adam nodded and helped himself to a seat in one of the leather armchairs in his father's office-cum-study. "What is it you're working on there, Pa?"

"This? Just a letter. Do you remember Mr. and Mrs. Shannon?"

Adam smiled. "Mrs. Shannon is the lady that makes the gooseberry tarts, isn't she?"

Ben had forgotten that. Obviously Adam hadn't. Lord, that had been a good many years ago. "That's right."

"We haven't seen them for a long time," Adam said.

"We got a letter from Les just after you left to go down to Packsaddle."

"If you got the letter that long ago and haven't answered it yet, then he's asked for something harder for you to deal with than just an exchange of news or the borrow of a simple loan," Adam correctly interpreted. His perception pleased his father.

"It isn't a loan he wants exactly," Ben said. "Les has invited us to invest in a railroad scheme he and some other fellows are putting together. I've thought it over, though, and I don't think I'll go in with him. Johns Bend has been a strong, steady source of good ore bodies. That whole area has been. It hasn't been a boom-and-bust cycle over there. But you never know when the veins will pinch out and just disappear. I don't know that the investment would be that good."

Adam grunted and stared into his steepled palms.

"What?"

"Oh, I was just . . . thinking."

"Yes?"

"That area has been producing for more than twenty years, right?"

"That's right."

"And there still isn't any railroad in that part of the country, right?"

"True."

"So all the gold shipped out of there has been processed right there, right?"

"Yes. What's your point, son?"

"I've been doing some reading, Pa. Did you know that a small stamp mill like I bet they have in Johns Bend only extracts thirty, maybe thirty-five percent of the gold that's in a given piece of ore?"

"I don't suppose I ever heard that, no."

"It's true enough. And another true thing is that modern ore processing can extract fifty-five, even sixty or sixty-five percent of the available mineral."

"Is that so?"

"Yes, sir." Adam looked up from whatever it was he'd been seeing inside the grasp of his hands. He smiled. "Think about it, Pa. Twenty-odd years of discarded mill tailings are lying there, and only half the recoverable value has been taken out of them so far. Why, it's kind of like free gold lying there on the ground and nobody wanting it, nobody thinking it's valuable. The only thing that keeps anybody from being able to haul those old tailings to a smelter for reprocessing with these better extraction methods is the problem of transporting all that bulk economically."

"What you're saying is . . . ?"

"Oh, I'm not saying anything, Pa. Not exactly. But it's like with me and my idea for a sawmill down south. I think it has enough merit that maybe it ought to be looked at a little closer before a decision is made."

Ben scratched the side of his jaw. "We do have stock holdings in the first three mining properties Les developed there," he mused aloud. "We grubstaked him when he and Chloe were starting out. Les gave us five or maybe it was ten percent of those claims. You could say that we already own a good amount of the tailings dumped over there."

"I would think a person could buy up tailings pretty cheap, Pa. About all he might want."

"Not once people understood why they were suddenly valuable."

"I wasn't suggesting—"

"I know you weren't, son."

"Anyway, Pa, I don't think you should turn Mr. Shannon down without looking into his railroad a little closer. I mean, a deal like that wouldn't only make those ore bodies and tailings more valuable, it would also mean steady traffic for the railroad too, wouldn't it?"

As usual, Ben thought, Adam was seeing the situation clearly. "Perhaps," he said, "I should write and tell Les I'll swing by Johns Bend and take a look at this railroad idea of his the next time I'm traveling through."

"Sounds sensible to me, Pa."

"I have to admit, son, that isn't the letter I'd planned to write."

"Whatever you think, Pa. You know I won't argue with you."

"No, you probably have a good idea here. The next time I go to San Francisco, I'll make a detour up to Johns Bend. It won't be all that much out of the way."

"Yes, sir." Adam stood. "I better make sure Hop Sing knows I'll be home for supper."

Ben frowned. "Maybe that will calm him down a little."

"What's Hop Sing mad about now?"

"Oh, you know how he is. He planned supper with Joseph in mind, then Joseph begged the afternoon off and rode down to see some girl that has him all google-eyed and his palms sweating."

Adam laughed. "That sounds like Little Joe, all right."

Ben wasn't laughing. "I'm not sure I approve of this one, Adam. Her father is a snake oil barker, and the girl dances in the tent show. I hope that's all she does. I . . . don't want Joseph to wind up being hurt."

"You know, Pa, Joe *is* almost grown. He hasn't seen much of the world outside of Virginia City and a few other places just as rough and crude and crazy. The wonder of it is that he hasn't been taught a hard lesson by some phony flirt already."

"I suppose you're right, Adam."

"Do you want me to talk to him?"

"No, that would only make him all the more determined to see this girl for what she pretends to be but isn't. You know Joseph. Let him hear the word 'can't' and he won't rest until he's proven you wrong. Or until he's battered himself bloody from trying to prove himself right."

"Yes, sir, that's Little Joe, all right."

Ben shrugged. "Sorry. I didn't mean to put any of this onto your shoulders."

"You didn't, Pa. And look, if you want to read up on the new gold recovery techniques, I can find some journals for you to look at. It's very interesting."

Interesting. Ben gave his oldest son a wry smile. Bless Adam's heart, he really did find such dry subjects as mining and metallurgy to be of interest."

"I'll let you know, son, thank you."

"Yes, sir." Adam grinned and went off in search of Hop Sing, while Ben returned to his letter writing. But the letter he was composing now was not at all the one he would have written had Adam not returned home when he did.

"Up a little more, little more, little . . . hold it. Now down. No, too much. Up . . . there!" With a grunt that was as much satisfaction as it was effort—after all, Hoss was providing the bulk of the effort involved here—Ben slid the heavy wagon wheel back onto its axle. "Hold it just a few seconds more, son, and I'll have this . . . there." He spun the hub nut onto the threaded steel at the end of the axle, working quickly while Hoss continued to hold the back corner of the wagon off the ground. "Are you doing all right, son?"

"Just fine, Pa. Except for my nose itching something awful. I wouldn't mind if you was to hurry it up just a little 'cause of that."

Ben chuckled. And hurried. He hand tightened the nut until it was nicely snug, then he said, "All right, Hoss, ease it down nice and slow."

"Whew!" Hoss let the weight down carefully. The new spokes on the old wheel creaked and groaned a little as they carried a load for the first time, but Ben's workmanship was sound and there was no danger the wheel would buckle now.

Ben looked up in time to see Hoss vigorously scratching the side of his nose. He began to laugh.

"What's the matter, Pa?"

"Nothing, son."

Hoss scratched some more, sniffed twice and shrugged. "You want me to get a wrench an' tighten that nut the rest o' the way, Pa?"

"No, I can do that while you go wash your face."

Hoss gave his father a questioning glance.

"Look at your hands, son."

The question on Hoss's broad face turned to astonishment when he looked down at his own massive hands. "Now where in tarnation . . . ?"

Both his hands were liberally smeared with thick, black grease the same approximate color and consistency of caulking tar. Obviously the grease had been on the frame of the wagon Hoss lifted.

"If you think that's bad," Ben said, "you should see your face. One side of your nose is covered with the stuff."

"You're funning me, Pa. Ain't you?"

"It was only a suggestion. You don't have to wash if you don't want to."

"Pa!" Hoss looked down at his hands again, then gingerly felt his nose. There was already dark grease liberally smeared there. His investigations only made it worse. "Pa, do I really . . . ?"

Ben grinned. "Yes, son. You really."

Hoss sighed. Then smiled. Ben always loved to see his middle son's good-natured smiles. "I think I'll go wash my face now, Pa."

"Good idea, son."

Holding his hands well out to the sides lest he touch anything—a clear case of locking the barn too late—Hoss ambled across the ranch yard toward the house.

Ben stepped inside the equipment shed and plucked a hub wrench down from a wall peg, then went back outside and began tightening the big nut. The wheel needed to be snug or it would wobble and cause undue wear on hub and axle alike.

He was nearly done when he heard the clatter of hoofs on hard earth and the crunch and grind of iron tires on gravel. He straightened, a sharp pain briefly reminding him that he wasn't quite as young as he used to be, to see a light rig rolling into the yard. He recognized the outfit. The wagon body was painted maroon trimmed in black, while the tarred canvas top was black with maroon fringes. The wheel spokes were mud-spattered white. The wagon belonged to Jeremy Isley's livery stable in Virginia City. It took Ben a few seconds to recall the name of the man driving it; he wasn't someone Ben normally did business with, although they had met on several occasions. It was Armand Blauhaus, a pawnbroker.

Blauhaus did not look entirely comfortable handling the reins of the hired horse. He leaned back to pull against the sweating brown's bit and pleaded more than ordered, "Whoa, horse, whoa."

Ben stepped out from behind the wagon where he'd been working and intercepted the brown, taking hold of the bridle cheek piece and uttering a few soft, soothing murmurs for the benefit of the horse. Blauhaus appeared quite relieved. He let go of the reins and removed his derby to mop the sweat from his brow, even though at this elevation there was rarely a day that was warm enough to make a man sweat in the absence of hard labor.

"Thank you, Mr. Cartwright. I thought I was having a runaway."

The horse hadn't been close to running away, Ben knew, but it would have been impolite to mention the fact. "No harm done, Mr. Blauhaus. Would you care to step down?"

"I would do, thank you." Blauhaus climbed carefully to ground level and seemed grateful to be there once his feet were safely on firm earth again.

Ben let go of the brown's bridle and found a hitch weight behind the seat of the buggy. He clipped it to the bit ring and set it down to secure the horse in place, then turned to offer a handshake to his guest. Blauhaus, anticipating the convention, was fussily removing his driving glove. Ben had a moment to look his unexpected visitor over.

Armand Blauhaus was a slight, short slip of a man, probably somewhere in his mid- to late fifties, and with only a few strands of graying hair remaining on top of his pate. He made up for the lack on high by cultivating a Vandyke and mustache. His whiskers, however, were invariably neat, tidy, and closely trimmed. But then, Armand Blauhaus was meticulously tidy at all times, about his person and—so Ben was told—his accounts. He was dapper if not always fashionable, preferring the tried and true to any impulsive extremes of fashion. Today he wore black trousers, gray cutaway, cream brocade waistcoat, maroon puff cravat—surely, Ben thought, that was coincidence; surely the man hadn't actually coordinated his wardrobe with the paint on Isley's rental buggies—and cream-colored spats over a pair of ancient but freshly blacked and polished lace-up shoes. All he needed to make the ensemble complete would be a malacca cane, Ben decided. Even as Ben was thinking that, Blauhaus reached into the driving box of the wagon and brought out a cane. Malacca. With a brass duck-bill head. Of course.

"Welcome to the Ponderosa, Mr. Blauhaus. Would you care to come inside?"

"I would." Blauhaus inclined his head a fraction of an inch. "Thank you."

Ben led the way, showing Blauhaus to a comfortable chair in the huge sitting room that dominated the ground floor. "Excuse me for a moment, please."

Blauhaus nodded again, and Ben went back to the kitchen. In comparison with his dapper visitor, he felt positively grimy. He quickly washed and asked Hop Sing to bring tea. It was much too early in the day to offer anything stronger, and Ben had the impression that this guest would prefer tea service to mugs of coffee. There was no sign in the kitchen of Hoss, which meant he must have seen Blauhaus drive in and, for some reason, slipped out the back way. Curious, Ben thought. He dried his hands and returned to the sitting room.

"I've asked my cook to bring tea," Ben said. "I hope that's all right with you."

"Very nice, very thoughtful, thank you." Blauhaus bobbed his head. He cleared his throat, removed his other glove and laid cane and gloves aside. He was sitting on the forward few inches of his chair, his back as stiff and straight as if he were a military cadet at attention.

"So, um, what can I do for you, Mr. Blauhaus?"

"I know you are a busy man, Mr. Cartwright. I will proceed to the point at once, yes?"

"Whatever you wish, Mr. Blauhaus."

"It is to save you time and difficulty that I come here, you see."

Ben did not see, yet, but he had hopes that he soon might. He smiled, nodded pleasantly, and waited for Blauhaus to get on with it.

He had to wait a bit longer because Hop Sing chose that moment to come in bearing a tray with formal tea service for two in ornate silver, their very best, complete with canned milk and refined sugar. Hop Sing, Ben saw, was putting on the dog here. But then Mr. Blauhaus seemed to have that effect on people, perhaps because of his own fastidiousness. Hop Sing put the tray down without a word and scurried off again, returning moments later with a plate of tarts that Ben hadn't known they had. Obviously Hoss hadn't known it either or there wouldn't have been any for company to share.

"Thank you, Hop Sing," Blauhaus said when Hop Sing poured the tea. Which was another thing Ben found to be of interest. He would not have suspected that Blauhaus would know the Ponderosa's Chinese cook. Nor, for that matter, vice versa. Hop Sing said something in Cantonese and bobbed his head, his pigtail flying. Blauhaus smiled—now surely the fellow didn't speak Chinese, Ben mused—and accepted a tart. Hop Sing finished serving the guest and passed tea tray and tarts to Ben with somewhat less ceremony.

"Now," Ben prompted when Hop Sing had gone, "you were saying something about the, um, reason we have the pleasure of your company today?"

"So I was, yes." Blauhaus smiled. "I came to you— one loving father to another, as it were—to discuss your son's account."

Account? One of Ben's sons had an account with the local pawnbroker?

Ben felt his jaw drop open.

There was nothing, simply nothing, he could have done to prevent it.

CHAPTER 3

Ben's shock was so complete, so overwhelming, that it must have been obvious even to as casual an acquaintance as Armand Blauhaus.

"Mr. Cartwright," the visitor blurted, "are you all right?"

"Yes, certainly," Ben responded without thought. "Or . . . I don't know." He grimaced. "What . . . that is to say, who . . ." His voice tailed away into an awkward silence.

"I've distressed you," Blauhaus said in an apologetic tone. "What did I do to . . . oh, of course. Sorry, Mr. Cartwright, so sorry if you misunderstand me. I am not here to collect a debt. No, no. Please forgive me if I gave that impression. Really, I mean if any of your family or employees were behind on payments—which none of them are, of course—that is to say . . . Mr. Cartwright, I am becoming confused myself at this point. May we start over?"

"Please do, Mr. Blauhaus."

"I am not here in my capacity as a lender, you see, but as a purveyor of, um, superior quality gemstones."

"I beg your pardon?"

"As a jeweler, Mr. Cartwright. I come to see you as a jeweler. Hopefully soon to be your son's jeweler, to be more precise about it."

"My . . . son's . . . jeweler," Ben repeated slowly, letting each individual word slide across his tongue as if he were tasting it. And not especially enjoying the flavor, if the truth be known. "May I ask . . . *which* son?"

Blauhaus smiled benignly and had a sip of tea before he responded. Ben was fairly sure that one sip required fourteen minutes to complete. The wait was agonizing. "Why, Joseph, of course," Blauhaus said happily. He reached inside his coat and extracted a slim case of exquisitely soft leather. He fumbled for a moment with a gold catch—it looked like the real thing and not merely polished brass—and spread the case open. "I have here, Mr. Cartwright, a selection of engagement rings of the very finest quality. I chose them myself, and I can assure you that I have brought with me only the very finest examples of the art. The diamonds . . . have you a loupe? Would you care to borrow mine . . . ? All are of white or blue-white hue, and the occlusions . . . well, you will simply have to judge those for yourself on a stone by stone basis. Naturally, there are occlusions. No matter what anyone else may try to tell you, occlusions are a perfectly normal occurrence, even in diamonds of this quality. You see that I am hiding nothing, not even the occlusions, while certain, um, others who may sell jewelry but who are not jewelers will pretend that such things do not exist. Those are the men—notice, I do not say gentlemen—who would resist any attempt by the customer to view their wares under the magnification of a loupe. I prefer that my customers learn to use a loupe so they can judge the quality for themselves. As you can see, I have nothing to hide, nor do I fear close examination. Now if I may, Mr. Cartwright, I will give you a brief overview and, with your permission, make a few suggestions. Then, of course, it will be up to you and Joseph to choose a ring of suitable quality and, um, price. Which I believe you will find to be entirely fair and competitive. And, frankly, much much lower than what is asked for those inferior rings my esteemed peer Mr. Cuddahey has been trying to palm off on your son."

Ben blinked. The initial shock was still with him, surrounding his head like mounds of goose-down pillows and
cushioning the meanings of Blauhaus's words even while
allowing most of them through.

It was as if he could snatch a phrase here, a meaning
there. He felt detached from them. Not uninterested,
though. It was more that he was numbed by what
Blauhaus was saying.

Oh, but the words and the meanings did sneak
through. A bit here, a bit there.

Rings. Engagement. Diamond. Engagement. Joseph.
Engagement. *Joseph*.

"Mr. Blauhaus," Ben said, snapping out of his confu-
sion.

"Yes, Mr. Cartwright?"

"You've driven out here to no purpose, sir."

"Oh? Don't tell me. Joseph has already made a purchase? Dear me. And I practically begged him to wait
until I could show my wares." Blauhaus smiled and
shrugged. "Oh well. He's a fine lad in all respects, Mr.
Cartwright. I wish him and his, um, young lady the very
best. My congratulations go out to him, and my very best
wishes to her. And I mean that sincerely, sir. I really do.
The sale of one small trinket is but a fleeting matter of no
consequence, but the joining of two young people in the
bonds of matrimony is a joy for all eternity."

"I am sure you do mean that with all sincerity, Mr.
Blauhaus," Ben said, wincing at the recollection of the
phrase having to do with all eternity. "But you still misunderstand. There can be no congratulations because there is
no engagement for him to be congratulated upon. Believe
me."

"No? How odd." Blauhaus shrugged again. "I've
misunderstood, then, as you say. Please accept my apolo-
gies, Mr. Cartwright."

What Ben really should give to Blauhaus was thanks.
He knew that, but of course was not about to admit it to
this person who, nice though he was, was not family and

not privileged to enter into any discussion as intimate as this.

"No harm done," Ben said. "It's all quite understandable, of course." Hmmph. Ben wished *he* could understand it, never mind Blauhaus. "Really, though, no harm done. Would you care for more tea? Another tart? Here, let me pour. You know, Armand, actually I'm glad you did misunderstand, since it's led to your visit. You haven't been to the Ponderosa before, have you? Such an oversight. I can't imagine how we've neglected having you out before now. You will stay for dinner, won't you? Please, I insist. You really must stay." Ben smiled. "All my sons will be back for dinner. They'll be very upset if they find they've missed visiting with you. You will stay then? Good." Ben's smile grew wider. Behind it he was wondering how in the *world* a father was supposed to handle this situation.

Ben climbed slowly, wearily, through the rocks and trees that sheltered the Ponderosa headquarters from the worst of the winter winds. Not that he had to think in those terms at this gentle season. Now it was solitude he sought here.

Four days had passed since Armand Blauhaus's visit. Not once in that time had any of the boys mentioned the pawnbroker's visit. Not once had any of the three of them asked why the gentleman called. Under other, less worrisome circumstances, Ben would have found that fact amusing.

Whatever the facts about that, Ben was not particularly worried. After all, all his sons were old enough to handle dealings of that nature if they felt compelled to do so. The implications were a reminder to Ben that perhaps he should loosen his purse strings with his sons. Just because he paid scant attention to pocket money did not mean he should ask them to do so as well. With him it was a habit born of his years at sea, when there might be neither need nor opportunity to handle cash for months at a time. Perhaps he had unconsciously expected his sons to adopt a habit that was not theirs to carry, and thus failed to see to their petty cash requirements.

That was a matter of no great importance, though, and one that could be worked out some other time.

For now his concerns lay with Joseph.

Lay with a most uncharacteristically silent and agreeable Joseph who for the past four days had said nothing about rings. Or engagements. Or even about going down to town. The young lady was languishing in Virginia City without benefit of Joseph's company these past few days and nights.

If Joseph, snared by Armand Blauhaus's visit, was now feeling too awkward and embarrassed to discuss the matter of the engagement ring with his father, then things had come to a pretty pass indeed.

Ben sighed and walked slowly along the high ridge where once, very long ago now it had been, he and Joseph's dear mother Marie once walked hand in hand, before Joseph's birth and for precious months afterward. It had been one of Marie's favorite spots, the brilliant blue waters of Lake Tahoe lying below their feet to the west, the rolling foothills and high desert plains to the east. The beauty she found here was the reason the ranch house had been built where it now stood. Its design had been largely a labor of her love, although Marie had not lived to see its completion. She died, so young, of a fall from a horse. At the time, she and Ben had been riding up to check on the progress of construction at the house.

And now Marie's own dear son Joseph was in need of . . . what? Maturity. That, really, was Joseph's only real lack. Ben's problem now was to protect Joseph long enough for time and experience to complete his education.

Joseph was mercurial, effervescent, filled with zest and enthusiasm, but limited as to the sort of wisdom one earns by way of hard experience.

Much though he himself would deny it, Joseph knew little of the world. Here at the Ponderosa he was surrounded by people who loved him. Even in Virginia City,

Carson City, and Reno he was virtually at home, surrounded for the most part by people who knew who he was and who did not want to offend his father.

There were exceptions to that norm, as Ben himself was now discovering. Apparently there were those entering Joseph's life now who would want to use the boy's inexperience so they could gain an advantage over him.

The Cartwright fortunes were, after all, considerable. Ben supposed it something of a miracle that his sons had not been ensnared in games like this before now. And now that the time had come, who should the target be but the youngest and least able to recognize deceit?

Ben reached the bole of a fallen pine. One he had sat upon with Marie years past? No. A more recent fall, he decided. He found a flat, smooth area and eased down upon it, drawing out his pipe and slowly loading and lighting it.

Modern technology was something to behold, he thought as he so casually extinguished a sulfur-tipped match and dropped it to the needle-covered earth. Twenty years ago a self-flaming Lucifer that needed neither flint nor glass would have caused a sensation. Now one was unworthy of comment. So far had man progressed. But not, Ben reflected, in the things that were truly important to mankind. Now it was easy to strike a fire. Yet it was not the slightest bit easier today for one man to trust another.

Was Ben misjudging this young lady who danced in tent shows and displayed her legs for the delight of paying strangers? He hadn't even met the girl and yet he was prejudging her to be unworthy of his son. Could he be wrong about that? Could it be that she—what was her name again?—could really be Joseph's truly intended, his life's one great helpmeet? If so, and he tried to stand between them, it should be the father who lost, not the beloved.

But if this girl and her father were only trying to use Joseph as a pipeline into the Cartwright pockets . . .

Ben sucked at the stem of his pipe, drawing the smoke deep into his lungs and savoring the flavors on his tongue, then just as slowly exhaling so the white smoke wreathed his head in the still air of the early evening.

The sun had already disappeared beneath the rim of the Sierras, and the bright waters of Tahoe were turning dark and severe in the shadowed valley. The sky over the distant Pacific was streaked red, gold, and purple. Ben stared unseeing toward the mountains and far beyond them, imagining the vast sweep of the great sea, and for a moment wishing for the simplicity of the sailor's life, with only the elements to conquer and only nature to fear. The land's troubles remained on land when a sailor committed himself to the sea, and there were times when a man could be tempted, oh so tempted.

He grunted softly to himself and turned to straddle the trunk of the fallen pine, dragging his attention away from the west and returning it to matters closer to home.

"Pa?"

"Adam. Come in, son."

"Hop Sing said you wanted to see me?"

"Yes. Sit down. Where are your brothers, by the way?"

"They're in the front room, Pa. Reading."

"Reading? Hoss? Joseph?"

"Yes, Pa. Reading."

"The *Police Gazette* no doubt."

"Dickens and Tennyson, I think. I could be wrong about that. Did you want me to . . . ?"

"Lord, no. Sit down, Adam."

"Yes, Pa." Adam settled gingerly onto the nearest chair. He somehow gave the impression of a small boy waiting for a whipping.

"Are Hoss and Joseph all right, Adam?"

"Pretty much, Pa. They're, well, kind of waiting for the other shoe to fall."

"How's that, son?"

"After, you know, after Mr. Blauhaus's visit."

"I see. They're waiting for me to blow up at them?"

"Something like that."

"Which implies I have reason to blow."

"Unless you're asking me a direct question, Pa, I'd as soon not say anything to that."

"No, I don't suppose you should." Ben took the glass stopper from a crystal brandy decanter. "Join me, son?"

"No, thank you."

Ben poured a small tot for himself and replaced the decanter on its tray. He carried his glass with him and settled into a favorite chair. "The reason I wanted to talk to you this evening, Adam, is that I want to ask you to do something for me."

"Of course, Pa. Whatever you want."

"I want you to take charge of the Ponderosa for the next month or so."

"Sir?"

"I know this is a busy time of year, but I'm sure you can handle it. You were going to go back down south to oversee the timber cutting, but there isn't any reason why Hoss couldn't handle that instead. All the timber has been marked, so he'll only have to make sure the loggers don't become overly enthusiastic in their cutting. He can manage that. The only other major job will be moving the livestock from winter pasture up to the summer graze. You can take charge of that."

"What about the crew, Pa? You've always done the crew hiring yourself."

"There's no reason why you can't do it, is there, Adam?"

A wisp of half-hidden smile played lightly at the corners of Adam's mouth. "No, sir, I can do it. I know I can."

"I know you can too, son."

The smile left its hiding place and became a full-blown grin. "Yes, sir," Adam said. "What, uh, about Little Joe?"

"Joseph and I, son, are going on a little trip."

"Sir?"

"I have some business to attend to in San Francisco.

Joseph will be coming along with me. And on our way back, I promised I'd take a side trip up to Johns Bend to see Les and Chloe Shannon, remember?"

"Oh, yes. That narrow-gauge railroad project. I remember."

"I'm sure you and Hoss can get along here very nicely without us."

"I don't know how nicely we'll manage, Pa, but I think we can get along. You, uh, do know that Little Joe has a lady friend down in town, don't you, Pa? He's pretty serious about her."

"Oh, I don't see any conflict, Adam. After all, real love can stand a few weeks of separation."

Adam gave his father a searching look that lasted long moments. Then he grinned. "Yes, sir. I think I see what you mean."

"I thought you might," Ben said as he reached for his pipe. "Are you sure you won't join me in a small brandy?"

"Maybe I will after all, Pa. Maybe I will at that." Chuckling, Adam rose and went to the sideboard to pour a small glass for himself and to refresh his father's drink. "Me and Hoss—excuse me, Hoss and I—will have things under control here, Pa. You and Joe take all the time you want." He laughed. "That San Francisco, it's quite the city. I wish I was going along with you."

Ben raised his glass in salute, and he and his oldest son shared a toast. To the future.

"Here she comes now, Pa. We didn't get the flag up any too soon." Hoss grinned and wiped his forehead, then climbed down the short ladder that was bolted to the side of the signal post. He had just displayed the red-painted wooden arm that would tell the engineer of the northbound Virginia and Truckee train to stop at the Cartwright siding.

Not everyone along the line had their own siding, but an exception had been made for the needs of the Ponderosa. The accommodation had been made, along with a block of stock in the railroad when it was capitalized years earlier, in exchange for a right-of-way easement across Ponderosa land. The Cartwright land holdings lay across the only economically feasible route between Carson City and the Truckee River valley where connection was made with the Central Pacific. Now, anytime the Cartwrights needed freight or passenger service on the Virginia and Truckee Line, they only needed to display the stop signal.

The familiar yellow cars steamed into view to the south, the engine trailing a haze of smoke, the cars rattling and swaying behind.

"Do you have everything, Pa?" Adam asked for perhaps the fourteenth time since they left the house that morning.

"I'm sure I do, son, thank you."

"You have Hop Sing's list," Adam said.

"Right here in my pocket," Ben said, patting the front of his coat. The list was incomprehensible to anyone but Hop Sing, but represented items, mostly spices, that were not available locally. When they got to San Francisco, Ben would give the list to Hop Sing's cousin Leo Chang, whose sister Beatrice worked at the Connor House where Ben generally stayed when in the city; she would give the list to another cousin, named Lee, who Ben had never met and . . . all of that was more complicated than Ben cared to follow; the point was that Hop Sing's relatives would find whatever Hop Sing needed and present the carefully wrapped bundle to Ben upon his departure from the hotel. Ben had no idea how or when payment for these things was ever made. He only knew that whenever he tried to pay the cousins for the contents of the bundles or for their time, they politely but firmly refused.

One other thing he suspected, even if he could not claim to fully know it. If ever he forgot the list or neglected to fetch the bundles home, there would be a mutiny in the household, and he would never hear the end of it from Hop Sing. That was a danger he did not care to risk. Adam had not had to worry about him leaving the precious list behind.

"I'm not even going to ask you, Joe," Adam said. "I can see that you've packed everything you own into those bags."

"Yeah, little brother. You need me to go along just t' carry all that for you," Hoss added with a glance toward the piled luggage, nearly all of which was Little Joe's. Their father had packed for the journey in one large bag and one small one. Joe was taking three large bags and a bundle.

"Now look," Joe began, then made a face and waved his hand in a show of disgust. "Why should I bother? You never listen to me anyhow."

"Of course we listen t' you, little brother. It ain't our fault if you don't never have nothing t' say."

Adam smiled and stepped in front of Joe, reaching out to tug at his collar and smooth the lapels of his brand new suit coat.

"Do I look—"

"You look just fine, Joe."

"This suit . . . ?"

"Is just fine too," Adam assured him.

"But you can see the creases in the trousers."

"By the time you top the mountains and start down for Sacramento, you won't be able to see a hint of crease in those pant legs, Joe. That cloth will wrinkle up soon and be just nice as can be, especially if you think to wallow around some when you're sitting there."

"You think?"

"I'm sure of it."

The problem, of course, was that a man with a crease in the cloth of his trousers was showing that his suit had come off some storekeeper's shelf and that he lacked either the substance or the sense to have his clothing tailored. In short, that he was probably no gentleman. In Joseph's case, his suit *had* just come off a store shelf. Once Ben decided they were going, there hadn't been time enough for a tailor to fit Joseph for a proper suit. And Joseph hadn't thought about the problem of the crease until they were leaving, or he likely would have had Hop Sing working late last night to iron the creases away. Now he was feeling self-conscious about his appearance.

"Time to say good-bye," Ben suggested as the engineer brought the short Virginia and Truckee train of mixed passenger and freight cars to a screeching, squealing halt beside the Ponderosa's small platform.

Ben gave Adam and Hoss each a handshake, and—never mind that people were watching—a bear hug as well.

"Don't worry about anything here, Pa," Adam said. "We'll take care of things for you."

"I know you will, son."

"I will too, Pa. You can count on the both of us."

"I know that, Hoss. I won't even have to think about the place while we're away. Except to miss you two. I expect I'll do a lot of that."

"Aw now, don't get that started, Pa," Hoss groaned.

Joe dismissed his big brothers with an air of studied casualness that he almost, but not quite, brought off. "See you later," was all he said to them. He kept his hands stuffed deep in the pockets of his new suit rather than risk having to shake or hug or any of that nonsense. He sniffed loudly and concentrated on kicking at a splinter on the platform planking.

"Right, Joe. We'll see you later."

"See ya, little brother."

"Yeah, 'bye."

"Good morning, Mr. Cartwright. Going to Reno, are you?"

"We are indeed, Bert."

"It's a fine day for it, sir. Can I help you with your baggage, Mr. Cartwright?"

"Thank you, but Hoss and Adam can manage."

The young men in question took the hint and jumped to get the bags and take them back to the baggage car, where the messenger and two guards were lounging in the open doorway.

Ben, and the train, waited until they returned; then he gave them each another handshake. "We won't be gone long. Six weeks, two months at the most."

"Don't you worry—"

"Take care of yourselves."

They smiled, impulsively hugged once more. Then Ben turned to the green-trimmed passenger coach. "After you, Joseph."

"Yes, Pa." Joe scurried up the steel steps, and his father followed at a somewhat slower pace.

The conductor signaled the engineer to pull away, then he too climbed onto the car. Up forward the engineer applied power to the driving wheels. The hitch couplings clanked and thudded as the slack was taken out, and the cars reluctantly began to roll again.

Joe had already claimed a window seat and was busy waving at his brothers on the platform.

Ben looked out at the sight of Adam and Hoss, their sturdy figures already becoming smaller as the siding fell farther and farther behind. He waved once, knowing the boys could not possibly see him, but giving in to the impulse in spite of that, for his own peace of mind not theirs. Then he settled onto the seat beside Joseph.

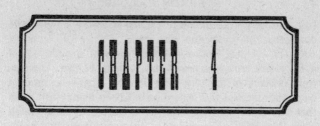

CHAPTER 4

Joe had been to San Francisco before. But the city hadn't seemed anything like this. Of course, he'd been younger then. Just a kid, practically. The last time was two years ago, and he'd been seventeen. Besides, Hoss had always been along before, and sometimes Adam. Those trips had been fun, but they hadn't been anything like this.

The horse-drawn streetcar—much more glamorous somehow than any old hansom cab—clitter-clacked along the fabulous bayfront. It was . . . exciting. To say the least. Ships' masts rose like a forest along the wharf, and bundles and bales of cargo were piled like miniature mountain ranges for near about as far as the eye could see.

There was a smell in the air that filled Joe's lungs and stirred his blood. It was a dank and heavy scent that was almost a stink, and yet was exhilarating. It smelled like dead fish and wet salt and old dogs. And life.

Pa said it was just that the tide was out and the mud flats were exposed to air, but Joe thought it was more than that. It was commerce he was smelling here. Commerce and all the big, wide world that was beyond this one bay, beyond even the whole Pacific Ocean.

Joe sat up straight on his seat when he smelled the

41

bay, and he got all the more excited when Pa signaled the conductor that their stop was ahead.

The Connor House was a castle right straight out of a fairy tale. Joe had never stayed there before. The last time he was in the city, with Pa and Hoss—he thought back and decided that Adam hadn't been along with them that trip—they were still staying at the old Monitor Hotel. There had been a succession of different places that Pa favored. The Monitor Hotel had been a nice one, if a mite stuffy and nose-in-the-air for Joe's tastes. He'd been sorry that it burned down. Now he was almost glad since that meant he and Pa were going to be staying at this grand and fancy Connor House.

There was a fellow, a man, with skin the color of old mahogany, standing outside the front doors. He was dressed head to foot in a uniform sort of rig complete with cocked hat, gold braid, bright buttons, buff leggins, and buff-colored lapels wide enough for two kids and a kitten to hide behind.

"Who's that, Pa? Some admiral or something?"

Pa looked like he was choking on something. "No, son, that's the doorman."

"Is he one of those black fellas you told us about?"

"Uh-huh."

"He looks like anybody else except darker."

"That's right, Joseph. He is like anyone else. Except darker. His name is Thomas." Pa smiled. "But you can call him Mr. Carter."

"Yes, Pa."

The streetcar came to a stop, and the conductor helped them gather up their luggage and transfer it all to the ground.

"Mistuh Cartwright, suh, how come you to be riding in this contraption 'stead of a propuh vehicle, suh? You. Scat. Just you get away from Mistuh Cartwright's things heah. Yo, boy. Quick now."

With a great waving of arms and pointing of fingers, Mr. Carter sent the streetcar conductor slinking away and summoned his own work force of dark-skinned boys, who swarmed out of the hotel, snatched up all the luggage in sight, and disappeared indoors like a horde of ants cleaning up a tidbit dropped on the picnic grounds. One moment things were there, the next they were gone.

Joe blinked, not entirely sure he should trust his eyes. Those boys—bellhops, Pa said, and for sure they hopped to it—were wearing less glamorous versions of Mr. Carter's admiral outfit. Joe could accept that, all right. Except for their caps. They were wearing caps that were, he could have sworn it, just like he'd seen on organ grinders' monkeys. The caps looked like little red sewing baskets turned upside down and held in place with narrow straps. Now, whatever would prompt someone to wear a sewing basket on his head? That was what Joe wanted to know. He shook his head. The Connor House was grand, but it was sure odd too.

"This way, Mistuh Cartwright, suh. Please come this way."

"Thank you, Thomas. And by the way, I'd like you to meet my youngest son, Joseph. Joseph, this is Mr. Carter."

Joe smiled, bobbed his head and stuck out his hand to shake. Mr. Carter gave him a funny sort of look—Joe couldn't begin to figure out what it meant—and hesitated for a moment before he carefully scrubbed his palm dry by rubbing it against the side of his fancy coat and then reached out to shake hands. Mr. Carter's hand was large and rough and warm. "My pleasure, young Mistuh Cartwright."

"Nice t' meet you, Mr. Carter."

Mr. Carter smiled and bowed and then turned back to Pa. "Allow me to help you inside, suh."

"Thank you, Thomas."

Mr. Carter held the door for them to pass through, and then, chin high, marched quickly ahead of them so he could announce their arrival—loudly; everyone in the lobby was informed that Messers Benjamin and Joseph

Cartwright of the Ponderosa ranch, Nevada, were in residence—to the pair of clerks at the front desk.

The clerks were dressed as grandly in their own way as Mr. Carter. Both men wore morning coats and mattress-striped trousers, although they were hatless. The taller of the two bowed as low as his position behind the counter allowed. "How nice to see you again, Mr. Cartwright. I've taken the liberty of having your things placed in your usual suite. Will that be satisfactory, sir?"

"Actually, John, I'll be needing something larger this time. This is my youngest son, Joseph. He will be staying with me and will want his own bedroom. Can you see to that, please?"

"Of course, sir. That will be no problem. We can accommodate you in Suite B, I believe." The tall clerk, John, smiled and bowed and at the same time reached out in the direction of the other clerk and snapped his fingers. The smaller clerk blinked once and bolted away. "Everything will be taken care of by the time you go upstairs, gentlemen."

There was something about John that Joe wasn't sure he liked. And he noticed that Pa told the fellow who he was but never did really make it into an introduction, so Joe guessed Pa felt something of the same. Still, John was efficient enough, and that was what he was here for, Joe supposed.

"Will you be going up now, Mr. Cartwright, or would you like messenger service first?"

"The messenger, I think. And we'll have brandy."

"Very good, sir." John bowed, and Pa went off to one side of the lobby—which wasn't as large as Joe might have expected but which made up for that by how plush and ornate it was, all covered with Oriental rugs and gilt columns and skinny, odd-looking potted plants that Pa said were little palm trees.

There was an alcove Pa took him to where there were overstuffed armchairs to sit in, a couple love seats with velvet upholstery, and two desks with spindly legs and leather inlaid writing surfaces. The hotel provided pens, ink, and tiny envelopes, where a body could sit and write out the addresses for a messenger boy to deliver engraved calling cards to show that one was in town and could be expected to call within the next few days.

"Will we be going to the brewery this trip, Pa?"

Pa smiled. "You remember that, do you?"

"Yes, sir." Joe grinned. "I liked Mr. Troyer."

"As I recall, he let you taste some of the product."

"Yes, sir."

"That was a long time ago. A fun time, though." Pa sighed. "Mr. Troyer died, you know."

"Mr. Phil did? Why didn't you tell—"

"No, no, I meant his father, old Mr. Troyer."

"Oh. I don't remember him, Pa. Just Mr. Phil. He's the one I liked so much."

Pa shook his head. "Sometimes I forget."

"Forget what, Pa?"

He smiled and shook his head again. "It isn't important." His expression brightened. "But I'll tell you what. We'll call on Phil at the brewery this trip. I'm sure he will be glad to see you again."

"Good. And the ships? Will the ships be in port now?"

"I don't know. Mr. DeShong can tell us."

Joe knew about rather few of the family's many business involvements, but there were some that he knew and cared about. The small fleet of sailing ships that carried timber from Oregon and Washington down to the lumber-hungry California markets were one of his father's greatest joys, and in truth Joe liked to see them too. As for the brewery, the last time he'd been there, Joe really had liked Mr. Phil awfully well. And he'd liked the product rather well also. The brewery was a Troyer family operation, just like the Ponderosa was operated by the Cartwrights as a family. Somehow—Joe wasn't clear on all the details—Pa had helped old Mr. Troyer get his start in the early days, and so there was some small involvement that Pa held in the brewery and in the bakery that had been the start of the Troyer ventures in California. All that Joe was sure of, though, was that he liked the folks involved and that Mr. Phil had given him his first sips of tart, bubbly beer. Matters of actual business Joe was perfectly willing to leave to Pa and to Adam. He had other things of greater interest to chew on. Especially now that he was a man grown.

"I, uh, don't suppose we could stop in and try our luck in one of the gaming halls one evening," he mused aloud as Pa was finishing up with addressing the envelopes and slipping his engraved cards into them for the messenger to deliver.

"Probably," Pa said, tucking the flap inside the front of one of the tiny envelopes and dropping it onto the tray with the others. "I was thinking we might want to take in some shows while we're in town too."

"Shows, Pa? Like with . . . dancing and singing and all that?"

"Mm-hmm." Pa reached for another envelope and dipped the nib of the pen into the inkwell.

Singing? *Dancing?* In Virginia City and in Carson City it was rumored that the most beautiful women in all the world were right here in San Francisco. And that some of the naughtier ones of them danced in public at the shows put on in certain of the city's night spots.

Surely Pa didn't mean for them to take in one of *those* shows. Did he?

Joe began to get even more excited than he already was, a condition he wouldn't have thought possible until now that it was happening.

Ben was becoming worried. Not a lot, perhaps. But worried nonetheless. His plan for taking Joseph's mind off that tent-show dancer back in Virginia City didn't seem to be working. Not, at least, that Ben could determine.

The simple truth was that Joseph was being unnaturally silent on the subject of Samantha Whittacker, who called herself—Ben grimaced at the thought—Sam.

Joseph hadn't once ever really discussed, not in so many words, his intended purchase of a diamond ring for this talented terpsichorean from ... who knew where. Hadn't discussed in any way, shape, or form his intentions toward the young lady in question.

Ben had hoped, among other things, that the time he and Joseph spent together during this trip to San Francisco would help prompt the boy to open up on the subjects of Samantha Whittacker and, if need be, of marriage, family, all of that.

This whole business, really, was enough to give a father heartburn. But the father was the only one who seemed to be experiencing any form of discomfort. Joseph careened gaily from one new sight to another with never a backward glance. Or at least never a somber comment.

Ben supposed that should be considered enough of a benefit, just knowing that for these past weeks in the city, Joseph's mind had been occupied with something other than Miss Whittacker.

Somehow that was not enough to lift Ben's spirits.

Not when Blauhaus had brought engagement rings to sell.

Not when Joseph was so unnaturally silent about that particular subject when in his father's company.

Any other time Ben could remember, on any other subject he could ever recall, Joseph would have been wide-eyed with excitement and as voluble as he was eager. The boy wore his heart on his sleeve, rarely held an emotion unvented or a thought unspoken. Whenever Joseph became enthused about something—an occurrence that normally happened at the rate of approximately four or five major enthusiasms per month—the normal result was a brightness in his eyes and an explosion of conversation. Quite frankly, the boy's mouth ran as fast as his enthusiasm on any given subject. Normally. Ben sighed. Not this time, it seemed. Not this time at all.

During this whole trip, Joseph had been eager to see, to learn, to do, to experience. He stood patiently throughout the fittings for his new suit, and now would likely have primped and preened in front of a mirror for hours if there hadn't been other activities of even greater interest available.

He explored every vat and hopper in the Troyer brewery, and chattered for hours with young David Thornton Kendall III—Ben had some small amount of difficulty accepting the idea that Davy was an attorney just like his father, but Joseph did not; D. Thornton Kendall had been the Cartwrights' lawyer for years—and listened with rapt attention while the family's San Francisco factor Alton DeShong reported on the smallest details and most unlikely rumors of every business venture he handled on behalf of Cartwright Enterprises. Joseph had been enthralled by all of that. And enthralled even more by the ornate gaming halls, the grand theaters and opera houses that his father took him to.

Practically every night for the nearly three weeks they'd been in the city, the two gentlemen from Nevada had put in an appearance at one or more of San Francisco's storied night spots.

Ben's unspoken hope was that something in all of this would burst whatever logjam it was that held Joseph's mouth closed on the subjects of Samantha Whittacker and marriage. He had hoped that the sight of an ankle more shapely than Miss Whittacker's or a smile even sweeter, a dimple dearer, a lip softer and more enticing, would somehow cause Joseph to open up and discuss with his father whatever his hopes and aspirations were as regarded the mysterious young lady whose father was a snake oil peddler and whose occupation was that of a dancer in a tent show.

Not that Ben opposed Joseph's desires, exactly. After all, he had yet to actually meet this young lady about whom he had heard little but imagined much. She might be quite wonderful, after all, and entirely worthy of Joseph's affections.

But, well, a father worried. That was it in a nutshell.

A father worried about his sons. Wanted to guard and protect them. Wanted for his heirs decency and honor and happiness.

And Joseph . . . Ben sighed again. The truth was that he had no idea, none, what Joseph's dreams were nowadays, what his hopes, his desires, his intentions. Had Joseph actually asked the girl to marry him? If so, it was not something Joseph had admitted to his father.

Had he not had time to ask the question before this unexpected trip west began? That, Ben concluded, was probably what happened. None of them had anticipated this trip. Ben himself would not have undertaken it so abruptly if it hadn't been for his concerns about Joseph and Miss Whittacker. And so Joseph was brought away before arrangements could be made for the purchase of a ring. Now that he thought upon it, Ben was certain Joseph would not want to ask so weighty a question as that unless he had the ring already in his pocket. So, no, probably there had as yet been no formal declaration between the two.

Could Joseph be keeping his silence out of some fear that the young lady might reject his troth?

Ben smiled a little. No, he quickly decided, that couldn't be it. Joseph's enthusiasms were such that the boy invariably believed the whole wide wonderful world shared them with him. If it was marriage he was bent upon, it would never occur to him that his suit might be rejected.

Then, as quickly as that thought came to him, Ben sobered again. Joseph hadn't expressed any desire to visit any of the jewelers in the city while they were here. Did that mean a ring had already been decided upon? Ordered, perhaps?

That could explain his son's seeming patience while they were away. He could be allowing time for the engagement ring to arrive in Virginia City. Then, when they were back home again, he would collect it and put forth his proposal of marriage to Miss Samantha Whittacker.

Ben groaned a little. If that were the case, then this entire venture was time wasted.

Unless Joseph did open up to him, asked for his father's advice on this most important of all decisions.

What had he done so wrong, Ben asked himself, that now, when Joseph needed him the most, the boy would not feel comfortable enough with his father's counsel to so much as seek it?

Where had he failed as a father?

What could he do now to correct the situation and—

"Pa."

Ben blinked.

"Pa!"

"Yes, son?"

"Are you all right, Pa?"

"Of course. Why do you ask?"

"You're sitting there looking like you just swallowed a cactus button, prickly spines and all."

"Was I?"

"Yes sir, you was."

"Were," Ben corrected.

"All right, you were."

"That's better."

"Maybe so, but you didn't answer my question."

"Yes, I did."

"If you say so, Pa."

"I'm fine, son. Really."

Joseph smiled. "All right, then."

Ben sighed. "We've done about everything we need to take care of here," he said. "We could start back home soon." He looked at Joseph closely, trying to gauge the boy's reaction to the news that they would be starting back. Back to Samantha Whittacker.

"Could we go to the Gilded Lily one more time before we leave, Pa?"

"If you like, yes."

"Tonight?"

"That would be fine."

"I'll wear my new suit," Joseph said, beaming.

This trip, for the first time in ... well, possibly for the first time ever, Joseph's father was completely unable to figure him out. Why *wouldn't* the boy open up to him?

CHAPTER 5

W e aren't taking the ferry?"
Ben shook his head. "Not this time." Joseph
smiled, but Ben couldn't decide if he should take
his son's pleasure at face value or not.

The quick and usual way home from the city would
be to take the Central Pacific–operated ferry across the bay
to Vallejo to make the rail connection east. Bypassing the
ferry in favor of one of the sternwheel steamers that plied
the American River meant a much slower trip than usual
would be in store for the travelers.

But to Ben, taking the sternwheeler meant he would
be able to spend that much more time on the water, which
he thoroughly enjoyed for its own sake, and meant as well
that he would have that much more time alone with Joseph
before the youngster was once again within the emotional
snares of Miss Samantha Whittacker.

Joseph, Ben suspected, might not have thought out
the additional delay involved here and could well be re-
acting solely to the novelty of riverboat travel.

Still, he seemed pleased enough for the moment, and
that was good enough for his father.

"How far will the boat take us, Pa?"

Ben took a look at the long, shallow-draft steam ves-
sel *Niels Haakinen* and tried without success to arrive at a

reasoned estimate. In the end he could only shrug and say, "It depends on how much water the river is carrying." Then he smiled and added, "That and the captain's nerve."

"Will we get as far as Sacramento?"

"Oh yes, I'm sure she'll take us above Sacramento."

"And after that, Pa?"

"After that we'll go overland the rest of the way, by coach if we can, or wagon if we have to. The road runs parallel to the river along there anyway. We'll be able to find something."

Joseph's smile turned into a grin. A trip like this was more than just a journey, it was an adventure too. A tame one perhaps, but an adventure just the same.

"You know," Ben mused aloud, "you might want to send some of your luggage ahead. We could ship it home by rail and have it waiting for us when we arrive. There would be less for you to carry that way; you know, when we transfer to the stagecoach or whatever."

"Oh, I wouldn't want to be without my new suits, Pa. And I for sure need everything in that bag there. And . . . well, I just don't think there's any of it I can do without until we get home, that's all."

"Do however you wish, son. Just so long as you remember it's apt to be you doing all the lifting and carrying."

"I don't mind that, Pa."

"All right, then, whatever you say."

They ignored the Central Pacific office where freight and passenger service could be arranged for points east—as far as Boston or Baltimore, if that was what one desired—and headed for the gangplank of the slab-sided and inelegant but lively *Niels Haakinen* instead.

Ben was fighting a losing battle. He couldn't keep his face straight.

"Pa!"

"Sorry, son."

"Well?"

"What?"

"Well, aren't you going to give me a hand?"

Ben laughed. "Oh, I think you're doing fine as you are, Joseph. Just, um, carry on."

The stagecoach messenger leaned down to accept another suitcase from Joseph's outstretched hands and transfer it onto the pile already accumulated atop the roof of the bright green passenger vehicle. Joseph turned and went back to the wharf to gather up the rest of his things and lug them the block and a half to where the coach was waiting. Ben handed up his own single bag and the oilcloth-wrapped bundle he was taking back to Hop Sing.

"That your boy?" the stage line employee asked.

"Yes, he is."

"Travels heavy, don't he?" The messenger sent a glance in Joseph's direction, turned his head aside and spat a stream of brown tobacco juice into the dusty road.

"I hadn't realized just how heavy until now," Ben admitted.

The messenger grinned and said, "Whatcha wanta bet he didn't think of it neither."

Ben chuckled.

"You want me t' go help him, mister?"

"Thank you, but no."

"Not for the money or nothing like that, just as a favor, like. I mean, I wouldn't mind doin' it."

"Thank you very much, but I think it's best if we let him manage on his own."

"Yeah, well, that's kinda why I asked. You know?"

Ben grinned and nodded. Down at the wharf where the *Niels Haakinen* had unloaded, Joseph was still busy trying to arrange the remainder of his things in his arms so he could complete the transfer with this one last load. He managed, but barely, having to balance his bags and bundles with all the precision of a juggler in order to accomplish it.

Ben truly hadn't appreciated just how much Joseph

had added to his luggage while they were in San Francisco. There had been the two new suits, of course. Joseph needed an extra bag for those alone. And then there were the new shirts to go with the suits. Stockings. Extra trousers. Shoes. Presents for Hoss and Adam . . . and several other presents that hadn't been mentioned in detail, presumably therefore intended for Miss Whittacker. Another bag had to be added to contain all those. There was also a derby hat in its own light but bulky pasteboard container. And that was on top of everything Joseph had insisted on bringing with him to start the journey. He had been carrying too much when they left the Ponderosa to begin with. Now . . . All in all it made for an impressive mound of baggage. So much that Ben almost sympathized with his youngest son's plight. But not quite.

The stagecoach messenger chuckled and spat again. And waited patiently for Joseph to stagger and stumble the rest of the way from wharf to coach depot so they could finish loading everything and lash a tarp over it all.

"Sure must be nice t' be young and full o' vim," the messenger commented.

Ben smiled and crossed his arms. If the stagecoach line was willing to be patient about this, so was he.

"Sign here, mister, or you can make your mark and I'll fill the rest in for you."

"I can sign, thanks."

"You, mister?"

"I'll sign for myself too," Joseph said. The clerk of the Bent Lodge in Johns Bend seemed impressed. Two customers in a row who had cash to pay for their room in advance, and could sign their own names too. When they'd first approached the Bent Lodge, Joseph had giggled at the name and commented on the hotelkeeper's sense of humor. A Bent Lodge in Johns Bend. Cute. That was until his father pointed out a signboard noting B. CAR-LISLE BENT, PROPRIETOR, EST. 1858, presumably referring to the time the hotel was established, not the proprietor.

The clerk—who might or might not have been Mr. Bent; he hadn't introduced himself—dipped his chin to peer over the top of his wire half-spectacle frames while he eyed the mountain of luggage that had been deposited on the front porch of the Bent Lodge. He looked at it twice and made no offer to help with the baggage. Ben wasn't sure if there were a connection between those occurrences or not, but he suspected there probably was. The man turned and took two keys down from a hook on the board behind the counter, slapping them down hard on the scarred wood beside the guest register.

"Room seven," he said. "Second floor front. It's the best in the house. Closest to the stairs too."

"That's very considerate of you."

The clerk nodded solemnly.

"Joseph, would you take our things upstairs, please?"

Joseph sighed. "Yes, Pa." He trudged outside and began gathering up his first load. This was going to take a while.

"Anything else I can help you with, Mister . . ." The clerk squinted down at the register, reading it upside down with the facility of long practice, and trying not to be obvious about it. ". . . Cartwaight?"

"That's Cartwright."

"Oh. Sorry."

"No harm. And yes, there is something you might help me with. We're here to visit an old friend. I assume he would be in his office at this hour, but I have no idea where his business offices would be nowadays." Ben smiled. "It has been quite a spell since I've been to Johns Bend."

"Not much ever changes here, Mr. Cartwright. Not very much at all, I'm afraid. Who was it you wanted to find now?"

"Lester Shannon. I assume you know him." Ben was watching Joseph trying to mount the staircase sideways. He was so heavily laden with suitcases that he couldn't fit into the stairwell in a normal posture, and had to turn sideways and crab his way up in order to make any headway.

There was only silence, and after a moment Ben quit admiring Joseph's labored progress and turned back to look at the hotel clerk again. The man was frowning.

"Is there something wrong?" Ben asked.

"Shannon, you say?"

"That's right. Les Shannon. You do know him, surely."

"Knew him," the clerk said crisply.

"Pardon?"

"Don't know him. Knew him. There's a difference."

"Yes, but—"

"Lester Shannon is dead, mister. We buried him. Last week I think it was. On Sunday. Sunday the week ago. Yes, I'm sure of that, now I think on it. Sunday a week ago. The whole town turned out for his services. Do you still want the room or not?"

Ben felt like he'd just been hit in the belly. "Les is dead, you say?"

"Dead and buried, mister. Now do you want the room or not?"

Ben didn't answer. He felt stunned. Les had been a friend. Not a close confidant, perhaps, but certainly a friend. And a friend of many years standing, at that. Now Les was dead. So unexpectedly. Ben's immediate thoughts, now that acceptance was swirling through his emotions, were of Chloe. How lost she must feel. How terribly alone. He had to find her. Tell her he shared her sense of loss. He turned and walked blindly away, leaving the hotel clerk unheard and unheeded at his back.

"Dead? Mister, I reckon. Blew himself up, he did. Tore him up so bad they could only tell it was him 'cause of the ring he was wearing, that's how dead he was. Mister, if you don't mind me saying so, you don't look so good. Here, let me pour you another brandy." The man

fetched down a dust-covered bottle from a shelf behind the
bar and poured a refill.

Ben knocked that one back atop of the first, the
warmth of the liquor spreading through his belly and acting to calm him.

"You okay now, mister?"

Ben nodded. "Yes, thanks."

"I didn't mean to say nothing to upset you, but you
did go an' ask me."

"It wasn't anything you said or did. Really. It's just
. . . such a shock."

"Ayuh. Always is, seems like. And Les, he was a
good man. Had lots of friends in this town, let me tell you.
His kind don't come along every day. He'll be missed."

Ben shuddered, thinking about what the bartender—
where better to seek information?—had told him. Poor
Les. Poor Chloe.

He had started out from the hotel toward the house
Les and Chloe so proudly showed him the last time Ben
visited Johns Bend, then realized that he as yet knew little
about Les's passing. And the answers to those perfectly ordinary questions might be extremely painful for Chloe to
have to give just now. Better, he had decided, to get his information first and then express his sympathies, hence this
visit to a saloon a block and a half from the Bent Lodge.
It was Ben's experience that in any community, the two
men most able to comment on community affairs would be
the bartender and the barber.

Now, with a shudder, he found he was not at all sure
he wanted the information he'd just been given. Les had
been blown—literally—apart. The mere thought of it was
sickening.

"You turned so pale there, mister, that for a minute I
thought we was gonna lose you too. But your color's
comin' back now."

"It's just . . . you know." Ben shook his head sadly.
"It's hard to believe, really. Les was always so careful.

And it certainly isn't like he was any stranger to blasting powder. Why, he used it for years and years."

The bartender grunted and frowned as he mopped up a damp spot on the bar. "Powder wouldn't o' done what was done to poor Les, mister."

"I'm sorry. I don't understand you."

The barman shrugged. "My opinion, mind. There's others as feel different. I expect giant powder has its dangers too. But it isn't so touchy as that stuff Les was using. I say it was Les's lack o' familiarity with these modern chemicals that killed him as much as any carelessness he mighta had."

It was Ben's turn to frown. "Are you saying it wasn't powder that Les was using?"

"That's what I'm saying, mister. 'Twasn't powder atall, but that chemical stuff niter . . . nitra . . . I can't remember the name."

"Nitroglycerin?" Ben prompted.

"That's right. Niter . . . what you said. Mister, you're lookin' pale again. You want another brandy?"

Ben shook his head and, his brow furrowing with concern, turned away from the bar. He took a few paces and dropped into a chair at one of the unoccupied tables in the saloon.

His thoughts were racing. Remembering.

Three years ago? Four? It didn't matter. Les had come to Virginia City to consult with some of the world-renowned mining engineers there about advances in timber shoring techniques. It had been only natural that he and Ben had gotten together several evenings to enjoy each other's fellowship. And one of the things Ben recalled Les talking about with another gent in the billiards room one of those evenings—getting into a drag-out argument was closer to the truth of it—was the use of nitroglycerin in mining.

All the weight of logic was on the Nevada gentleman's side. Nitro was cheap and efficient. Overwhelmingly more powerful than coarse blasting powder, it allowed the drillers to achieve results with holes a sixth the size required for powder. Cutting the size if not always the depth of the holes meant a significant savings in time and therefore expense. The savings in the cost of labor alone could be enormous. Why, a drilling crew using nitro could prepare two, sometimes three, blasting shots in the same time, and for the same pay, that it would take to prepare one shot with powder. A mine being carved with nitroglycerin—or now with the even newer and much more stable dynamite charges—was plainly and simply far more cost efficient than one operating with old-fashioned blasting powder. The Nevada miner had all the facts and figures to support his claims on the subject, and they were undeniable.

Les, however, was not to be swayed by logic. Certainly not that night. Nitro was fickle, finicky stuff, he claimed, and he was quite plainly frightened of it. And even though he was long past the point of having to go underground and act as his own powder monkey then—and this, Ben remembered now, was several years past—he would ask no man to do a job for him that Les would not have been willing to do for himself. And that included the handling of nitroglycerin. Les would not touch a bottle of it himself, nor would he bring any of the treacherous stuff onto his property for another to mishandle. Giant powder had been good enough all his life, Les declared to the Virginia City mine owner that night, and it would continue to be good enough until Lester Shannon was dead and gone.

Well, Ben ruefully thought, now Les Shannon was dead and gone indeed. And now this bartender was telling him that it was nitroglycerin that killed him. How horribly ironic, Ben thought. If only Les had stuck by the hidebound—but safe—convictions he'd displayed that night, tonight Chloe Shannon might not be a widow.

It was a sad, sad situation.

Ben took a moment more to just sit and regain control of his emotions, then paid for his drinks and headed once more for the Shannon home. He was doubly glad now, though, that he'd stopped at the saloon first. It would have been much too painful for Chloe to have told him the things the bartender did.

With a sigh in his throat, and his heart heavy in his chest, he tugged the bell pull beside the opulent stained-glass front door to the Shannon home.

In all the years Ben had known the Shannons, Chloe had hardly changed. Except, that is, for a certain shading of gray in her hair, and that was an area in which Ben had no room to be judgmental. Chloe Shannon was short and plump, her features appearing to have been molded from smooth balls of pastry dough. Generally she was every bit as jolly as her form might suggest. Ben doubted he had seen her angry—not sad, mind, but angry—more than . . . well *ever,* now that he thought on it.

Until now, that is.

Chloe answered the ringing of the doorbell with a scowl as she snatched the door open and lifted an accusing finger in the general direction of Ben's suddenly wide-open eyes.

Both Chloe Shannon and her caller drew back and stiffened in quick alarm. Ben recovered first, snatching his hat off and starting to bow even though this form of entirely unexpected greeting had him decidedly off balance.

Chloe gasped, blinked, lowered her now trembling finger. "Ben? Ben Cartwright. Is it really you?"

"I wrote to Les a month ago that I'd be coming by, Chloe, but I never thought . . . I mean, I certainly had no idea that . . . Chloe, I am *so* sorry about Les. Truly I am."

She acted like she hadn't heard, or anyway hadn't comprehended. "It is you, Ben. Heaven's sakes, it is. Come in, Ben. I'm sorry if I . . . that is to say, I never meant to . . . oh, dear." She blinked some more and seemed to shiver. "Come inside, Ben. Please."

She guided him to the parlor of the home the Shannons had been so proud to show off when it was first built. Ben was careful to avoid the chair that had been

Les's. Chloe's was still drawn close beside it, so that the two of them could share the use of a single footstool. Les's pipe rack and humidor of tobacco still sat on a tiny table beside his chair. One pipe, an old but much favored meerschaum, lay amid dark dottle in an ashtray, its bowl still packed with gray-tinged ash from the last time Les smoked it.

"Sit down, Ben. Can I get you something? Coffee, liquor, something to eat?"

"Nothing, Chloe, thank you. The question really should be what can I do for you. You know, I hope, that you have my sympathies. This news," Ben shook his head, "it is shocking. Awful. I can't begin to tell you—"

"I know, Ben. Thank you."

He sighed. "I know how terrible your loss has been."

Chloe reached forward and patted Ben's wrist. "When most people tell me that, dear friend, I know they mean well but that they don't fully understand what they are saying. With you it is different. I remember how it was with you and Marie. I know how much you still miss her. You really do understand, don't you?"

Ben nodded. He still missed Elizabeth and Inger too, but Chloe and Les had known only Joseph's dear mother.

"Does the sense of loss ever go away, Ben?"

He shook his head. "No. But over time it becomes easier to bear. A little and then a little more."

"I have that to look forward to anyway, then. Thank you. For your honesty most of all." For just a moment her round, normally serene features twisted in a brief show of the pain she tried to hide. Then she recovered and sat back in her chair, smoothing the apron that lay over her lap. She managed a smile. "Les always said you were the most honest man he was ever privileged to know, Ben. Did you know that?"

Ben shook his head again.

"I can't tell you how many times he said that to me."

"I take that as a high compliment, Chloe, and I would

have to say that Les was extraordinarily honest himself. But then he was a good man in many, many ways."

"Yes, he was, Ben." She pulled a bit of calico cloth from the pocket of her apron and dabbed her eyes to dry them.

"Are you all right, Chloe? I mean . . . of course you miss Les, but . . . you know. Other than that," he finished lamely.

"Certainly, Ben, but thank you for asking."

"Forgive me if I'm intruding, but when you came to the door just now, you acted like, well, like you were upset with whoever you thought was calling."

"Oh, it's just that I thought it was someone else. Obviously."

"What can I do to help, Chloe?"

"Nothing, Ben. Really."

And that was absolutely all he could get her to say on the subject. Since he did not wish to cause Les's widow any discomfort, he let the subject drop and exchanged it for something that would be of greater interest to Chloe. For the next hour and a half the two of them sat in Les and Chloe's parlor and talked about the old days when they were all, the Shannons and the Cartwrights alike, young and vigorous and filled with the excitement of challenge and promise and opportunity.

Those had been good days, genuinely so, and soon Chloe warmed to the memories. Soon she was smiling and occasionally even laughing as she and this old friend thought back to the joys, and to the foibles, of their struggling youth.

The afternoon was spent much more pleasantly than Ben would have anticipated, considering the purpose of his call here, and it was reluctantly that he remembered his manners and left before he might become a burden on his still grieving hostess.

"Give my best to your sons, Ben," Chloe said as he took his leave.

"I will, of course, Chloe, but I'll be in town for a few

days more. If you wouldn't mind, perhaps we could visit again."

"I'd like that, Ben. Very much."

He smiled and bent low over her hand, then walked away, his face carefully masking his feelings. How sad it was that poor Chloe had to remain alone in this huge, fine house that she and Les had built.

At least, despite all else, he had had his boys, with whom he could share life and hope, joy and sorrow, since the deaths of his beloved helpmeets. Chloe and Les had not been blessed with children. And now that one of them was gone, the other was so terribly alone.

Ben felt sadness as he left the Shannon house, but also an appreciation of the gifts that had been granted to him, family being first and foremost among them, and indeed perhaps the only one of God's gifts that truly counted for anything.

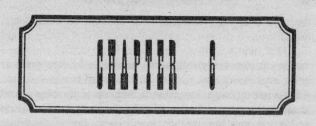

CHAPTER 6

Joe looked at the pile of luggage with a sigh and a bit of a groan. Something was definitely wrong here. There couldn't be this much of it that was his. Surely Pa was putting one over on him somehow. If only he could see through the trick that was being used ...

He grunted softly and concluded that even though there was so very much that had to be carried downstairs again, the result would make the effort worthwhile, for Joe was anxious to start for home now. The trip to San Francisco had been wonderful—in ways that Pa knew and in a few more that he didn't—but Johns Bend was a bust as far as Joe was concerned. There was nothing in this fading old camp to hold anyone's interest. There was an opera house, but it was boarded up and held nothing now but cobwebs and memories. Joe knew that for a certain fact because he'd peeked in through some gaps in the boards over the windows. Dust and mouse droppings were about all there was to be seen inside the musty old building now. The point was, the quicker they started for home, the better Joe would like it, and never mind how much luggage he had to shift in order for that happy event to occur.

He took another look to make sure everything was ready. There were only two stage runs between Johns Bend and the railroad each day, and if Pa got back from his visit with Mrs. Shannon soon enough, they could still be in time to catch the evening coach. Near as Joe could figure it, that would put them into Reno station sometime in the early morning tomorrow, and home by, say, noon or a bit after. With any kind of luck, he could be in Virginia City visiting with his friends tomorrow evening. And wearing his next-to-best new suit too. That San Francisco tailor had done him mighty proud. He took a quick gander in the hotel room mirror, shot his cuffs and struck a chin-high, chest-out pose. Noble, he judged. Mighty noble indeed, if he did say so.

"Joseph?"

Pa! He'd come in so quick and unexpected that Joe hadn't realized until too late that—

"Do you have something in your eye, Joseph?"

"No, sir."

"Something wrong with your back?"

"No, sir."

"Then why are you standing there like that? You're puffed up like a pouter pigeon. Are you sure you're all right?"

"Fine, Pa." Joe felt a rush of warmth into his cheeks and fumbled for something, anything, to explain away the posturing. "I was just . . . breathing, Pa."

"Breathing?"

"That's right. Deep breathing." Once he'd found a hook to hang his explanation onto, he quickly warmed to it. And to avoid lying to his father, he, well, breathed. Deeply. "You should try it, Pa. Real deep now. In." Joe breathed in. "Out." He exhaled. Loudly. "Fills the old lungs, see, and makes you feel good. Come on, Pa. Try it. In . . . out . . . in . . . out." Joe heeded his own instructions, and after a moment his father mimicked the example Joe was setting. "In . . . out . . . in . . . out. Doesn't it make you feel good?"

"Maybe. A little."

"Sure it does. In . . . out." With each "in," Joe went up onto his tiptoes as if filling himself so full of air he was growing lighter. Then as he exhaled he came down again onto his heels. "In . . . out."

Pa smiled and shook his head. "Wherever did you hear about that one?" he asked.

Joe grinned and shrugged. "Some fella." Which was true enough. He'd seen some fella do this, for sure. Of course it hadn't been in Johns Bend and it hadn't been all that recent either. It was last summer—he remembered the incident perfectly well—in Virginia City when Big Nose Charlie White was training to meet Howard Hard Hands Hawkins for the middleweight combined championship of the California and Nevada mining districts. Hawkins was the Comstock champ, while Charlie White represented California. White was an advocate of deep breathing as a health-giving measure, while Hawkins preferred running to the top of Sun Mountain twice each day as the basis of his training regimen. The efficacy of deep breathing suffered a setback when Hard Hands Hawkins knocked Big Nose Charlie White out in the eighteenth round of the bout, and Joe hadn't thought much about the method since then. But it came in handy again now. "Feels good don't it, Pa?"

"Not bad," he admitted.

"The trick is to breathe real deep, real deep, that's right. On your toes. In . . . out." Joe grinned and swung his arms in a windmill motion like Big Nose Charlie used to do when he was through breathing. His father quit the exercise without the additional motion.

"Did you see Mrs. Shannon?" Joe asked. "Is she doing all right?"

"I saw her, but I'm not sure how she's doing. Of course it's much too soon for anyone to know. It takes some time for the impact of the loss to be felt. Right now her feelings have been numbed by the shock of it all, I suspect. It could be weeks or even months before she begins to adjust."

"That's a shame, Pa."

"Yes, it is, son. I remember when your mother—" He stopped, his features twisting from the pain of that long-ago loss, and Joe felt a sharp pang of sorrow; for his father and, to be honest about it, somewhat less, for the mother he could not really recall.

"While you were gone," Joe said, wanting to change the subject, "I checked with the man at the desk downstairs. There's a coach this evening at half past six. We have plenty of time to make it if you're ready."

His father gave Joe a quizzical look. "Did you think we would be leaving so soon, Joseph?"

"I just ... you know ... I thought with Mr. Shannon killed and everything ... well, I just thought there wouldn't be any reason to be staying here anymore."

"I see. Are you so anxious to get home?"

"Not ... I mean ..."

"You can go ahead if you like, Joseph. You could take a crew down to the flats and gather those colts, I suppose. That needs to be done soon. They need to be gelded and started in harness. I intended putting you in charge of that anyway. There is no reason why you can't start the job without me."

"No, I, um, just didn't know what you wanted t' do, Pa. I'm in no hurry to get back." He might have felt some eagerness for the task if it had involved breaking young horses to saddle. At least there was some fun in that, some excitement and some thrill. But getting horses started in harness was merely tedious and time-consuming. It was, bluntly, work. And even a place as dull as Johns Bend was preferable to that.

"Good," Pa said, "because I want to stay here a few days more. I want to make sure Mrs. Shannon will be all right."

"Of course she will, Pa. Mr. Shannon owned half of Johns Bend. Everybody knows that."

"So they do, I suppose, but it isn't the lady's finances that concern me. When I first arrived, Joseph, Mrs. Shannon seemed very upset when she answered my ring. She calmed down when she saw who I was, but the fact remains she was quite upset to begin with. I don't want to pry, son, but I do want to satisfy myself that she is all right before we leave."

"Whatever you say, Pa."

"If you're sure, Joseph. You're free to go on ahead of me if you like."

"Yes, sir. Thank you."

"And in any event I suggest we go downstairs to supper. They're serving a roast this evening, I believe. I could smell it when I came through the lobby just now. Are you ready to go down?"

"Yes, sir. Right with you." Joe gave himself one more quick and surreptitious inspection in the mirror, then followed his father into the hallway and down the stairs.

Joe propped his right foot on the polished brass rail that stretched along the front of the massive, carved walnut bar. He felt pretty good, his belly warm and full after a good supper, and now with a foaming, slightly bitter beer in front of him. Pa wouldn't have minded if he'd ordered a brandy instead, but Joe hadn't developed a taste for the biting flavor of brandy. A plain beer was enough to satisfy him.

"Cigar?"

"No thanks," Joe said to the bartender. That was another taste he had yet to acquire.

"When you're ready for a refill, speak up."

"Thank you, sir."

The barman nodded pleasantly and retreated down the length of the long, handsome bar.

"Hauling this in without a railroad must have been some job," his father mused.

"It must have been," Joe agreed. And it was true. The wooden bar was massive, probably weighing upward of a ton. It was all of one piece, though, and would have presented some freighter with quite the challenge to overcome. That unknown freighter had managed to bring the bar in intact, but the back-bar mirror either had not survived or was never attempted, for instead of the normal lone large mirror section, there was an expanse made up of many small mirrors set into a framework that almost but not quite matched the color of the walnut around it. Even so, whoever hauled the bar in over twisting mountain roads had done a fine, proud job.

Pa finished off his brandy with a sigh of pleasure and began to fill the bowl of his pipe from the leather tobacco pouch he always carried. "Ready to go back to the hotel, son?" he asked.

"I'm not sleepy yet, Pa. Would you mind if I stayed here a spell?" Joe had his eye on the gaming tables which were active in the back end of the saloon. A friendly game was kind of fun, he'd long since determined.

"Stay if you like, then. I'll leave the lamp trimmed low and the door open. Mind you're quiet when you come to bed."

"I won't be long, Pa."

"One thing, Joseph."

"Yes, sir?"

"Remember what I've told you about gambling with strangers."

Joe felt his cheeks grow warm again. Just a little. "Pa! You don't have to treat me like I'm some little kid. You know?"

His father smiled and reached up as if to ruffle Joe's already curly hair. Then he thought better of the gesture and at the last moment brought his hand down to take hold of Joe's shoulder and squeeze it lightly. "I know, son. It's just that fathers can't help but be concerned. Even when their sons are all grown up."

"I won't be late, Pa."

"Good." His father winked at him. "Good night, son."

"G'night, Pa."

His father paused long enough to light his pipe from a candle on the bar provided for the purpose, then ambled out into the night.

Joe smiled expansively at the sight of the busy saloon

and its patrons. He fingered the coins that lay in his pocket, trying to recall just how much he had with him at the moment. All he possessed, that was for sure. It was just that he couldn't remember how much that was. No matter. He felt lucky tonight. Really lucky.

Carrying the beer with him, he drifted back in the direction of the gaming tables.

CHAPTER 7

Movement seen in the mirror before him caught Ben's attention. He straightened, wiping the blade of his razor on the hand towel, and turned with a smile. "Good morning, Joseph. Did you sleep well?"

Joseph yawned and blinked. He was seated on the side of his bed, his dark hair tousled and unruly and his bare legs so pale and hairy he looked somewhat like a chicken in serious need of further plucking.

"You got in earlier than I expected last night," Ben persisted. "Is everything all right?"

Joseph nodded, yawned again and began knuckling his eyes so vigorously it looked to his father as if it should hurt.

"Come out ahead, did you?"

Joseph smacked his lips, paused, finally shrugged, the gesture barely perceptible.

"Not ahead," Ben said.

Joseph shook his head and made a face as if he had an exceptionally sour taste in his mouth. And for that matter perhaps he did.

"You lost," Ben said.

Joseph nodded.

"Much?"

Joseph grimaced.

His father smiled. "Cleaned you out, did they?"

"You could say that," Joseph admitted, his voice husky with sleep.

"Everything?"

"Uh-huh. Everything short of the clothes on my back an' the boots on my feet. I think they'd've taken them too, except my stuff wouldn't've fit any o' them."

"Learn anything from it?"

Joseph gave his father a sheepish look. "Yes, sir. Next time I'll listen to what you told us."

"In that case, son, the lesson was worth its price. Now if you're feeling up to taking some breakfast with me . . ."

Ben finished shaving while Joseph stumbled his way through the morning routines, then the two of them went down to the hotel dining room. It amused his father to see that Joseph's appetite was unaffected by his recent reversal of fortunes. The boy ate as if he were in training to compete with Hoss in a hotcake contest. When they were done, Ben gave Joseph a ten-dollar gold eagle and told him, "I don't want you to be broke, but I don't want to see you waste this either."

"No, sir."

"I'm going to be making some calls on several of Lester Shannon's friends here in town. You're welcome to come with me if you like, but you don't have to."

Joseph rubbed his chin. He hadn't taken time to shave before they came downstairs, and his beard stubble was obvious even if it was not particularly heavy. "If you don't mind, Pa, I won't go with you."

"Care for a suggestion?"

"Yes, sir."

"Judging from the way you look this morning, Joseph, I'd say you should find a barber instead of trusting the steadiness of your own hand."

Joseph's grin flashed, and for the first time since waking, he looked himself. "I'll do that, Pa. Promise."

"All right, then. I'll see you later."

"Yes, sir."

Ben dropped his room key off at the desk—he probably should have given it to Joseph, but hadn't thought to—and went out into the early morning sunshine. At this elevation the mornings could be brisk at any time of year. Today the air was just pleasantly cool and the sunlight nicely warm in contrast. Ben knew the way to his destination. He had been there several times before in Les Shannon's company.

A sign painted on the door glass in gilt lettering read: JOHNS BEND INTELLIGENCER, CIRC. 720. Ben went inside.

The newspaper office consisted primarily of one large room with a counter at the front separating the public from the workroom portion, which was dominated by a small press, racks of type, and pile upon pile of baled newsprint. The only person in evidence was a slender young man wearing eyeshades, sleeve garters, and celluloid cuff protectors. He was bent over a metal tray and was using tweezers to set type at a slow and somewhat awkward pace. The young man looked up at the sound of the door opening. "Can I help you, sir?"

"I'm looking for Mr. Vickers. That is, assuming Henry is still editor here."

"He's still the boss, but you won't find him here at this hour, mister. He always stops at the Canterbury to take his coffee first."

"The Canterbury." Ben thought for a moment, then brightened. "Of course. I remember now. A block down and two over? Best tasting sweet buns this side of Boston?"

"Yes, sir, that'd be the place all right."

"In that case I'll try to catch him there. Thank you."

Ben had been to the every-morning coffee gathering at the Canterbury Café once before. With Les, of course. That had been years earlier, and Ben had forgotten about it. All the better class of Johns Bend businessmen were in the habit of taking their coffee there at the time. It seemed they still were. He nodded a good-bye to the young newspaperman-in-training in the *Intelligencer* office and walked the few blocks to the Canterbury.

The Canterbury was large, as cafés went. But then, restaurants were in great demand in the mining camps, as few miners had families with them and even fewer would admit to liking their own cooking. A decent restaurant in any mining camp had to be considered a solid investment. In any event, after not too many false turnings, he found his way to the Canterbury.

A good three-quarters of the tables were occupied at this hour when most businesses in town would be open. The clientele for the most part consisted of men wearing coats and ties rather than a workingman's rough apparel. Ben stood in the doorway for a moment to allow his eyes to adjust to the dimness indoors and to give him time to spot the gentleman he'd come to see. There, in the far corner, he recognized him after several seconds.

"Show you to a table, sir?" a young woman offered.

"Not right now," Ben said. "I want to say hello to Mr. Vickers. And the gentleman on his right. Is that . . . ?" It was on the tip of his tongue, but he couldn't quite lay claim to the name.

"That would be Mr. Keith," the waitress said.

"Of course. The banker." Ben gave the young lady a smile and a wink. "Thanks for saving me some embarrassment."

"My pleasure, sir."

Ben made his way through the tables and stopped beside Henry Vickers, Mr. Keith—Ben thought the banker's first name was George, but was not positive about that—and a gentleman Ben had never met before. All three locals were in their late forties to early fifties and had the appearance of businessmen who were prosperous and well settled in their careers.

When Ben greeted Vickers and Keith by name, Vickers looked up, frowned in concentration, and after a second or two admitted, "You have the advantage of me, sir. I know we've met before, but—"

Ben introduced himself.

"Of course. Forgive me, Mr. Cartwright. You were Shannon's mentor and longtime friend, weren't you? Of course. I remember now how pleased he was when you visited. Join us, won't you?"

Ben took the chair that was offered, and the newspaperman finished the round of introductions. "This is Tom Keith, our mayor and president of the Miners and Merchants Bank." It was just as well he hadn't counted on remembering that the fellow's name was George, Ben conceded. "And this distinguished gentleman here is Craig Albritton. Craig is a lawyer. Also quite the gambler."

Albritton smiled and reached across the table to shake hands. "They are pulling your leg, Mr. Cartwright. They've already exhausted themselves pulling mine. You see, we match coins every morning to see which of us pays for the coffee and sweet rolls. I've managed to lose to these sharps every morning this week, and twice last week as well. I suggest you put little credence in anything either of them may tell you."

"Thank you for the suggestion, Mr. Albritton. Mr. Keith, I believe I've had the pleasure of meeting you before, sir."

"Quite so," the banker agreed. "Les introduced us. Mr. Benjamin Cartwright of the Ponderosa ranch, Virginia City, Nevada. Let me see, that would have been, what, summertime . . . five years ago? Something like that."

"You have a remarkable memory, sir."

"Not really. You see, I am the one who issues the drafts against our accounts, Mr. Cartwright. I've made out drafts in your favor as a stockholder in the Shannon enterprises every quarter for years and years now." His smile faded. "Oh, say now. I hope I haven't loosed any cats you wanted kept in the bag about that. I should have thought before I spoke."

"No harm done, Mr. Keith. I've never seen any reason to hide my association with Les Shannon. Far from it."

"Aye, we can all agree about that," Vickers put in. "He was a good man, Lester Shannon. We'll all miss him. This whole town will."

"Hear, hear," Keith added.

Ben and Craig Albritton mumbled their concurrence.

There was a moment of awkward silence, then the men bent to their coffee and rolls and put those thoughts behind them. The waitress brought coffee to Ben without being asked, but he declined the suggestion of a sweet bun to go with it.

"You're missing the best pick-me-up in town, Mr. Cartwright," Vickers said.

"So I understand, but I just now finished breakfast. And please call me Ben. It's too early in the day for formality."

"If you'll return the compliment," Vickers said, and the others said as much for themselves as well.

The coffee proved to be steaming, aromatic, and deliciously rich in flavor, far and away the best Ben had had since he left home and Hop Sing's cooking.

"What brings you to Johns Bend, Ben?" Keith asked.

"I came to see Les, actually. Had no idea about his accident, of course. I was shocked when the fellow at the hotel told me."

"We were all shocked by it," Henry Vickers said. "You should read my editorial this week. It's a tribute to Les. I saved the type and am having a few copies printed on fine rag paper, if you're interested. That was Tom's idea."

"When Henry told me what he intended, Ben, I thought it would be fitting for Chloe to have a copy. We're having one put under glass and framed. A keepsake, so to speak."

"That was thoughtful of you, Tom. And yes, I would like one too, Henry."

"I, um, have to tell you, Ben, that I'm giving the

prints away but am asking for donations from those who accept them."

"Donations? Certainly. What is this for, a memorial of some sort?"

"Much more practical than that, Ben. The proceeds will be deposited into Chloe's—that is, into hers and Les's—bank accounts."

"That way," Albritton injected, "she needn't know where the money comes from. She might be embarrassed otherwise."

"Craig thought of that angle," Vickers said.

"But I don't understand," Ben said. "Les was a very successful businessman. Surely Chloe has been left in comfortable circumstances."

The Johns Bend gentlemen were the ones who seemed embarrassed now. Finally Tom Keith responded, head down and staring at his fingernails, his voice low and sad. "You must understand that as a banker I cannot say anything about a client's affairs, Ben. But since you are a stockholder in the Shannon enterprises, I can, well, discuss with you the state of your own investments. If you see what I mean."

"I appreciate the niceties of the situation, Tom."

"Good. Well . . . as I was saying, you, um, you shouldn't look forward to any disbursement of dividends this quarter, Ben. Nor, I would hazard, ever again."

"No! How . . . ?"

The banker shrugged. For reasons that Ben did not understand, Keith was looking now at Albritton.

Craig Albritton seemed very uncomfortable. "The timing of Les's death . . . it couldn't have been worse, Ben. I am . . . was, that is . . . Les's attorney. I was also his partner. One of them. In a business venture. We had—Les and several others of us—a dream. We wanted to bring a railroad into Johns Bend. A short-line, narrow-gauge railroad linking Johns Bend and seven other communities—all active mining communities with excellent production records—with the Central Pacific mainline."

"Les had written to me saying something about that," Ben said. "He seemed quite excited by the prospect. In fact, he invited me to join you gentlemen as an investor. That was one of the things that brought me here."

"Really? Les hadn't mentioned that to me. Perhaps he had to the others. No matter, of course. At this point it is all problematic. The project is dying on the vine. And so is Les's investment, mine, all of us. The trouble is that the rest of us will have a chance to recoup. Poor Les won't. And he—I really shouldn't tell you this, I suppose, but Tom does say you are a stockholder—Les had pledged his entire holdings in exchange for railroad shares. Worse, the production levels of his mines have been falling. We are out of development capital for the railroad, and the mines are failing." Albritton shook his head. "There will be very little for Les's estate to pass to Chloe, Ben. I hate to say that, but it is true. Perhaps if Les had lived . . . But we will never know, will we?"

"No, I suppose not." Ben was scarcely aware of the gentlemen at the table with him now. This news was shocking, to say the least. Chloe, that dear woman, destitute? After all the years of Les's labors, all his successes? That seemed really quite incredible. "I don't know what to say, gentlemen."

"Do you still want a copy of the editorial, then?"

"Yes, of course. Put me down for . . . I don't know, a hundred dollars?"

"That is most generous of you, Ben."

But having uttered the figure, Ben saw now that it was anything but generous. It was a piteously feeble amount. A sop to his own conscience rather than a genuine attempt to assist a good friend's grieving widow.

There had to be something he could do for Chloe that would be more effective than this.

There just had to be.

Joseph was not in the hotel room, nor could he be found downstairs. Ben bought a copy of the *Intelligencer* and settled into one of the featherbed-deep armchairs in the lobby.

The editorial eulogy Henry Vickers spoke of was mawkishly sentimental but no doubt heartfelt and sincere. Probably Chloe would find comfort in it. Someday.

Ben read Vickers' editorial several times, then returned to the front page and read the local paper through. Henry Vickers was a man who liked to trumpet good news and shy away from dire warnings. That much was obvious. Even so, it would have taken a magician's abilities to keep any editor from sounding sour notes as to the future of the town. The mining news carried in the current edition of the *Johns Bend Intelligencer* was uniformly . . . cautious. Not bad, but stark in contrast with the other writings in the small newspaper. The absence of full-blown optimism stood out here like warnings of doom might have in other places. Or at least Ben was finding this to be so. Perhaps he was only exaggerating.

He grunted, filled his pipe and smoked in comfortable solitude while he finished reading the paper. Eventually, as lunchtime approached with still no sign of Joseph, Ben folded his newspaper and laid it aside. He stood, his knee joints cracking in protest after being idle so long, and went outside.

"Chloe, I have a problem."

"Oh, Ben, I'm sorry. Can I help?"

He smiled. "I hate to eat alone, and I can't seem to find Joseph at the moment. Would you do me the honor of joining me?"

"Why, I would be pleased to, Ben. Come in. I'll have something on the table in no time, and—"

"Now, Chloe, asking you to go to the trouble of cooking for me isn't at all what I had in mind, and you know it. What I was thinking of was a nice meal out somewhere, with a waiter to do the carrying and a chef to do the cooking. And with a change of surroundings too. If I had to guess, I would say you've been inside these four walls every day since Les died. Now haven't you?"

"Yes, Ben, I suppose I have."

"The change will be good for you, then."

"What will people think, Ben? A fat and dowdy old hen like me being seen on a gentleman's arm so soon after—" She swallowed, wanting to be bright and cheerful but having some difficulty managing it.

Ben patted her wrist. "It would take a very small mind for anyone to see scandal in two old friends having a meal in public, that's what I think."

"I'd have to change, Ben. I couldn't possibly go anywhere looking like this."

She looked perfectly fine so far as Ben could see. All she needed was to put on a hat. Her dress was entirely appropriate for daytime wear. Still, he knew better than to tell her that. She would insist on changing regardless. "I'll sit right here on your porch and enjoy watching the world pass by, Chloe. Take your time. I'm in no hurry."

"All right, Ben. I'll do it. Give me five minutes, just five, and I'll be with you."

"That sounds good. Five minutes it is." He smiled and nodded and, out of mild curiosity, glanced at his pocket watch.

Thirty-eight minutes later Chloe came back to the door ready to go. Ben considered her speed something of an accomplishment.

By the time they had finished dessert and were lingering over final cups, coffee for Ben and rose-hip tea for Chloe Shannon, Ben still hadn't come up with any sensible plan for bringing up the rather personal and private subject of finances with his old friend's widow. Fortunately Chloe did it for him.

"It is only fair for me to tell you, Ben, that you shouldn't expect dividends from our properties this year. Not even the Shan-Rock." The Shan-Rock was the largest and best producing of the mines Les had developed in the early days of the Johns Bend discoveries. It was, or had been, the foundation of all his later successes.

"No, Chloe? Why is that?" He saw no point in telling her about the discussions he'd had earlier with Les's friends in the business community.

"I know Les told you about the plans for our railroad, Ben. We discussed it over and over before he finally decided to write to you and invite you to participate. You know he wouldn't have done that if he hadn't believed, really and firmly believed, that the investment would be sound."

"I know that," Ben agreed.

"Well, the railroad plan is bogged down now. It may or may not ever be built. And Les pledged most of what we own—our mining properties, that is—to the railroad. He held back a portion of the Shan-Rock that he thought should be enough for us to live on fairly comfortably until the railroad began to pay off. But now production at the Shan-Rock is falling. Not dramatically, I suppose, but enough that it barely covers our—my—commitments to the railroad venture. There is nothing . . . that is to say, I don't think you should expect to receive any dividends this year. Not from the Shan-Rock nor . . . what others of our properties do you hold an interest in, Ben?"

"Do you know something, Chloe, I can't actually recall. I have it written down somewhere at home, but I don't recall any of the names. I wouldn't even have been able to remember the name of the Shan-Rock if you hadn't brought it up first, although now I don't see how I could have forgotten."

"I suppose it doesn't matter anyway, under the circumstances, Ben. I . . . I'm sorry. I know Les would have been mortified. If he'd . . . you know." If he'd lived long enough to realize the extent of his fall. No wonder Chloe couldn't bring herself to say that aloud, Ben thought.

"Tell me more about this railroad plan, Chloe. I mean, if Les thought it was a sound investment before, then I'm sure it's a sound investment still. Perhaps—I don't know—perhaps I can do something to help the venture over whatever the difficulty is now. Surely it would help your situation—and for that matter my own, since as you say I do own shares in several of your ventures—if the railroad comes to fruition."

"I don't understand all of this railroad business myself, Ben. Les talked to me about it, of course. We discussed everything we got into our whole lives long. He always did that for me." She looked a little weepy for the first time since they'd sat down to lunch, but managed to keep it under control. "Even though he was so good about telling me everything, Ben, it's all I can manage to understand a fraction of what he would explain to me about the mining. And I couldn't comprehend much about that either except after years and years of exposure to it all. When it comes to this railroad thing, well, I'm still a babe in the woods about that. Les told me, but I don't really know what any of it meant. Would you like me to introduce you to his partners? I'm sure they would be glad to tell you anything you want to know. Especially when I tell them you may be interested in investing. May I tell them that, Ben?"

"Certainly."

"Fine. We can stop in at Neal Hubbard's office when we leave here, if you like. It's right on the way."

Ben smiled. "That would be fine, Chloe." She carefully folded her napkin and laid it on the table to signify she was ready to leave. Ben stood and helped Chloe with her chair, dropped a coin onto the table to pay for their dinner and then some and gave Chloe his arm.

"Thank you, Ben. I haven't been out of the house since . . . except for the funeral service, of course . . . and I . . . well, thank you. Perhaps I needed this outing much more than I realized."

"Thank you for the company, Chloe."

"Turn left at the end of this block, please. Neal Hubbard's office is on the second story of the bank building there. I can introduce you and leave you there to talk with him."

"You'll do nothing of the sort. I will accept the introduction, but Mr. Hubbard and I can have our chat after I've taken you the rest of the way home."

She pooh-poohed the suggestion that Ben go so many blocks out of his way just to see her home again, but it was clear that she was pleased too.

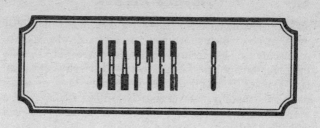

CHAPTER 8

When Ben returned to Neal Hubbard's office, the businessman was not alone.

"Come in, Mr. Cartwright. Have a seat. Would you care for something to eat? Coffee? Perhaps a little nip to take the chill off? No? As you wish, then. Lucas, this is Mr. Cartwright. Mr. Cartwright is an old family friend of the Shannons and, as I understand it, holds a very small stock position in some of poor Les's properties. Mr. Cartwright, this is Lucas Dadley. Mrs. Shannon said you are interested in our little railroad venture, so I thought you might want to visit with Lucas too. Lucas, Les Shannon, and I are—I should say were—the principals in the railroad."

"I see." Ben shook hands with Dadley and accepted the chair Hubbard pointed him toward. "It's very kind of you gentlemen to give me your time, thank you." He smiled and nodded and pulled his pipe from his coat pocket.

While he was loading the bowl of the pipe, he had a few moments in which to look over these men who had been Les's business partners. The two seemed an odd pair. Neal Hubbard was by far the more imposing. Tall and lean and craggy, Hubbard had a distinguished, almost Lincoln-esque appearance. The man's suit was impeccably tailored and his shirt collar crisp. He had a thick mane of hair as white as new-fallen snow, and a spindly pair of pince-nez spectacles dangled from a cord around his neck. Despite the color of his hair, he was not a particularly old man. Ben guessed Hubbard to be considerably short of Ben's own age, possibly not yet into his fifties. Dadley was a marked contrast to Hubbard. Where Hubbard was lean and smooth, Dadley was blocky and abrupt. Dadley was a squat, powerfully built man with bulldog jowls and a habitual scowl. His hair was a helmet of blue-black curls, and even at this early hour he was in need of a second shave for the day. He wore an overlarge shirt with the necktie pulled loose from the collar. Tufts of dark hair escaped from confinement at his neck and both wrists, and the backs of his hands were so hairy as to seem furred. Dadley appeared to be forty or thereabouts.

Perhaps typically, it was Dadley who came right to the point. "I'm a busy man, Cartwright. What is it you want with us?"

Ben's smile was a shield against Lucas Dadley's truculence. "It isn't so much that I want anything, Mr. Dadley, as that I am concerned about Mrs. Shannon's wellbeing." The smile became all the more gentle and soothing. "I'm sure that is something we all three share, is it not?"

"Yeah, I suppose we do," Dadley conceded.

"And if my own interests are involved, well, I am equally sure we can all put that aside for the time being," Ben said, guessing that these businessmen would do no such thing. More than likely they would ascribe his interest to his own profit potential rather than any concern for Chloe Shannon's comfort. That, at least, was Ben's impression. He would have been quite willing to be proven wrong on the subject.

"Of course," Dadley said. "Never would have thought otherwise."

"Not for a moment," Hubbard said.

Ben grinned. Fine. They were all cheerfully, politely,

and with good grace lying to one another. But in a nice way. Things could have been worse.

"So tell us, Mr. Cartwright, just what was it you wanted to know?" Hubbard asked.

"The status of the railroad plans, for the most part."

"Naturally. That would affect your investments in the Shannon affairs."

"You do understand my concern," Ben said. It appeared he was right. These birds placed self-interest to the fore. Fair enough.

"Of course we do." It was Hubbard who had taken over the conversation at this point. "I can tell you—that is to say we can tell you—that the High Sierra Short Line is proceeding apace."

"Apace," Ben said, mouthing the word slowly as if to examine the flavors it produced.

"Everything is still in the works," Dadley said. "But slow. Real slow right now."

"But moving forward," Ben pressed.

"Yes, indeed. Forward. But slow."

"Which means I can't really expect an immediate turnaround in the, um, dividend situation."

"Not really," Hubbard said. "After all, Mr. Cartwright, think about it. We haven't even begun laying track yet. And . . . I don't mean to intrude upon your personal affairs, but Les was, after all, our partner. We certainly are aware of his, uh, situation. The simple truth of the matter, Mr. Cartwright, is that Les pledged to the railroad all the production proceeds from the Caroline, the Mobeetie, the Tosh, and the Whist properties. Plus most of the income from the Shan-Rock. Which of those did you say you have holdings in?"

"I don't recall that I did say," Ben told him.

"Yes, well, that doesn't matter anyway. The point is, we are struggling to create renewed opportunity here in Johns Bend, Mr. Cartwright. Les believed in this as firmly as Lucas and I do. The three of us together hoped with this railroad to extend the life of Johns Bend and half a dozen other towns very much like it by making it possible to earn profits from the lower quality ores that are beginning to become common here. We believe in what we are doing, Mr. Cartwright. And if you think you can come in here, a virtual stranger, and find fault with us for—"

"Whoa. Mr. Hubbard, please. I want to do no such thing. If I've given that impression, please accept my apology. My interest has to do with Chloe Shannon's welfare, and my own as a matter of secondary importance. I only want to be able to walk away from here with the feeling that Chloe's future is in capable hands."

"Capable remains to be seen, Mr. Cartwright. But if good intentions count for anything, you will find no quarrel here."

"I don't think I could ask for more than that, gentlemen."

Hubbard smiled. Lucas Dadley grunted.

"Would the railroad be any quicker to succeed if there were a fresh infusion of cash?" Ben asked.

"Oh, I suppose." Hubbard smiled again. "After all, I can't think of any business that wouldn't benefit from some extra cash. But that isn't likely to happen, Mr. Cartwright. Not with the production values of our mines on the decrease like they are. Our income is more likely to decline than to rise. Any other expectation would be unrealistic."

"You misunderstand me," Ben said. "I wasn't indulging in wishful thinking. I was pondering whether I should accept the invitation Les extended to me by mail earlier this year."

"Invitation?" Dadley asked.

"Yes. An invitation to join you gentlemen as investors in the—what did you call it?—the High Sierra Short Line Railroad."

Dadley's scowl deepened into something approaching real anger. "We voted on no such offer, and that means there wasn't no such offer ever made. I don't know what you're trying to pull, mister, but—"

"Easy there, Mr. Dadley. I'm not trying to 'pull' anything, and I have no idea what you gentlemen have or have not voted on. I'm merely mentioning that Les Shannon wrote to me and asked if I would be interested in investing in your railroad corporation. I wasn't able to respond to that invitation while Les was alive, but you could say that I had been keeping my options open, such as they might be. If you aren't interested in—"

"Now now, Mr. Cartwright. And you, Lucas, calm down. I think we're getting off track here. Mr. Cartwright, Lucas didn't really mean to imply that you are trying to pull anything on us or anyone else. Please understand that Lucas sometimes overreaches himself when he speaks in haste. And Lucas, you should know better than to say things before you have time to think them through. Of course Mr. Cartwright wasn't accusing us of anything. Were you, Mr. Cartwright?"

"No, certainly not."

"For our part, Mr. Cartwright, I hope you will understand that Les never discussed this offer—I should say alleged offer—with either of us. If he told you we were seeking more investors, he was in error. And if you think you can force us to accept some unsubstantiated offer like this one, if you think you can make us take you in as a partner when—"

"Please. You are reading much more into this than I intended. To begin with, I wouldn't say Les put it as strongly as to say you were 'seeking' anything, Mr. Hubbard. And what he did say wasn't so much an offer as a suggestion. There was nothing formal in his letter to me. Not that that matters anyway. I was only wondering if a little more investment capital would tip the balance in your favor. And Chloe's." Ben's smile was disarming. "I meant nothing more than that, I assure you."

"Well, all right, then," Hubbard said, seemingly satisfied.

"Just so you have it straight, Cartwright," Dadley added, "we don't want no more investors. None."

"I have no quarrel with that," Ben said.

"Good. Because when this thing starts to pay out, we don't want to have to split it any more ways than necessary."

"That seems entirely reasonable," Ben said. "Do you mind me asking, out of consideration for Mrs. Shannon's well-being, just how many stockholders there already are in the High Sierra Short Line?"

"That's none of your affair, Cartwright," Dadley snapped.

"Sorry. I was only curious," Ben paused for a moment, then judiciously added, "since you two gentlemen seem to be determined to reject investment capital without consulting any of the other stockholders." He smiled. "Forgive me if I fail to understand the way business is conducted here, but ... is it proper for you to do that?"

"Get the hell out of here, you—"

"Lucas!" Hubbard barked, cutting Dadley off. "Sit down and be quiet. Please. Mr. Cartwright, I think it would be best if you were to leave now. And in the future, sir, you really should watch yourself. It isn't a good idea to bait Lucas, you see. Not a good idea at all. Please go now. Please."

Ben stood, not at all sure how he should regard these men Les had chosen to stand in harness with, and made his way out of Neal Hubbard's offices.

CHAPTER 9

J oe eyed the cloverleaf roll that remained in the bread basket. The waiter had brought only two apiece, and Joe already ate both of his.

"Don't you want your roll, Pa?"

"What? Oh. No, go ahead if you like."

Joe snagged it before his pa might reconsider. He was lucky Hoss wasn't with them or he would have done well to get one roll out of the basket. He peeled the soft wedges apart and slathered them thick with butter, then popped the smallest into his mouth whole. Whoever baked for the Bent Lodge did an almighty fine job of it.

"Tell me something, Joseph, have you ever known anyone who didn't want more money?"

Joe swallowed and shook his head. "I don't think so. Wait a minute. Maybe I have at that. Clete Burr. You remember him, don't you?" Clete was what was politely called eccentric. Otherwise known as loco. He owned, and apparently wanted to own, nothing but the rags on his back. He would perform odd jobs, but only in exchange for a meal or a corner where he might curl up to sleep. He never accepted payment for his work. Clete showed up in Carson City or neighboring Virginia City most summers. Each fall he would disappear, presumably drifting south ahead of the winter. He possessed neither a coat nor a blanket. "I tried to give Clete money more than once, but he wouldn't take it. Acted like it would dirty him if he touched it."

Pa's expression indicated that wasn't exactly the response he'd wanted when he asked the question.

"What's your point, Pa?" Joe asked.

"I keep thinking about Les's partners."

That was no big surprise. Pa hadn't talked about much else since he'd come back to the hotel this afternoon.

"They really stick in your craw, don't they?"

"They do for a fact, son."

"You think there's something wrong with them?"

"I'm not sure. I mean, they seem fine in some ways. But what they tell me and what Mrs. Shannon tells me are two different things. They say everything is moving along just fine with the railroad and they don't need any help. She is under the impression that the project has virtually collapsed and that all Les's properties will be lost."

"What does Mr. Albritton say?"

Pa sat up straighter in his chair. "Why didn't I think of that?"

"Think of what?"

"Asking Les and Chloe's lawyer, that's what."

Joe felt a flush of pride. It sounded like Pa was really pleased with his suggestion.

"Of course, a lawyer isn't supposed to discuss a client's affairs. But there may well be some light he can shed on this." Pa smiled and slapped his thigh. "I'll ask him, Joseph. Thank you."

"Any time."

The waiter came to see if the gentlemen were interested in dessert. Pa was anxious to quit the dining room and go off to find Mr. Albritton, but Joe was sure interested. Especially when the fellow said there was dried apple pie still warm from the oven.

"Go ahead and have your pie, son. I'm going to see if I can find Mr. Albritton."

"If you're sure you don't mind me staying back—"

"Not at all." Pa paid for their supper, the dessert included, and left. He went in such a hurry that he left his tobacco pouch lying half underneath the napkin he'd hurriedly tossed onto the table beside his plate. Joe ate the pie—it was every bit as good as it'd sounded—and took the leather pouch upstairs with him.

Once in the hotel room, he commenced to feel antsy. Pa and Adam could sit by themselves for hours at a time as content as content could be if they had a book to get lost inside. Joe liked to be out and doing things. And anyway, he hadn't any books with him here. What he would have liked was a nice card game, kind of like he'd had last night, except possibly with a better outcome. Those old boys last night sure had seen him coming. He hadn't wanted to go on so much about it afterward. If Pa ever went and mentioned it to Adam and Hoss, he'd be in for some ragging for sure. Those sharps he played with last night, though ... they'd roped him in, tied him up, and picked him clean as a Sunday chicken. It was pitiful. Worse, it was his own dang fault. Pa had taught him better than to let himself be taken in by a set of whipsaw artists like that. What they'd do to a fellow was toll him in and lull him to sleep by letting him win a few hands. Then when he thought the luck was running with him, they'd take back everything he'd "won" and whatever else he had in his pockets too. That was just exactly what they'd gone and done to him last night, darn them. What he really would like to do now would be to—

Joe snapped his fingers and, alone in the hotel room, let out a little yip of laughter.

Why not?

Grinning like a possum in a corn patch, Joe began shaking the tobacco out of his pa's pouch, dumping the cut-leaf, rum-cured tobacco onto the top of the dressing table.

He was still grinning, and in addition to that was humming a sprightly tune under his breath, when he let himself out of the room, careful to lock the door behind him, and went skipping lightly down the staircase to the lobby.

He had one stop to make. Then, by golly, he thought he'd just go and play some more cards tonight.

Joe leaned against the bar for support. His legs were rubbery, his knees wobbling this way and then that. He resolved that difficulty by placing both forearms flat on the bar surface and supporting much of his weight that way.

"Beer," he said, blinking and grinning. A bubble of spittle appeared at the corner of his mouth. He seemed not to notice.

The bartender gave him a close look, then shrugged and drew a foamy brew from the tap.

Joe chuckled and loudly slapped a nickel down onto the bar surface. He picked up the beer and drank off the top half like he was in grave danger of thirsting to death, then smacked his lips and wiped the sleeve of his coat—his old coat, not one of the new San Francisco ones—across his mouth. "I needed that." He cackled and took a smaller drink.

The barman gave him a sour look and turned away in search of someone more pleasant to wait on.

Joe belched and, picking up his beer, turned to search the room with wide, staring eyes. "You. I remember you." He made his way with a cautious, rather stiff-legged gait to the table where a group of men were playing cards. Joe was roughly half the age of most of the men at the table. "Sure, I 'member you fellas," he said pleasantly.

"Good evening, Joe," one of the gentlemen responded.

"Can I—" His face twisted into a scowl. "What was your name again, mister?"

"Carl, Joe. My name is Carl."

Joe beamed, and swayed slowly from side to side. "O' course. Carl. My friend Carl. We had us a nice time las' nigh', Carl. Didn' we?"

"Yes, I would say that we did, Joe."

"Can I have a nice time with you again tonigh', Carl?"

"Do you think you should, Joe? You overplayed your hands last night, as I recall. If you have anything left, perhaps you should hang on to it. What d'you think?"

Joe grinned. "I think I feel lucky t'nigh', Carl. That's what I think."

"Gentlemen?"

The others at the table nodded their assent, and Carl pointed to an empty chair. "Take a hand, if you like."

"Thanks, Carl." Joe lightly touched the back of one chair after another as he marched slow and solemn around the table to the vacant spot. He plopped heavily onto the chair and had some difficulty dragging it closer to the table once he was sitting on it. The only man at the table who cracked a smile was one who hadn't been there the night before. This evening's honoree as pigeon, Joe concluded.

"Wha's the ante?" Joe asked, his voice just a touch louder than was necessary.

"Same as before, Joe. Small stakes. This is just a friendly little game."

"Good." Joe grinned. "Real good." He reached into his trousers pocket and brought out a handful of silver that he dumped onto the table in an untidy heap. Then he fumbled inside his coat for a small pouch made of soft, supple, handsomely tanned leather. He held it in his palm for a moment as if gauging its weight, then plucked the draw cord free and dipped two fingers inside the pouch. He belched once, his face red and perspiring, then he brought a small gold coin out of the pouch and added that to the loose change already on the table before him. When he tried to return the pouch to his coat it slipped from his stiff fingers and fell to the floor with the solid, chunky, telltale thump of very heavy coins. Joe swallowed, covering his mouth with his hand to suppress another burp, then leaned down in search of the fallen pouch.

"Here y'are, Joe."

"Thanks." He blinked. "Thanks a lot, huh?"

The gentleman returned the pouch to him, and Joe tucked it away in the inside coat pocket. "What'd you say the ante was again?"

He smiled. So did the other gentlemen at the table.

"A f-f—" He shook his head and tried again. "A f-flush, gennelmen."

"Beats me, Joe. You, Hal? Barry? Anybody beat a flush? No?" Carl shrugged. "That's your third pot in a row, Joe. You were right. Your luck really has changed tonight."

"Sure has," Joe agreed. He raked the pot in, having to use both hands to pull the pile of loose silver and gold coins to him.

He hadn't been keeping close track, but as near as he could figure, he'd recovered everything he'd lost last night and a little bit more.

More to the point, and again as best he could figure it, he had pretty well used up the come-on phase of this preplanned chicken plucking.

The sharps at the table, Carl and his partners, by now should figure they had him nicely wrapped up and tied down, lured in by this extraordinary run of good "luck" and ready to greedily push now for high profits.

Joe wasn't vindictive. Much. He gave them their moment of pleasure. He pawed through the small coins for a moment, then reached inside his coat and pulled out the heavy pouch he'd displayed earlier.

That was just what the gentlemen would have been waiting for. Once he was willing to risk the big money, they would be ready to pounce. And take it away from him slick and smooth as a snake swallowing a boiled egg.

"Gentlemen," Joe said, "I surely do thank you."

"What d'you mean, Joe?"

Joe smiled at him. "Why, Carl, I mean I thank you. I mean I've enjoyed this evening even more'n I did last. I mean I think it's time to cash in and go to bed. That's what I mean when I say that I thank you."

"But you can't—"

"No, Carl?"

"I mean—"

Joe grinned again. He hefted the pouch in his palm, enjoying the feel of it and the dull clanking sounds that came from it.

Then he loosened the drawstring and upended the pouch over the table, spilling out a cascade of dull, gray lead washers onto the green baize surface.

"What the . . . ?"

Joe, whistling and nonchalant as if unaware of the distress he was causing, dumped out the worthless washers and began stuffing the pouch instead with his winnings.

Set him up, would they? Sucker him in and pick him clean, would they? And then think they could do it *again?* Huh! They deserved this lesson in turnabout being fair play.

"Thank you, gents." Joe dropped the pouch into his pocket and stood, his voice and posture somehow no longer suffering from the influence of drink. He winked at them. "Mayhap we can do this again tomorrow."

With that he turned and sauntered out of there.

CHAPTER 10

I'm sorry, Ben. You know I can't discuss a client's affairs with anyone else."

"Nor would I ask you to."

"But, um, as Tom so ably noted this morning, there is nothing wrong with me discussing that person's own prospects. Yours, for instance, as a shareholder in certain mining properties in this district. And naturally I would be free to speak of my own affairs." Craig Albritton winked and motioned toward Ben's empty glass. Ben nodded, and Albritton took up the decanter to pour another brandy. They were relaxing in the comfort, and the privacy, of the study in the lawyer's own home. Mrs. Albritton, a slender woman with a warm and gracious smile, had retired soon after welcoming her husband's guest.

"I certainly don't want to intrude, Craig, but I've become more and more concerned the more I've thought about this. This morning you told me, and again this afternoon Chloe did, that the railroad is unlikely ever to be built. I believe you even said point-blank that the lack of development capital is the problem. Is that correct?"

"As a stockholder myself ... I handled the partnership and the incorporation papers, you understand, and it is common enough for the attorney of record to be awarded a small stock position in exchange for services rendered and, um, a board position. Anyway, Ben, since I am myself a stockholder in the corporation, I am free to discuss my own investments and my own prospects. There is nothing unethical about that. And in truth, I would have to say that I hold very little hope of ever seeing dividends from my Short Line shares."

"I see. And the investment capital . . . ?"

Albritton shrugged. "What can I tell you? Les and I both thought the plan was an excellent one. When Neal and Lucas came to us with the proposal, we both thought it a superb opportunity. After all, how often in a man's career does he have a chance to serve his community and enrich himself at one and the same time? Seldom, I can assure you. Both Les and I truly believed this to be just such an opportunity. Frankly, I still think it should be." He threw his hands up. "What can I say? It simply isn't happening the way we thought it would. We—possibly I shouldn't say this, but Tom assures me that you have a legitimate interest in this by way of your investments in the Shannon properties—we have all put in every cent we could manage. In fairness I should exclude myself from that. As a minority shareholder, my assessments were the least of anyone's. Les held the largest block at thirty-five percent. Neal and Lucas each are in for thirty. I have the remaining five percent of the shares."

"So no one man holds a controlling interest," Ben observed.

"Control is not what we were seeking," Craig Albritton said. "Everyone agreed that decisions should be reached by consensus, not fiat."

"That sounds like Les, all right."

"Very much so," Albritton agreed, "although—" He stopped in mid-sentence, obviously thinking better of whatever it was he had been about to say. "Never mind. Sorry."

Ben nodded and took a small sip of the smooth, warming brandy. He set his glass aside and reached into his coat for his tobacco pouch, then frowned.

"Is something wrong?"

"Not really. I seem to have misplaced my tobacco."

"No problem. Try mine." Albritton was out of his chair before Ben could refuse. He brought a large humidor over and set it at Ben's elbow. When he removed the tight-fitting cork lid, the room was infused with a rich, sweet, fruity aroma. The tobacco itself was dark and moist. Its flavor when Ben had it alight was somewhat more delicate than his accustomed taste, but certainly was pleasant enough.

"What were we saying?" Ben asked as he puffed at the stem of his briar, wreathing his head in a cloud of smoke that smelled deliciously edible.

"We were talking about the prospects for the rail-road."

"Oh, yes. I believe you mentioned that the line needs more capital."

Albritton smiled. "I said no such thing, Ben. Which I suspect you remember quite good and well."

"Didn't you? My mistake. Sorry."

The lawyer chuckled but did not pursue it any further. "You know, Ben, I don't know you very well at all. But I knew Lester Shannon since the first day I arrived in Johns Bend. He was more than a client. He was one of the best friends I ever hope to have. And I know the high regard Les had for you. Everything he ever told me about you suggests that you would not be the sort who would want to come in and pick through the bones of Les's enterprises in search of personal gain."

"I should hope not."

"Then let's come right out with it, Ben. Something is bothering you here. You keep nibbling away but not really asking the things you want to know. So let's do it this way. Ask me, Ben. Ask me anything you wish. First lay a coin on that stand beside you. A retainer fee. A penny will do. That's enough to make you one of my clients so that I can reasonably invoke the limitations of client confidentiality if anyone wants to know what we've discussed here this evening. Then you ask me anything you like, just as bluntly and forthright as you know how. I in my turn will tell you anything I can that does not violate the confidences of any other client to whom I am obligated. Does that sound fair?"

Ben drew on the pipe for a moment. Then he nodded. "It does, Craig. It has the same ring of fair play and honesty that I would have expected from Les Shannon." He smiled. "Or from one of his friends."

Ben leaned back in the overstuffed leather armchair and pondered for a moment. It was not that he lacked for questions to ask. The thing he wondered about was how best to phrase them and in what order they should be asked.

After that, once the conversation reopened, Ben Cartwright and Craig Albritton sat in the lawyer's study for some hours longer.

The levels in both the brandy decanter and the tobacco humidor were both rather seriously reduced before the two men finally parted for the night and Ben made his way back to the hotel.

Ben met with Craig Albritton at the lawyer's offices the following morning promptly at eleven. Even though the work day was not yet half gone, Albritton already had a full day's work completed. At least Ben considered it so, and Albritton confided that he had brought in his wife as an amanuensis to help get everything done as quickly as possible.

"Even the copies?" Ben asked.

"Everything," Albritton assured him, "just like we discussed last night. Copies for each party and for the court filing."

"And an extra set to submit to the partnership?"

"Especially that," Albritton said.

"Well then, let's go see if we can make this happen."

The lawyer gathered his sheafs of barely dry papers together and placed them into a thick briefcase. He motioned for Ben to precede him, and the two gentlemen went out into the midday sunshine.

"Ben, Mr. Albritton, how nice to see you both."

"May we come in, Chloe?"

"Of course. Please do. May I offer you some lunch?"

"No, but perhaps we can take you out after we've completed our business here," Ben said, then added with a smile, "in celebration, so to speak."

"Celebration, Ben?"

"An appearance of celebration, actually."

"I don't understand," the plump, graying widow said.

"That's what we want to explain, Chloe."

The lawyer coughed into his fist, obviously more than a little uncomfortable with his role in this. "It, um, was Mr. Cartwright's idea, really. Although I do concur with it. Completely so. I, uh, added a few notions of my own, in fact."

"A few notions indeed," Ben retorted. "Your Mr. Albritton here is brilliant. So much so that it seems almost a shame for him to have gone into law. He would have become legend if he'd chosen to be a criminal instead."

"Ben! Please don't say things like that."

"Sorry, Craig, I was getting just a bit carried away, wasn't I?"

"Both of you hush," Chloe Shannon pleaded. "Why, I don't understand a single thing either one of you is saying."

"No, I suppose you wouldn't," Ben conceded. "Can we all sit down, Chloe? First we have some things to discuss with you. Then, if you agree with what we have in mind, there are some papers for you to sign."

"All right, then," Mrs. Shannon said. "I trust the both of you. I certainly shall listen to whatever it is you want to tell me. But really. You two. Showing up here unannounced like this and acting . . . like a pair of small boys with a secret to share, that's what you remind me of."

"Mm. Not so far off the mark as you might think, Chloe," Ben said.

"Will you tell me now, please?"

"Yes, of course."

Chloe Shannon sat with a fresh, crisply starched white apron spread over her lap. The gentlemen callers began to speak, first Albritton and then Ben. As they talked they became more and more animated and excited, one interrupting the other and then that one interrupting back again while Mrs. Shannon patiently listened.

"Right away, Mr. Albritton."

"And you will see to it yourself, Herbert?"

"Yes, of course, Mr. Albritton. Just as you wish."

"It's just that I want to make sure everything is done right, Herbert, and you always get everything exactly as it is supposed to be."

"Thank you, Mr. Albritton. Nice of you to say so, sir." The slightly prissy Clerk of Court accepted the documents the lawyer handed him. He also accepted the filing fees that Ben Cartwright handed over. "Let's see now," he said, thumbing quickly through the papers, "we have transfers of fee simple deeds, claim, um, another claim here, stock certificates, another claim, another deed, more stock certificates . . . everything seems to be in order, Mr. Albritton. I can get to them immediately after lunch, sir. The filings will be completed before the close of business today, and all the dates of record will be as of today. Is that what you wanted, Mr. Albritton?"

"That is exactly what we wanted, Herbert, thank you."

"Very good, sir. And you, sir, the recording fees for all this should total sixteen dollars and, um, eight-five cents."

"Would it be out of line for me to suggest you keep the change from that double eagle and buy yourself a drink?" Ben asked.

"Oh, I couldn't do that, sir." The man sounded positively hurt by the idea. "That wouldn't be at all right." He hurriedly produced a metal cash box and made change, then filled out a receipt form and gave that to Ben too. "Was there anything else I might do for you gentlemen?"

"No, Herbert, you've already done everything we might wish for," Albritton said. Which was mostly the truth. What the Clerk of Court hadn't yet done he soon would. Albritton had assured Ben of that. Last night, in fact.

"Good day, then, gentlemen. And I promise you, I'll see to these filings myself just as soon as I return from lunch." Herbert was smiling and already backing away toward the rack where his hat was hanging. He seemed in something of a hurry now to dash away for his dinner, although until Albritton and this newcomer to Johns Bend arrived, the man had exhibited no great rush to order whatever the special of the day was at Harry's Eats.

Albritton and Ben said perfunctory good-byes and got out of there so they would not delay Herbert any longer than was necessary. After all, it was understood in Johns Bend that the two best ways to broadcast news in the community were either through the pages of Henry Vickers' *Intelligencer* . . . or by telling Herbert Carou. And of those two, it was equally well-understood that telling Herbert was the quicker, if not quite so accurate as dealing with the newspaper.

"What do you think, Ben?" Albritton asked once they were on the street again. "Dinner?"

"I think we're entitled to some rest now, Craig. But it will be my treat. I insist."

"Very well. In celebration of a good day's work."

"It's a shame Chloe wouldn't join us."

"I can understand why she would rather not," Albritton said. "Right now she is probably wondering if she's done the right thing here, if she may have betrayed Les's memory somehow, and all those years of hard work he put into this town."

"So long as you hang on to the papers in that portfolio, she needn't worry about that," Ben put in, pointing to the briefcase where, in addition to copies of the documents placed on public record at the courthouse, there was one brief but critically important paper that was carefully *not* recorded.

Albritton smiled. "As a lawyer I suppose I shouldn't say this, and if you ever repeat it to anyone, Ben, I'll swear you are a liar . . . but any word written on paper can be turned upside down or inside out, and we both know it. Mrs. Shannon's greatest safety doesn't lie in anything we three signed today; it lies in your integrity and goodwill. It was your word, Ben, and not my legal powers, that convinced her to go along with all this."

Ben shrugged and grunted. But in truth he also felt quite flattered. "Come along, Craig. Where would you care to go for dinner?"

"Would the Canterbury be all right with you, Ben?"

"Fine."

Albritton grinned. "We can give Herbert's tale-spinning an early start."

"Then by all means, let's hurry."

Tom Keith saw the two gentlemen enter. He waved to get their attention and held up one finger in a gesture indicating "one minute, please," then leaned forward to say something to the man in overalls who was seated in front of his desk. The bank president said something else, smiled, and repeated the "one minute" signal, this time to the customer. Then he left his desk and came out into the lobby.

"Craig, Ben, don't rush away, either of you. I'd like a moment with you."

"Actually, Tom, we stopped by to see you."

"Good, excellent, have a seat. Barney, bring some coffee for the gentlemen here, would you? Make yourselves comfortable. I won't be long." He smiled and bobbed his head, hurrying back to the customer he'd abandoned in his office.

"Looks like the word is already getting around, doesn't it?" Ben observed.

"It certainly does," Albritton agreed.

After all, they had left the restaurant not ten minutes earlier. The bank president hadn't been there, but he certainly was acting like he'd heard that Ben Cartwright was the new owner of all of Lester Shannon's mining properties, stock shares, and other assets.

A young man wearing sleeve garters and celluloid cuff protectors took time away from his duties to bring coffee to the visitors, then with eyes averted scurried back to his ledgers. The coffee smelled bitter with age, and Ben set his aside without tasting it. Instead he pulled out his pipe and filled it. Funny thing, though. Surely it was only his imagination, but lately his tobacco tasted like dust, as if somehow contaminants had gotten into the pouch along with the tobacco. It had tasted like that ever since yesterday, when he'd misplaced the pouch, although surely that was only coincidence. Still, a poor pipe was better than no pipe. Ben tamped the bowl with care and lighted it. Craig tried the coffee and made a face, rolling his eyes and quickly setting the cup aside. He too reached for his pipe.

The man in the overalls came through the lobby, and Tom Keith was right behind him. "Craig, Ben, won't you come in now, please?"

Tom Keith very rarely closed his office door. He did so now. "All right, darn it, I have to know. Are the rumors true?"

"Rumors?" Albritton asked with feigned innocence. "What rumors would those be, Tom?" Then he gave himself away by grinning.

"It is true, then," Keith said. "Good for you, Ben. I can't imagine why you've done this, taking over an operation that has already collapsed, but you certainly found a way to rescue Les's widow, didn't you?"

"Oh, I hope we've done more than that, Tom. I hope we've found a way to revive Les's holdings."

"Is that a fact, Ben?"

"There are no guarantees, of course, but that is what Craig and I came up with once we put our minds to it."

"Just what is it that you intend, then?"

"Obviously you already know that Chloe agreed to sell out in my favor. Everything has been signed and by now should be recorded. And you can expect her to deposit a draft against my San Francisco bank. That is one of the reasons I wanted to stop by here this afternoon, Tom. I want to verify the draft for her. She may or may not elect to transfer the funds here"—in fact she would not, as they had already discussed, but there was no need to go into that with the Johns Bend banker—"but there should be no problem establishing a drawing account here, should there?"

"Of course not, Ben. I already know your reputation and, shall we say, your standing in the California and Nevada financial communities. Naturally I will honor any note with your signature on it."

"Thank you, Tom. That, as I said, was one of the things I wanted to mention. The other is that as a bona fide stockholder in the High Sierra Short Line, I believe I should be entitled to inspect the corporation's accounts. Wouldn't you agree with that?"

"Certainly I would agree, Ben, but . . ."

"But what, Tom?"

The banker looked first at Ben, then at Craig Albritton. "You didn't know, Craig?"

"Know what, Tom?"

"The railroad's banking affairs were moved away from this bank a few days after the corporation was chartered. Miners and Merchants was the initial repository of record, true, but the stockholders voted to move their accounts almost at once. I assumed you knew that, you being one of the shareholders and everything."

Albritton flushed. "I didn't know, Tom. I'm sorry. Why didn't you say something?"

"I didn't think . . . well, you know. I thought you already knew about it."

"I certainly did not. Where are they banking if not here?"

Keith shrugged. "I've no idea, Craig. The accounts here were closed and the deposits taken in cash. Have you paid any assessments since?"

"Certainly. We all have. Les, Neal, Lucas, me ... we've all kicked in several times since the initial stock offering."

"In that case, Craig, I might be able to find out where the railroad accounts are being maintained now. Assuming you paid your assessments by check."

"Yes, I did."

"Good. Those checks will have been returned to us. All we have to do is look on them to see what bank received the disbursement to the railroad's account."

"You could do that?"

"On your checks, certainly. There is no reason why I can't discuss your own checks with you. Naturally I couldn't discuss Les's checks with either of you, not even with you, Ben, since your purchases today do not give you privilege into Mrs. Shannon's personal accounts. But I can tell you whatever I know about your own accounts, Craig. I take it there is a reason for all of this?"

"Ben still believes ... Why am I telling him this, Ben? You go ahead. It was your idea."

"Not all of it by any stretch of the imagination," Ben protested. "Not that that matters. The point, Tom, is that I still believe the railroad to be a sound investment and a genuine opportunity for success. I think all the arguments Les put forward in his letter to me remain true today, despite his death. And I would like to see this venture through to completion if at all possible. If not," he shrugged, "then the sensible thing will be to withdraw and salvage the mining properties. As it is, they are being bled into a project that may or may not have any future. I want to see a railroad built and operating or else see the mining revenues reverted to normal business practice and income."

"That sound sensible enough to me," the banker said. He winked. "Especially if that would mean those revenues would flow through Miners and Merchants again. As it is, everything coming out of the Shannon—excuse me, now the Cartwright—mining properties runs onto my balance sheets and right back off again. As a banker I would much rather see those funds remain on deposit here in the community."

"In that case, Tom, I hope we can count on your cooperation," Ben said.

"Indeed you can. Starting right now. If you would excuse me, I'll go right now and take a look through our file of canceled checks. That should tell you where the railroad accounts are being kept nowadays, Craig." The banker left the office.

He returned some ten minutes later. He was frowning.

CHAPTER 11

D amn you, sir."

"I beg your pardon."

"Don't give me any of that high-and-mighty, nose-in-the-air nonsense. You know. Damn you, I said, and damn you I meant. You are interfering. It won't do you any good, not any good at all." Neal Hubbard had accosted Ben as soon as he stepped outside the bank building. But then Hubbard's offices were on the second story directly over the Miners and Merchants Bank. The businessman either saw Ben and Albritton enter the bank himself or was tipped to their presence by some third party. Either way, he was waiting, ready to pounce as soon as Ben reached the wooden sidewalk.

"Are you referring to my business investment?" Ben asked.

"Investment? Nonsense. I daresay you are attempting to defraud that poor widow, my own dear departed partner's widow. What did you pay her? A few pennies on the dollar? You are a vulture, sir. A leech and a vulture."

Ben tried to picture an animal that was both a leech and a vulture at one and the same time. The possibilities were amusing, but improbable.

"I intend to have the law on you, sir. We won't let you get away with this. You can't come in and rob a poor widow like this. The good citizens of this community will see to your comeuppance. Count on it."

Ben smiled. "Really, Mr. Hubbard, you shouldn't allow yourself to become so overwrought. It's bad for the liver, don't you know. Causes all manner of palpitations, I'm told. You should calm yourself. And now that we are partners—"

"Partners! That will be the day. You are no partner of mine, sir. You never will be."

"Protest all you wish, but I am indeed a partner of yours. As soon as Mr. Albritton is finished in the bank there, he will be delivering your copies of the paperwork involved. And it is true, as you undoubtedly already heard. I have indeed bought Lester Shannon's business holdings from his widow. Including all the shares he held in the High Sierra Short Line Railroad. You can ask Mr. Albritton to explain it to you. He is Mrs. Shannon's attorney of record, and a shareholder and attorney of record for the railroad too. He handled all the transfers of ownership, and it is all duly recorded with the Clerk of Court. You and I, Mr. Hubbard, are partners. Whether you like it or not."

"Never," Hubbard declared. "You will never be any partner of mine."

Ben opened his mouth to deliver a scathing retort. Then thought better of it. Calm, he told himself. Pour out honey, not vitriol. That can be so much more pleasant in the long term. For everyone.

"Regardless of what you may think at the moment, Mr. Hubbard," he said in a soothing tone of voice, "I can assure you that I mean neither you nor the railroad any harm. I believe in what you and Les and Mr. Dadley tried to accomplish here. I only want your plan to succeed. I do hope you will believe me about this. I only want what is best for the railroad and for the communities it will serve. I only want to help."

"We don't want you, Cartwright. We want nothing to do with you."

"But I only—"

"No. I won't listen. I don't have to listen. It's very simple. You are butting in where you are not wanted."

"Oppose me if you wish, Mr. Hubbard, but I am a partner now, and I do intend to help."

"You are no partner of mine. You never will be."

"I am, sir, like it or not. Mr. Albritton will advise you about that. Must I remind you, sir, that I am now the largest shareholder in the venture? I hold, all legal and above-board, a thirty-five percent share in the railroad. I am entitled to a full inspection of any and all records, reports, minutes of board meetings, financial affairs ... everything."

"You will get nothing from me, Cartwright. Nothing."

"Then I will have to secure an injunction, Mr. Hubbard. I am entitled to protect my own legitimate interests. And I shall, sir. For openers, Mr. Hubbard, I want you to tell me where the financial records and bank accounts of the railroad are maintained. I want you to tell me why checks paid to the railroad as assessments against costs have been cashed at a San Francisco clearinghouse instead of being deposited into regular banking accounts. Can't you see how that looks, man? Why are you allowing something like that to give an appearance of impropriety when there can be no need for it? Surely it doesn't matter if someone, especially your own shareholders, knows where the bank accounts are maintained. Just tell me, Mr. Hubbard. I truly don't wish to be your enemy in this matter. I really do only want to help you see your dream become reality. Just like Les would have done if he hadn't been killed in that explosion."

Ben's plea fell on ears that were not deaf but which certainly were hostile.

Better, perhaps, if they had been deaf instead.

"I already told you, Cartwright. You are no partner of mine and you never will be. I accuse you. I accuse you of trying to defraud my dead partner's widow. And I give you fair warning. Either you abandon this attempt to mix into my affairs, or I shall have the law take a hand. I'll have you arrested and charged with robbing Mrs. Shannon of her late husband's estate. Mind what I tell you, Cartwright. This thing stops right here and now or—" Whatever else he might have said went unspoken as Craig Albritton came out of the bank and inadvertently stepped onto the sidewalk between them.

"Neal," Craig said pleasantly, as yet unaware of the tension between Hubbard and Ben Cartwright. "I was just about to come up and see if you were in. You can save me the climb." He looked down and began rummaging through the papers in his briefcase in search of the document copies that had been prepared for the railroad partners.

Neal Hubbard snorted angrily and stormed away without a word for the lawyer who was also one of the railroad partners.

"Did I say something wrong, Ben?"

"Not that I know of, Craig. I'll tell you one thing, though. Your friend Mr. Hubbard has a real knot in his tail over the idea of me coming in as a shareholder. Huh. You'd think I was trying to ruin things for him instead of helping."

"He'll see things differently once I explain it to him, Ben," Albritton said. "Don't worry about a thing. Neal will come around. You'll see." The lawyer smiled. "Why, before this is all over, I'll wager Neal Hubbard will be singing your praises and thanking me for helping to bring you into the deal."

Ben was not so certain about that, but did not dispute Albritton's view on the subject. It was a wager he really should have accepted.

This was just about as good as it got, and Ben knew it. He sat in a reclining position with his eyes closed, his ankles crossed, and his hands comfortably folded over the flat of his belly. He was not asleep, but he was not far from it either. His cheeks and neck stung slightly from the moist, steamy heat of the barber's towel. Nearby he could hear the rhythmic shhhhh-pop, shhhhh-pop of a razor on the strop. Ben sighed with contentment and tried to ignore the faint beginnings of an itch in the small of his back; he really did not want to sit up and scratch just now.

A bell chimed as the barbershop door was opened, and Ben could hear boot steps at the front of the room. A puff of cool air swept in and ruffled the edges of the sheet draped over him from nape to knees.

"Hello, Dave. Wanting a trim, are you?"

"No trim, Johnny. I'm looking for a fella."

"That so?"

"Ayuh. Fella about, oh, yea tall. White hair. City dressed."

"This fella have a name, Dave?"

"Ayuh. Cartwright."

Ben opened his eyes. "My name is Cartwright." Both the barber and the man named Dave were already looking at him. "You knew that already, I take it?"

"Kinda thought maybe," Dave admitted.

"What is it you want, sir?"

"Mr. Cartwright, I don't know as you'd really want me t' answer that. Not here where Johnny can listen in."

"No?"

"No," the man named Dave said, pulling a wallet from inside his coat and opening it to display a lawman's star-in-wreath badge.

"I see," Ben said, not really seeing at all but trying to be polite about the matter. "Must I leave before I'm finished here?"

"You ain't under arrest, Mr. Cartwright, if that's what you're asking. You do what you think best. But, uh, I'd ruther if you was t' pull that sheet back a mite so's I can see your hands. If you don't mind, that is."

It occurred to Ben that the marshal, or deputy, or whatever his official title might be, was standing with his thumbs hooked into his belt so that his hand was never more than a few inches from the butt of his revolver.

"Johnny," Ben said, "why don't we do this later? And you could remove the sheet if you would be so kind."

The barber nodded, unpinned the sheet from around Ben's neck and pulled it away.

"You ain't carrying," Dave observed.

Ben smiled at him. "No, but I couldn't think of any reason why you should have believed that if I'd mentioned it at the time."

"Don't suppose I woulda," Dave agreed.

The barber unwound the towel from Ben's cheeks and neck—funny how a sensation that had seemed so warm and comforting only moments earlier he now found to be just damp and clammy—and Ben sat upright in the chair.

Better able to get a look at this unexpected visitor now, Ben saw a man in his mid- to early thirties, lean and pale, with the splotched and unhealthy look of the consumptive. He wore a huge mustache and a ratty scrap of chin whiskers. His suit was much worn and slightly shabby, but his shirt was clean and his collar crisp and spanking new. Shirt and collar alike were buttoned high at the throat, although he wore no necktie. His hair was a dull and lifeless chestnut hue that lay in a tangle on top and was cut so close as to appear almost shaved from the ears downward. A gun and holster dangled from his belt near the buckle. In spite of the armament, he looked more like a bank clerk than a marshal.

"You're Mr. Benjamin Cartwright of Nevada?" he asked once Ben was on his feet.

"That's right."

"I'm Dave Ossamer, Mr. Cartwright. Town marshal o' Johns Bend."

"Pleasure to meet you, Marshal Ossamer."

"Likewise, I'm sure. Whyn't you come along to my office, Mr. Cartwright? No charges, mind. I just want a few minutes t' visit with you. In private, I think might be best."

"As you wish, then." The barber held Ben's coat for

him, and he slipped it on, then said, "We'll finish this up later, Johnny."

"Yes, sir, Mr. Cartwright."

Ben followed Marshal Ossamer outside and two blocks down to City Hall. The county courthouse, where presumably there would be a sheriff's office and where Ben and Craig Albritton had gone earlier to record the transfers of title, was some blocks in the opposite direction. The marshal's office was in the basement of the City Hall building. There was a large room with several desks and a few extra chairs, and arranged along the back with stonework walls, stone floor, steel plate ceiling, and steel bars, were four small jail cells, all of them empty at the moment.

"Have a seat, Mr. Cartwright."

"Thank you."

"I don't keep no coffee here. Can't drink it myself, upsets my stomach something awful. I could pour you a little goat's milk if you want, or water. I got water."

"Nothing, thanks." Ben pulled out his pipe and began to load it.

"No offense, Mr. Cartwright, but I'd ruther you didn't light that. I can't be around smoke much. It's like fire in my lungs."

"That's a shame."

"Well, it is and it ain't. I don't allow no smoking in my jail. Funny how that makes some fellas think twice about doing something they might could be arrested over. They don't mind the lockup so bad, but they don't wanta be without their smokes. In a way you could say it cuts down on crime in Johns Bend."

"Useful," Ben observed.

"Yes, sir. Sometimes things are. Like sometimes it helps to have a talk instead o' jumping up an' doing things without you first think about what t' do."

"We're talking about today now, are we?"

"You could say that we are, Mr. Cartwright." Ossamer had been pacing slowly back and forth while Ben sat. Now he stopped beside his desk and slid up onto it so that he was sitting on the desk surface with his legs dangling free. "No offense intended, Mr. Cartwright, but I never in my life heard o' you before today. Now all of a sudden I ain't hearing about much of anything but you."

"I can see how that might be ... food for thought."

"Exactly. First somebody tells me you've bought out Mr. Lester Shannon's estate lock, stock, an' barrel. Then somebody else says you're over to the bank demanding t' see Mr. Neal Hubbard's personal accounts—no, you don't have t' correct me about that one, sir, I already found out that there was an exaggeration. Next thing, Mr. Neal Hubbard is screamin' in my face about how I'm supposed t' arrest you for stealing from the Widow Shannon, an' at the same time Miz Shannon's lawyer Mr. Albritton is saying that ain't so and ... Mr. Cartwright, for a fella I never heard of before, you sure have managed to make my day a interesting one."

"Yes, I can see what you mean. There has been a ... divergence of opinion, one might say."

"Divergence of opinion," Ossamer repeated slowly. "That's a real nice way t' put it. I'll remember that, thank you."

Ben waited.

"I already been to talk to Miz Shannon. Nice lady. I liked her husband too. Heckuva nice fella, Mr. Shannon was, always friendly. Always a good opinion o' everyone. Stood up as my sponsor to join the Elks Lodge. And Miz Shannon, when my Eleanor died it was Miz Shannon that washed her and laid her out and got all the other ladies in the church circle t'gether to set with her until the burying."

There was a point to all this, Ben was sure, even if he didn't know what it was.

Ossamer swung his legs and peered into the distance for a moment before he went on. "Miz Shannon, she tells me Mr. Shannon thought more o' you than just about anybody on the face o' God's green earth. Is that true, Mr. Cartwright?"

"Les and I were old friends. Good friends too, I would say. I trusted Les completely, and I believe he trusted me. As for that other, well, I would think that to be gilding the lily somewhat."

"Uh-huh." Ossamer looked off beyond the ceiling again. "D'you have any idea what I'd do 'bout someone that stole from a lady like Miz Shannon, Mr. Cartwright?"

"I think I have some idea, yes."

"She tells me you're all right, Mr. Cartwright. On t'other hand, Mr. Hubbard, he tells me you ain't. And he's a respected businessman in town here. Has the ear o' the town council, an' they're the gentlemen that hired me. They can fire me anytime they want too. If you get my meaning."

"I believe I do, Marshal."

"Yes, sir. So let me ask you right out, Mr. Cartwright, eyeball t' eyeball, man t' man. What is it that you get out o' all this?"

"What do I get out of it personally?"

"That's it, Mr. Cartwright. What was it that made you go an' buy up Mr. Shannon's property?"

"Shouldn't that be obvious? I was trying to help Mrs. Shannon."

"Is that right?"

"Yes, it is."

"You come in here not knowing Mr. Shannon is dead—so you say—an' when you find out he is, you buy everything he owned just as a favor for his widow . . . so you say."

"So I do say," Ben agreed calmly.

"How is it, Mr. Cartwright, that you just happened t' have the money on you that you could do that? I mean, I didn't ask Miz Shannon how much she got, but I'd guess all that property would come pretty dear."

"I didn't arrive here carrying a large amount of cash, Marshal. I arranged for the purchase—and you are quite correct that the exact amount Mrs. Shannon received for her property is none of your business—by way of a draft against a bank in San Francisco."

"That so?"

"You can verify it with Mr. Keith at the Miners and Merchants Bank if you wish."

Ossamer nodded and turned away to find a notepad and pencil on the desk. He took a moment to jot down some notes, then looked up again. "You told folks you didn't know Mr. Shannon was dead before you got here."

"That's right, I had no idea. I came to see him in response to a letter he sent me some . . . oh, it's been more than a month ago now, I believe, well more than a month, I'm sad to say. Perhaps if I'd been quicker to arrive—"

"You have any proof of that, Mr. Cartwright?"

"I probably still have his letter in my desk at home. I don't recall throwing it away. But I don't have it with me. Is that important?"

"I don't know, Mr. Cartwright. I'm just tryin' to get a handle on things, so t' speak. Just kinda talkin' in circles t' see if I can make sense o' things in a general sort o' way."

"Forgive me for disputing you, Marshal, but I'm getting the very strong impression that you have something entirely specific in mind here."

"I didn't say that, Mr. Cartwright."

"No, nor did you have to. The things you're asking me now have nothing to do with my purchase of some mining properties and railroad stock shares. Are you casting about in search of a motive for . . . foul play? Or worse?"

"I didn't say that either, Mr. Cartwright."

"You didn't have to, Marshal. You mentioned earlier that you and Les were lodge brothers. You also implied that you attended the same church. Would you say that the two of you were close?"

"I might say that we were. Not that it's any business o' yours."

"No, but most of the other men I've met here were friends of Les's in a business sense. I take it your friendship was on a personal level."

Ossamer shrugged.

"I think . . . Marshal, forgive me if I'm reading too

much into this, but perhaps there is something nagging at you. Possibly the same thing that has been nagging at me whenever I think about Les's death. The sort of thing that a friend might know where a business acquaintance would not."

"And what would that be, Mr. Cartwright?"

"Lester Shannon hated and feared nitroglycerin explosives, Marshal. I know that for a fact. He refused to have anything to do with nitroglycerin or even with dynamite. He insisted on using blasting powder. Only powder. He used to say that economy was the reason, that powder cost less than dynamite. But the full truth was that he was afraid of nitro. He told that himself because we were friends and didn't mind if our weaknesses became known. But with business friends he always explained it away by saying the powder was cheaper to buy. Did you know that about Les, Marshal? Did you know why he refused to use nitro or dynamite in his diggings?"

Ossamer didn't say anything. He didn't have to. His expression was answer enough.

"Tell me something, Marshal Ossamer. Did Lester Shannon die in a mining accident? Or was his death no accident at all?"

Again there was no answer.

"Whatever it is you are driving at, Marshal, you won't find me standing in your way. In fact I'll be glad to help you any way I possibly can. No matter the consequences, to myself or to anyone else."

Ossamer peered off through the ceiling for a while and then, without turning his head or looking back toward Ben again, he said, "Thank you for coming by, Mr. Cartwright. Maybe we can talk again sometime."

"Any time, Marshal," Ben said, standing and reaching for his hat. "Good day."

Ossamer didn't answer. When it became obvious that he wasn't going to, Ben quietly slipped out of the office and headed back to the Bent Lodge.

CHAPTER 12

P a was spitting mad. Well, what passed for spitting mad. With Pa that wasn't so easy to tell. Sometimes Pa was at his maddest when he got his quietest. In this case it was a down-deep sort of burn that said Pa was fixing to dig his heels in and turn scrappy. That was sign that Joe knew how to read, and it was all there to be seen right now. Luckily, none of it was directed on him.

"That pusillanimous so-and-so," Pa said in a deceptively even tone. "He called the law on me, Joseph. He refused to allow me access to the records of a company in which as of this afternoon I am the major stockholder—a fact which he knew quite good and well—and then on top of that he actually filed a complaint against me with the law in this town. Incredible!"

"Yes, sir." Joe steepled his fingertips and slumped a bit lower in the hotel room chair so as to make himself comfortable for the long term. Now that Pa was wound up and spouting, Joe suspected he might be in for a long term indeed.

"And it turns out that the law here, this Marshal Ossamer, was a friend of Les's too. Unless I'm misreading him completely—and I don't believe that I am—he has his own suspicions. I think the marshal believes Les may have been the victim of a deliberate plot on his life. He was

121

willing to think me responsible for it or I doubt I would have known that, but that is what I gather from the questions he was asking me this afternoon. He isn't sure that Les was murdered, but he certainly has doubts.

"Then to top it all off, when I left the marshal's office this afternoon, I went over to the Shan-Rock mine to inspect my new property. And do you know what, Joseph? They wouldn't allow me in. Even when I told them who I was. No entry. By order of the superintendent, some fellow name of Burke. Harrumph! We'll just see about that."

"They didn't believe you?"

"The simpleton on duty there this afternoon wouldn't so much as tell me what he did or did not believe. All he would do was repeat that he had his orders and no one was allowed in or out without this Mr. Burke's approval. He was a real muttonhead, this one. So I left. What else could I do? It was either leave or get into a fistfight with him, and I didn't think that would accomplish anything in the long run. So I left and marched right over to Albritton's office for him to go back with me and verify to those idiots that I was indeed the new owner. But by then Albritton had closed his office and gone off for the evening. So I came back here. But tomorrow morning, first thing tomorrow morning—"

"I'll go with you, Pa."

"Actually, Joseph," Ben cleared his throat, "there is something else I want you to do."

"Yes, sir?"

"All I intended, you know, was to come here to visit with Les and discuss an investment opportunity. Then I wanted to help Chloe if I could. Now . . . well, now I'm thinking there may be much more to this than meets the eye, what with the marshal's suspicions and the railroad partnership's intransigence."

"You think they're related, Pa?"

"No, not really. In fact, the more I think about it, the more inclined I am to think the marshal is wrong about Les's death involving foul play."

"How's that, Pa? You've commented yourself about Mr. Shannon not wanting anything to do with nitroglycerin explosives."

"True, but I've been giving that some serious thought since I spoke with Marshal Ossamer earlier. You have to keep in mind that this railroad was important to Les. He had everything invested in it, just at the very time the production of his mining properties was beginning to decline. The railroad would overcome that, according to what Adam tells us, and surely Les must have known that too. Having a railroad to haul the ore so it could be refined by way of these new processes would have made a tremendous difference in the productivity of Les's mines. It would increase his income even if the ore bodies were deteriorating. With that kind of incentive, Joseph, it's entirely possible that Les would have decided to ignore his own prejudices and go ahead with the use of nitro. After all, the drilling is quicker and more efficient with nitro. He might have thought the possible benefits outweighed the dangers. And knowing Les, he might very well have decided to try the nitro out for himself before he asked any of his men to use it. My inclination at the moment, Joseph, is to discount the marshal's concerns on that subject. On the other hand, I do have doubts about the efficiency of the railroad planning. Why else would Hubbard and Dadley want to deny me access to the records? Quite a lot of money has been put into this project. I think it's entirely possible that those two have been guilty of some sort of mismanagement. They might well want to hide that knowledge from a stranger like me. Not that they will get away with it. If necessary I'll get a court injunction forcing them to open the books for my inspection."

"You can do that?"

"Easily."

"Even though we're strangers here?"

"With Craig Albritton and Chloe Shannon standing behind my request, I'm quite sure I can get the injunction.

Then we shall see if the railroad will continue or if the corporation should be dissolved."

"Why would you want to dissolve the corporation, Pa?"

"If the railroad plans can't be completed, then it only makes sense to disband the project and return the income from the mines to Chloe."

Joe sat up a little straighter on his chair. "I think I'm beginning to get the idea of what you're up to, Pa. No wonder those fellows don't want you rooting around in their cellar. Not if you could mess them up like that."

"Well, I won't mess them up, as you put it. Not without good cause."

"I know that, Pa, but they wouldn't. They got no reason to think you'll go ahead and do what's best for the railroad. Why, they're likely to think you just want to take the profits from the mines and never mind if the railroad ever gets built. That's what I might think if some stranger came and muscled into my deal. Take the cream off the top an' run with it."

"Good point, Joseph. I'll have to remember to assure them otherwise. If the railroad is still a viable plan, by all means it should be built and put into service. I must let them know that I mean that."

"You said there was something you wanted me to do in the meantime?"

"Yes. I would hope for the cooperation of the gentlemen here, Joseph, but I won't count on it. That's where you come in. I want you to carry a letter for me."

"Sir?"

"I want you to go back to San Francisco, Joseph. I want you to speak with Mr. DeShong about our problems here. It seems the railroad's bank accounts are not kept here in town, and no one, not even Mr. Albritton, knows where they are maintained. No one, that is, but Mr. Hubbard and possibly Lucas Dadley. All we know is the name of the brokerage house in San Francisco where the assessment drafts have been converted into cash. Where the cash goes after that . . . we haven't a clue. I'm hoping that with his contacts in San Francisco, Alton DeShong can find out where the High Sierra Short Line bank accounts are maintained. I don't need any privileged information, you see. Just the name of the bank or banks that hold the accounts. I can get access by way of a court order, but first I must know what to ask the court to grant. I need the name of that bank."

"That's all?"

"That will be quite a lot."

"You just want me to go down and ask Mr. DeShong to ask around for you."

"That's right."

Joe grinned. "I can handle that, Pa."

"Of course you can."

"I can leave first thing in the morning. There's a stage scheduled out at a quarter past seven. It connects with the Central Pacific in time for the night coach to Vallejo."

"That would be just fine."

Just fine, Joe thought, and he was still thinking so hours afterward when he lay wide awake on the hard, hotel mattress trying to go to sleep but so wound up from thinking that he couldn't manage to drift off. Just fine. Sure, it would be fine. Why, there wasn't one single thing in the errand Pa wanted him to do that a stamp and an envelope couldn't handle just as easy.

Get the little boy out of the way, that was more like it.

Why, that was purely unfair.

Pa didn't believe there'd been any foul play about Mr. Shannon's death. But he wasn't going to trust that belief so far that he'd allow his youngest, the baby, to stay around here. Drat it, why'd they always insist on thinking he was some kind of wet-behind-the-ears kid? No, send the baby off outta the way. Just in case.

And those railroad partners. They'd already called the law on Pa once. Who knew what they might be up to next?

Pa didn't want him underfoot. Didn't trust him. That was the truth of it, the way Joe saw it. Just plain didn't trust him to handle himself.

Well, maybe they'd just have to see about that.

Pa wanted Mr. DeShong told about the situation and asked to come up with the name of some silly bank? Fine. Like Joe already figured out, that was something that could be taken care of with a stamp and an envelope.

As for the situation here in Johns Bend—that was something Joe could take care of his own way.

All he had to do now was figure out just how to go about that.

He lay with his eyes wide open and staring in the darkness, hands laced behind his neck while he pondered how best he should go about handling this in a mature and rational manner.

CHAPTER 13

Ben saw Joseph off—along with all his vast store of luggage—on the morning stage south, then made his way back, not to the Bent Lodge, but to the Canterbury Café. Craig Albritton was not there. In fact, Ben did not recognize a single soul in the place. Apparently the breakfast crowd and the mid-morning coffee coolers were a completely different group. Ben dawdled over his meal to make sure Albritton had ample time to open his office.

Even so, there was no sign of the lawyer at the office by nine o'clock. Grumbling, Ben turned away. His passage was blocked by a stocky man built with the beam, if not the grace, of a square-rigger. The fellow was half a head shorter than Ben and stood athwart his path with hands on hips and a belligerent attitude.

"Is there something I can do for you?" Ben asked.

"If you're Cartwright there is."

"I'm Ben Cartwright."

"I'm Fitzhugh Burke, and I know more than you or any man about the workings of the Shan-Rock mine. Or for that matter, the rest of 'em too. I've worked underground in every mine Lester Shannon ever owned, mister. The Shan-Rock, the Caroline, the Mobeetie, all of 'em. I know 'em. I know 'em inside and out. And Mr. Shannon, he made me his superintendent, he did. He told me the job was mine to keep. So don't think you can come in here and fire me this way. I won't go, I won't. Mr. Shannon gave me this job his own self, and he meant me to keep it. I already seen a lawyer. I got rights. You try an' fire me, mister, you got a fight on your hands."

"Fire you! Wherever did you get an idea like that?"

"Mr. Hub—never mind."

"Mr. Hubbard told you that I intended to fire you? Surely you know better than to listen to rumors like that, Mr. Burke. I bought the Shannon properties, yes, but it certainly doesn't follow that I would want to fire everyone now. That would be stupid, wouldn't it?"

"That's what I was telling you. It'd be real stupid."

Ben smiled. "We are in agreement about that."

Some of the truculence faded from Burke's expression. "You ain't gonna try and fire me?"

"Not without good cause, certainly, and I know of no cause. Yet."

"Mr. Hubbard said—"

"Mr. Hubbard was, ahem, in error."

Burke grunted. "Reckon I made a mistake, huh?"

"Only a small one of no consequence."

"Yeah, well, they said you was at the Shan-Rock yesterday, wanting in."

"That's right."

"Guess I'd best have a word with my boys, eh?"

"That would be good, yes."

"Look, Mr. Cartwright, maybe you and me, we could kinda take a step back an', you know, start over?"

Ben smiled again. "I'm sure we could, Mr. Burke."

Burke grinned and literally, physically, stepped a pace back, turned around and came forward again, this time with his hand extended. "Mr. Cartwright, sir, I'm Fitzhugh Burke, and it's my pleasure t' make your acquaintance, sir."

Ben accepted the offer of the handshake much more readily than he had welcomed the scowl before.

*   *   *

"All the way down, Benny."

"Yes sir, Mr. Burke." The lift operator shifted on his stool and spat a stream of brown juice into a rusty tin can that served as a cuspidor by his work station. "Level eight, it is. Grab hold, Mr. Cartwright. It's a long way down."

Ben took hold of one of the thick cables, smearing his hands with thick, gooey grease, but glad for the support a moment later when Benny threw the lever on the steam donkey that controlled the hoist, and the huge steel bucket dropped freewheeling into the hole that was the Shan-Rock mine.

Ben's stomach felt like it was still at the surface even as the bucket continued its controlled fall through a Sty-gian shaft, the darkness broken only now and then as lanterns and oil lamps flickered past.

"How far is it that we're going, Mr. Burke?" Ben asked, quite acutely aware of the tightness in his throat that made it difficult to speak.

"Not so far really," Burke said, as calm and unruffled as if they'd been seated in the lobby of the Bent Lodge. "Bottom level is twelve hundred foot, more or less. That's the eighth level we've opened. Right now we're working eight an' seven an' doing a little cleanup work on six. One and three are played out complete. The others could still be worked some, but the ore has most pinched out in them an' they don't pay real well. Not worth the trouble any more unless things get awful tight. Or the price o' gold goes up. Which ain't likely to happen, the way I hear it."

"No, I suppose not," Ben agreed. Unlike the more volatile silver, gold prices had been stable for years. Ben knew it was highly unlikely there would be any significant change in the value of gold during his lifetime. Perhaps not even during that of his sons. "I was told the production values are down," he said, wishing this downward plunge would soon end.

"That's right. I got the figures in the office up top. You can go over 'em whenever you're of a mind to. But you got 'er right to begin with. The old Shan-Rock is still paying—don't think it isn't—but it ain't producing like it used to. Used to pay sixty-five, seventy dollars a ton. Now it's closer to forty. And that ain't the profit, mind. That's the recovery. Wages, upkeep, all the operating expenses got to come out of that. And o' course the deeper we go, the more it costs to produce the ore, what with having to lift it all in this here bucket. It all takes time and man-power. You, uh, know about that stuff, do you?"

"Don't worry, Mr. Burke. I understand about the costs of doing business."

"Yeah, well, mining ain't like most other businesses. Mining is touchy. So are miners. You got t' know men if you want to get along underground."

Ben knew something about mining. He was a partic-ipant in several mining ventures in the fabled Comstock close to home. He also knew something about men, how-ever, and he suspected that Fitzhugh Burke would prefer to think that his knowledge was superior to that of his new employer. Which of course it was. Burke's pride, Ben sus-pected, was such that the man would be happier if he thought he possessed an overwhelming advantage. That would help restore the confidence that had been shattered when Neal Hubbard made him believe he was to be fired. Ben wanted to be particularly careful about ruffling Burke's feathers here, because it was his hope that he would soon be able to return control of the Shan-Rock to Chloe Shannon. Ben himself did *not* want to be saddled with the responsibility for properties in Johns Bend, Cali-fornia. He was well aware of his role as a caretaker, there-fore. Not only did he not wish to fire Burke, he intended to preserve the status quo in this and the other mines as much as was humanly possible.

There was a stomach-wrenching jolt as somewhere far overhead the lift operator began to apply the brake on the donkey motor. Ben felt the cable stretch—or was that only his imagination?—and the rate of fall quickly slowed.

They descended at a speed Ben judged to be a brisk

walk, if anyone could walk up or down a vertical wall, past a brightly lighted platform where a line of ore carts filled to overflowing with lumps of perfectly ordinary-looking gray rock sat waiting. A man wearing a carbide lamp strapped to his cap waved and gave them a cheery greeting as the bucket went by.

"That's level seven," Burke said helpfully. "Looks like Ray—he's shift foreman on seven—looks like Ray has a load t' go up."

"In this same bucket?" Ben asked.

"That's right. We only got the one bucket an' the one hoist. Everything in or out, it has t' go this way."

"What if the cable breaks or the steam donkey breaks or something?"

Burke grinned and, as the bucket came to a lurching, swaying stop at the bottom of the shaft, pointed to a rather rickety-looking wooden ladder that was spiked into the solid rock of the shaft walls.

"You can't be serious," Ben said.

"Anybody don't wanta climb out, he's welcome to stay down long as he wants. O' course, you never know how long it'll take t' get things fixed whenever something busts. You just never know."

"It does happen then?"

"O' course it happens. I wouldn't call it common, but it happens time t' time."

"And the men have to climb out on that ladder."

"Ah, this hole ain't so deep. Some places they run two, three thousand foot down. Now that'd be a climb." Burke chuckled.

Ben shook his head and laughed, but he knew what Burke said was true. There were mining districts where a measly twelve hundred feet would be considered a scratch in the dirt. As for climbing out in the event of equipment failure or, God forbid, trouble in the hole, the Comstock by now had become so interconnected that more often than not a crew stranded in one mine could simply find their way into a competitor's drifts and ask for a lift. But that was there. And this was Johns Bend, not Virginia City. Ben tilted his head back and stared up the dark, ghostly shaft.

"Watch your step, mister."

Ben brought his gaze back to where it should be and saw a bearded man in lamp cap and clothing impregnated so full of gray rock dust that the fabric had lost all color. The miner was steadying the suspended ore bucket with one foot while he reached to take the visitor's arm. Here, of course, a misstep would not have been so serious. The bottom of the main shaft, littered with chunks of stone and gold ore and ancient lunch wrappings, was no more than twenty or so feet beneath the bucket. At any other level a fall from the bucket would be instantly and irrevocably fatal.

"Thanks." Ben stepped onto the platform and Burke followed close behind him.

"Clear," Burke said.

The miner stepped to the side and took hold of a cord that Ben had noticed ran the full depth of the shaft from top to bottom. The fellow gave it a sharp tug, and a bell attached to it rang briskly.

"That tells the hoist man the bucket's empty again," Burke said. "There's a bell, see, up top and on each an' every drift level. Tug the cord an' all the bells ring. That way everybody can listen in an' know how the bucket's moving."

Almost instantly the bell rang again, this time without the level eight man touching it. It rang several times, paused and rang several times more.

"The first series asked Benny for an ore hoist, the second one told him it's level seven asking."

The bell chimed twice more.

"That's Benny acknowledging and saying he'll put the bucket at seven."

"How does the lift operator know where the bucket is?" Ben asked.

"Easy. Markings on the cable. Let out so much cable, the bucket's got t' be so far down."

"Of course. Simple." There was a clank and the bucket was drawn up out of sight. Ben started over toward the platform, intending to lean out so he could watch it rise toward the seventh level.

"I wouldn't do that if I was you, mister," the level eight miner said.

"No?"

"You do what you want, of course, but rocks fall all the time. Tools and stuff gets kicked over the edge of the other levels up higher. You stick your head out there to look, mister, you're real likely to get a face full of rock. But like I said," the fellow grinned, "you do what you want."

"Thanks for the advice, friend."

"Any time." As if to emphasize the worth of that advice, there was a dull clatter and a stream of broken ore bits fell past the open platform.

"They're dumping the carts now," Burke said. "Pouring the ore out of those carts you saw, into the bucket. You can hear if you listen close."

They waited in silence for a moment to give Ben time to listen if he wished, then Burke picked up a lantern and motioned for the new owner to follow.

It was cool inside the mine. Not cold exactly, but brisk. Ben suspected it could feel cold after ten or twelve hours of working underground, however long a shift was in the Shan-Rock. He asked.

"Ten-hour days. I used to tell Mr. Shannon twelve is better, but he insisted on ten. Said the two hours at the ends was needed for dust to clear after the blasting shots was fired anyhow, so tens would do. If you want, Mr. Cartwright, we can go to twelves. Just say the word. I think we should. Always have thought so."

"I wouldn't think it would be a good idea to expand the payroll costs now with production falling."

"Nobody said nothing about more pay, just more

hours. These boys already get top wages. Three dollars a day. Won't many of them move along if we make the workday twelve hours instead o' ten. And any that goes will be easy enough replaced. Most places work twelves anyhow."

"For the time being," Ben said, "we'll leave things the way Les had them."

"Whatever you say. Just let me know if you change your mind."

"I will, thank you."

The tour was interesting enough, if not quite so new to Ben as Fitzhugh Burke might have believed. There was little difference between the mining here and that in Virginia City. If anything, it was easier here. The native rock was much more stable here, so shoring timbers did not have to be nearly so elaborate as in the Comstock. And there was far less moisture here. In the Comstock district the walls and floors seeped water constantly, and it was a struggle to keep the mines pumped free of its intrusion. Here the rock was nearly dry.

As in any hard-rock mine, the process was simple and logical. A drift, which is a hole that does not bore all the way through a mountain—unlike a tunnel, which is a hole that goes through something from one end to another—is run beneath the desired ore body. Then the miners burrow *up* to the ore, allowing gravity to do much of the work involved. The opening created by the upward-slanted ore removal is called a stope. Once blown out of the stope face, the valuable ores are separated and taken away on carts riding on rails made of steel or, mostly, wood. The Shan-Rock used steel carts and wooden rails. The unwanted matrix rock is then dumped in a previously emptied stope, and the miners follow the ore veins wherever they might lead.

The process was all quite comfortably familiar to Ben as he trailed Burke through the Shan-Rock.

"What's this?" he asked once as they passed a section of wall that was closed off with carefully laid stone mortared into place with cement. He hadn't seen anything remotely like that anywhere else in the mine.

"We don't go in there no more, Mr. Cartwright."

"No?"

"It's where Mr. Shannon had his accident."

"I see."

"We brought up what we could, but . . . it was pretty awful in there. Real bad. Mrs. Shannon, she said something about maybe putting a plaque here or . . . I dunno. Whatever. O' course, that was before you bought the place. I guess we'll do whatever you want, Mr. Cartwright. But the boys, I think they'd feel pretty bad if you was to want to open that stope again. Hope you don't mind me speaking free. I just thought you oughta know."

"Yes, of course."

"The ores wasn't so good in there that you'd ought to want to go in again anyway."

"We'll certainly leave it closed then, Mr. Burke. And I'll try to remember to ask Mrs. Shannon about that plaque."

"That'd be nice, sir. Real nice." Burke cleared his throat and resumed the guided tour through the depths of the Shan-Rock mine.

Ben felt a chill as he passed the sealed portal behind which Les died such a horrible, violent death. But then, it was cold so far below the earth's surface. He should have thought to bring a sweater or overcoat, that was all.

CHAPTER 14

It was after dark when the freight wagon rolled into town. By that time every bone in Joe's body was hurting in one form or another. Practically since dawn he had been pounded, pummeled, bounced, and shaken, first on the stagecoach south, and then on the wagon coming back north again.

At the railroad he'd taken time to ship his luggage east and a long letter west, then he'd barely been in time to speak with the driver of the big wagon that was transferring sacks of flour and cornmeal from the railroad to merchants in Johns Bend.

There hadn't been time left over for him to get any lunch. And frankly he hadn't thought about it at the time anyway, as it was then well short of noon.

Well, that was certainly a dim and distant memory at this point, and he still hadn't had a chance to eat. Not even a proper breakfast this morning. It had been early, and he hadn't been especially hungry. All he'd had to eat this whole day long was a pair of sweet rolls before he left Johns Bend, and a piece of jerky this afternoon. He'd had to practically beg the freighter to get the man to part with that bit of jerked beef.

Now Joe's stomach knotted and churned with hunger in addition to the other pains of travel.

When the wagon rolled to a halt behind the J. C. Reardon Mercantile, Joe waited until it came to a complete stop, then vaulted over the side to land with both feet planted firmly on solid footing. He'd had quite enough jolting and jostling in the back of that wagon for the time being, thank you.

He stood with his feet braced wide apart and took a moment to stretch, loosening cramped muscles, then reached into the back of the wagon and lifted out the lone bundle of spare clothes that he'd saved out from all the luggage he'd shipped back home to the Ponderosa.

"Hey," the freighter called angrily. "Where d'you think you're going?"

"Supper," Joe told him. "I'm hungry."

"D'you see all we got to unload here?"

Joe grinned. "Sure do."

"Well, grab a sack and get to it, boy."

Joe took another look at the thick, hundredweight sacks of meal, then looked back at the man driving the wagon. "Remember this afternoon when you were having your dinner? Remember what you told me then?"

"Nope."

"You said if I'd wanted a lunch, I should've brought one along."

"So?"

"So I reckon I'll carry off this wagon all the sacks I put onto it. Which would be just this one," he hefted his clothes bundle, "not any of those. Thanks for the ride." He turned and started walking away.

"Hey! You!" There was a thump as the driver jumped down off the wagon, then the sound of running footsteps.

Joe stopped and turned to face the angry driver.

"You owe me."

"Do I?"

"You're gonna unload those sacks, boy, or I'll take my whip to you."

For the first time Joe's expression lost its teasing amiability. "I expect maybe you will," he said softly. "If it turns out you're man enough."

The driver frowned. "I didn't mean—"

"No? What did you mean, then?"

"I just . . . you know how it is."

"No, tell me."

"I . . . aw, never mind."

"Thank you for the ride," Joe said, his voice still soft.

"Ye—uh . . . yeah." The driver turned away, mumbling something under his breath, which Joe figured he was better off not hearing anyway, and went back to his rig at a pace that was just barely short of a scurry.

Joe slung the bundle over his shoulder and strode out in search of a workingman's café or restaurant where the chuck would be cheap and filling. He was careful to skirt a block wide of the Bent Lodge, though. It wouldn't much do for him to be spotted in town now that he'd gone to all this trouble.

Joe fingered his chin, then probed between the two middle buttons on his shirt to scratch his stomach. He hoped that itch was caused by a stray bit of straw and not by some little passenger he might've picked up during the night.

He'd spent the night in a cold but otherwise fairly comfortable rick of barley straw at the back end of the livery stable. It wasn't a first-class hotel accommodation, but all it cost was a dime bribe to the hostler so he'd look the other way.

This morning Joe needed a shave and a hairbrush and he itched all over. But his belly was warm and full from a huge mess of oatmeal and coffee—all a body could hold of each for a nickel—and his newfound pal, Harlan, assured him things were looking up.

Joe and Harlan had met at the café earlier. Harlan was nursing a hangover fit for framing so it could be admired by future generations—or so he said, anyway—and was drawn into conversation by a combination of awe and repulsion as he watched Joe eat.

"I swear, neighbor, I never seen anybody wrap hisself around porridge so quick. No, don't do that no more, not where I can see." He screwed up his face and made a gagging noise. "Eeeyuu! Don't. I can't stand no more of this."

Joe grinned at him and took another big bite, cleaning out his second bowl and quickly reaching to refill it.

"You're cruel, neighbor. Got a heart of stone in you," Harlan said, squinting his eyes near closed and holding his coffee cup under his nose and breathing deep as if to steam the hangover away.

"Got no heart at all," Joe said agreeably, "but a big appetite. That comes from having brothers. A fellow has to learn to defend himself at the table when he has brothers, older ones especially."

"Got brothers, do you? So do I. Younger ones in my case."

"No doubt you taught them all they need to know in a situation like this. Pity you didn't learn some of it for yourself while you were at it. Pass those raisins, please. Don't you want a few more?"

Harlan made a face again. "Please! I tried to eat a raisin in the first bite I took. It scampered off my spoon. That was enough for one morning, I think."

"The prices we pay, eh? Was last night's fun worth all this?"

Harlan laughed. "It must've been. Not that I can remember any of it. But it was expensive enough."

"Oh?"

"Aye." Harlan leaned closer and confided in a rasping whisper that could have been heard half a block away. "I woke up so broke this morning, I don't even have the wherewithal t' pay for this wretched meal. One more cup o' java and I'll slide outta here. Watch me and learn." He winked broadly and laughed, then sobered a little. "Good morning, Charlie."

"I'm gonna break your neck, Harlan. See if I don't."

The whisper had indeed been overheard. Now the proprietor of the café, a man bigger than Joe and Harlan combined, was standing behind the seated Harlan. He had a firm grip on Harlan's collar.

"He's joshing you, Charlie," Joe put in. "I told him I'd buy this morning. That's why he's kidding around like this. He really isn't going to pay, but not the way it sounds."

"You mean that, boy?"

"Sure thing. Here." Joe dug deep into his pockets and came out with a half-dime, a three-cent piece, and two pennies to pay for both their breakfasts. The bruiser named Charlie grunted, and let go his hold on Harlan.

Once Charlie was gone, Harlan broke into laughter again. "I owe you, don't I?"

"Naw."

"Yes I do, and Harlan Kane never forgets a favor nor a friend. Which I expect you are now, like it or not."

Joe grinned and stuck out his hand. Which was how he came to become acquinted with Harlan, and which was how he came now to be standing in a line of men waiting outside the guard shack at the Shan-Rock mine.

"Are you sure they're hiring?" Joe asked for probably the twentieth time.

"Sure they are. The Shan-Rock is always hiring. Why, I bet I've hired on with them eight, ten times myself."

"How come so often?"

"Part of it's my own dang fault," Harlan confessed. "I get a couple dollars ahead and I try to turn it into a fortune at the faro tables. That ain't so bad unless I win a little. Then I kinda get lost for a week or three. Time I know what's what again, I don't have a job no more. The rest of it," he shrugged, "ol' Fitz Burke is a funny bird. Every so often he takes a notion to get mad at some guy. There's no help for it then but to either quit or get fired. Once Fitz gets it in his head that he's down on a guy, the guy is gonna wind up gone, one reason or any other. It don't mat-

ter what he does to try and stop it. Fitz won't listen to reason once he gets started in on a guy."

"That doesn't seem fair."

"Fair? Who's talking fair? I'm talking three dollars a
day and all the rock dust you can eat."

Joe laughed.

"Funny. Sure. But it ain't all that bad. Fitz is notional,
but he has to have *some*body down there to get the job
done. He'll hire a guy back even if he's just fired the same
guy a week ago. To tell you the truth, I think Fitz doesn't
remember one guy from another. We're all just lumps of
muscle and sweat so far as he cares. Foreman and bosses
he calls by name. Everybody else is Bo to him. So don't
take it personal when he can't remember your name. Just
tell him you're Bo. It won't matter anyhow."

"All right. But do you think I can get the job?"

"Sure, no sweat. I'll vouch for you."

"But you said—"

Harlan laughed. "Trust me."

"Whatever you say."

"Name?"

"Harlan Kane. Hell, Fitz, you remember me. I
worked under you here two years ago. Or was it three? I
was your lead spiker then."

Harlan, Joe observed in silence, had told him not
twenty minutes ago that he'd worked in the Shan-Rock
two or three *weeks* ago loading ore carts for Superintendent Burke.

"Yeah, sure, I remember you. Good man. Good
worker."

"That's me all right, Fitz." Harlan turned his head
enough to give Joe a wink. "I've come up in the world
since then. Me and my partner Bo here, we're a team.
Drilling team. Best damn drillers you ever seen, that's us."

"Yeah? Got your own tool dresser?"

"Not with us. He went off and got married."

"Dumb," Burke said.

"Yeah, but you can assign us a good dresser. We don't mind."

"You're the singlejack man?"

"That's right. I swing the hammer and Bo here spins the drill for me. We can punch a hole in rock easy as that guy over there sticks a knife into a pork chop."

"Three bucks a day," Burke said.

"Fitz!" Harlan sounded positively wounded. "We're a tip-top drilling crew. First-class work and nothing but. Guys like us are worth at least four dollars."

"Three bucks."

"Three and found."

"Three or get the hell out of here."

"It's a pleasure to be working for you again, Fitz."

Burke grunted. He leaned to the side and peered suspiciously at Joe. "What'd he say your name was again?"

"Bo," Joe said. "Bo . . . Burns." It wasn't exactly a lie. Not the Burns part anyway. It was his middle name. It had just occurred to him that it might not be a good idea to be tossing the name Cartwright around too casually. Not since a Cartwright just turned up as the new owner of the place.

Harlan give him an odd look and then a shrug. But then at the café Joe had given Harlan his real name. There hadn't been any reason not to at the time. Now . . . now it was a good thing Harlan didn't seem to care. Bo Burns it was. For as long as his pal Joe wanted, and without any silliness like asking for the reasons why. Harlan, it seemed, was easy to get along with.

"You ready, Bo?"

"For what?"

"For to go to work, of course."

"Now?"

"Yes now. When'd you think? C'mon over here. You can stash that stuff of yours with the hoist operator and draw a lamp to use. When we come up after our shift, I'll take you over to the boardinghouse. Ten bucks a week, but they feed pretty good and everybody's working the same shift." Harlan grinned. "Trust me."

Joe chuckled and said, "Why do I get the idea I oughta turn around and run instead?"

"Hey," Harlan said with a show of utter innocence, "are we pals, Bo, or what?"

"Reckon you haven't steered me wrong yet."

"Not that you know about," Harlan agreed cheerfully. "C'mon now, we better hustle or we'll miss that bucket down."

CHAPTER 15

When a second business day dawned with no sign of Craig Albritton at the lawyer's locked and shuttered office, Ben went looking for the man. There was no one at Albritton's home, and by that time it was almost mid-morning anyway, so Ben next tried the Canterbury Café for the every-morning coffee crowd. Albritton was absent from his usual table, nor was Tom Keith in his accustomed spot, but Henry Vickers was there holding forth.

"Sit down, Ben. Join us." The newspaperman made the few introductions necessary. In addition to Vickers, the table included a mining engineer named Armstrong, Dr. Willard Monroe, and another lawyer named Victor Curtis.

"My pleasure, gentlemen."

"Believe us, Mr. Cartwright, the pleasure is all ours. After all, you're the sensation of the month," Armstrong said pleasantly.

"I?"

"Certainly. The mysterious financier from afar who whisks in and gobbles up the best mining properties in the district all in one sudden transaction. How could you be other than a sensation?"

Ben smiled. "I hadn't thought about it quite like that. But I do take your meaning. Should I apologize?"

144

"Heavens no. I'm sure we are all grateful for the excitement."

"To say nothing about sticking a thorn into Neal Hubbard's side," the doctor added in a dry voice.

"The rumors must be flying fast and furious."

Dr. Monroe exhibited a thin smile as he bent to his coffee cup. "The rumors are fast. The way I hear it, it's Hubbard who's furious."

"That wasn't my intention," Ben said.

"Good Lord, man, don't apologize. You'll ruin my enjoyment of the situation if you feel badly about it."

"I take it you don't particularly care for the gentleman in question?" Ben asked.

The doctor harrumphed and grunted but didn't otherwise answer. Armstrong took it upon himself to do so instead. "Willard and Neal got into a disagreement over a game of cards one night and—"

"Disagreement nothing," Monroe snapped. "The SOB was bottom-dealing me, I tell you. I saw him. Even if no one else did, dammit, I distinctly saw him do it. Twice. Once might have been my mistake. Twice was most definitely his."

"We know, Willard. You don't have to convince us."

The doctor harrumphed loudly again and shifted from side to side on his chair in an attempt to contain himself.

"You should understand, Mr. Cartwright, that Willard is one of the few gentlemen of substance in the community who are what you might call independent from Neal. Most of us are, or can be, affected by his displeasure."

"SOB," Monroe mumbled under his breath.

"Even Willard isn't completely immune from punishment. If you want to call it that. Willard had been retained as company doctor by nearly all the mines in Johns Bend before his disagreement with Neal. Since then more than half of them have dropped their association with him."

"Can you imagine? Now some little know-nothing of a schoolboy drives over twice a week all the way from

Harptown to hold a clinic. A clinic! I ask you! With my patients. Can you imagine it?"

"That's terrible," Ben said for the sake of politeness. He glanced across the table to Victor Curtis, who was remaining pointedly silent through all of this. Ben suspected there was a reason for that. Probably a reason having to do with client loyalties. After all, there couldn't be too awfully many lawyers in a town the size of Johns Bend, and Ben already knew that Craig Albritton was not Neal Hubbard's normal counsel.

"Where do you stand, Henry?" Ben asked. "I noticed you've been quiet so far."

"As always, Ben, I stand squarely atop the proverbial fence. A newspaperman can't take sides, you know. Fair and impartial treatment for one and all."

Armstrong snorted. The doctor rolled his eyes. Victor Curtis laughed aloud.

"Go ahead. Keep it up. See if I suffer your abuse any further. Ha! See if I buy you coffee anymore." Vickers was smiling when he made his threats.

"Don't tell me you lost again, Henry," Ben said.

"They're cheating me, Ben. I don't know how they do it, but they're cheating me. Don't ever play cards with them, I warn you."

"Everything I know I learned from that SOB Hubbard," Monroe said.

"Come to think of it, Willard, they do say that it takes a cheat to catch one."

"Well, I had to support myself through medical school some way, didn't I?" Monroe said with a grin.

"Ben, ignore these imbeciles. We have to talk."

"We do?"

"If I hadn't run into you by this fortunate chance, Ben, I would have been looking you up today anyway. I need a story for tomorrow's edition of the *Intelligencer*."

"And what would I have to do with that, Henry?"

"Come now, Ben, be serious. You know quite good and well you are the talk of the town. So let's put paid to the rumors. Give me the truth of your business interests here, and I'll put it into the paper for all to see."

Ben shrugged. "There isn't anything exciting I can tell you, Henry. It's a very simple situation. Mrs. Shannon was in possession of certain valuable properties that she was not, um, inclined to operate or manage by herself now that her husband has passed away. I made an offer, which she accepted. The properties are simply a business investment." Ben's expression was bland and agreeable. Never mind that it was at this very table that he'd learned Chloe Shannon was destitute and that her "valuable properties" were not able to provide her with any sort of livelihood. Nor did he choose to mention the railroad project for the time being, if only because none of the other gentlemen at the table had brought it up. He assumed they surely must know about it. But if they preferred to leave it out of the conversation, then perhaps he should follow suit.

"That isn't much of a news story, Ben."

"I told you it wouldn't be."

"I can get half the front page out of this, but I was hoping for more."

"Henry, surely you can't milk this for more than a paragraph. Can you?"

"Wait until you see his story tomorrow, Mr. Cartwright," Armstrong said. "You'll only recognize yourself if he remembers to spell your name right."

"No fear," Monroe said. "Henry isn't likely to start anything new at this late date."

"If we can be serious for a moment, gentlemen, has any of you seen Craig Albritton today?" Ben asked. "I've been looking for him for the past day and a half, but his office is closed and his home seems to be empty too."

"Sorry, Ben, I haven't seen him."

"No. Sorry."

"He's in Bryceville," Victor Curtis said. Ben was not sure, but he thought there was something of a sharp edge to the lawyer's tone of voice when he spoke.

"Oh?"

"On business. He's been asked to handle a civil case over there."

"What case is that, Vic?" Armstrong asked.

Curtis gave the engineer a glowering look.

"Not Crown Corporation's suit against the Royal Flush? I thought you were supposed to handle that."

Curtis's expression was sour indeed. For the benefit of the others, Armstrong explained, "It's a claim dispute, but a rather nasty one. The owners of the Crown say they followed a clear vein onto Royal Flush property. That would be quite all right. But the Royal Flush says Crown's vein pinched out twenty feet short of the boundary and the Crown is trying to poach into the Flush's ore bodies. That wouldn't be legal. Then to make matters worse, after Crown broke through, the Royal Flush began dumping rock into the Crown's stopes. There were some real brawls for a time, and the Royal Flush hired some bullyboys to raid the Crown crews. There have been charges of ore theft on both sides, and one hears there has been a lot of high-grading going on. The case has become quite a mess, with witnesses bribed and others disappearing and I don't know what all else. The only ones who are sure to win in the long term are the attorneys. Which I had clearly understood Victor here would lead on behalf of the Royal Flush. Not so, Vic?"

"I'd just as soon not talk about it," Curtis said.

"You say Craig is over there now?" Ben asked.

"That's what I heard, yes."

"Do you know how long he will be away?"

The lawyer shrugged. "They were scheduled to file motions this week. After that . . . Bryceville is in another county, understand, so I haven't seen their calendar . . . it depends on when the judge wants to proceed. If the judge wants time to take the motions under advisement, it could be months before Craig has to go over there again. Or he could be busy straight through for the next three weeks or more. I really couldn't say."

Ben frowned. He needed Craig Albritton's help to gain access to those records.

Unless Neal Hubbard or Lucas Dadley had a change of heart.

Which meant, of course, that he needed Albritton's help.

Ben pushed his chair back preparatory to leaving the table of friendly gentlemen, then abruptly was stopped.

"You're right about one thing, Willard," Curtis said. "Neal Hubbard is a sonuvabitch."

Ben raised an eyebrow.

"Hubbard is on the board of directors of the Royal Flush Mining Company," the lawyer unhappily explained. "He's the one who told me I could expect their business. I spent most of this past month researching precedents and laying out my arguments. Now the company turns around and retains Craig instead. You try to figure it out. I sure can't."

No reason at all, Ben thought. Except that it got Craig Albritton out of town just at a time when he was needed to poke a sharp stick into Neal Hubbard's affairs.

Not that there was necessarily any connection between the two. Of course not.

And if someone wanted to believe that, Ben thought, why, he had some really valuable mining properties to sell them. Cheap.

CHAPTER 16

J oe stopped and leaned against the wall for a moment while he pulled an extra-deep breath into his lungs.

"You all right?" Harlan asked.

"Yeah. Sure."

"Look, you, uh, you have been underground before, haven't you?"

"Sure. Lots o' times." Which was maybe an exaggeration if not exactly a lie. He had been underground before. But never all that deep and never for so very long.

His mistake had been when he looked up. There was a whole, entire mountain up there above his head. A whole, entire mountain of rock. For just a second there Joe'd been convinced that the weight of all that rock was pressing down on him. Crushing in on his chest so that he couldn't breathe.

Just for a second.

That had been more than enough.

"You look kinda pale."

"I'm fine, Harlan. Really."

"Okay, if you say so."

"I do." And it was pretty much true. He did feel much better now. All he'd needed was a reminder that he could breathe down here.

But Lordy, if all that weight, that whole entire mountain of it, ever *was* to come down . . .

Like a ladybug on a railroad track. That's just about what it would be like. There wouldn't be enough left of him, or any of them, to make a good smear of red color. Joe shivered.

"It is kinda cold, ain't it," Harlan said.

"Yeah, a little."

"Watch your step there, Joe. Mind the track."

In some places the drift was barely wide enough for the ore carts to pass through, in others it would comfortably accommodate four men walking abreast. Harlan Kane ambled along through this dank, unnatural underworld as casually as if he were in his own parlor. Joe followed close behind him, not wanting to become separated from Harlan in the maze of drifts and unlighted stopes that lay buried deep within the mountain.

"This way, Joe." Harlan turned sideways to squeeze past a line of parked carts, then disappeared without warning.

"Hey!" Joe hurried to catch up. Harlan had stepped through a low portal leading into another stope, this one smaller than most.

"Here." Harlan thrust an armload of drill bits at him. Joe hadn't remembered how heavy a drill can be. But then it was also true that these bits were much thicker than the ones he'd seen employed in the Comstock district. Those were little thicker than an inch, just over the diameter of a dynamite stick. Some, the drills used to prepare nitro shots, were even smaller. These clunky, heavy old things were two inches or more across at the head. But then, blasting powder, being less powerful than the modern materials, required a bigger hole.

Harlan gave Joe the drills, then picked up the singlejack hammer that he would spend the next ten hours swinging. All in all, Joe was just as pleased to not have Harlan's job.

"Hope we get a good tool dresser," Harlan said. "I hate trying to work with dull drills."

Joe grunted an acknowledgment. He hoped he sounded like he knew what he was doing here, but in truth most of his knowledge about drilling came from the Fourth of July contests where the top drillers from each mine in Virginia City competed in trying to punch holes through a slab of granite. The winners earned a cash prize for themselves and a keg of beer to share with their shift mates. From a spectator's point of view, it had all been exciting enough. Now Joe was wishing he'd paid a little closer attention to what the men were doing.

Once again he followed Harlan back along the main drift, this time encumbered by sixty or so pounds of tool steel. They came to a large stope, lighted by lanterns all around, where the members of the day shift were gathered.

"Harlan, what the hell are you doing back here?"

Harlan grinned. "H'lo, Rolly. Nice to see you too."

"Don't tell me you're drilling this time?"

"That's what the man said."

Rolly gave Joe a doubtful look. "Do I know you, bub?"

"I'm Harlan's twister. Name's Bo."

"Really?"

"Close enough that it'll do."

"Yeah, well, whatever. Just give me a fair shake and I'll give you the same. The best advice I can give you is to listen to me first. And Harlan never."

Harlan grinned like he'd just received a compliment. "You got a dresser for us, Rolly?"

"Cooter. You're it."

"Aw, Rolly. I gotta?"

"You gotta."

"I won't get no bonus if Harlan's drilling," the tool dresser complained.

"Cooter, you haven't earned a production bonus since you been here. Why complain now?"

"It's a point. I s'pose."

The tool dresser came over and stuck a hand out to Joe. "The name is Barcoot. Lee Roy Barcoot. You can call me Cooter."

"I'm Joe. Joe Burns. The Bo part was just made up."

"Are you boys gonna spend the day jawing or do you figure to give me a day's work for your day's wage?"

"We got a choice, Rolly?" Harlan asked.

Rolly bent to pick up a chip of rock. He threw it at Harlan and got a grin in return. "Straight on to the end, boys. Take the rise on your left. And make sure there's holes enough to make the powder monkeys happy before your shift is over. You know what's what around here."

"Yes sir, Cap'n Rolly, sir, anything you say, sir." Harlan snapped to attention and executed a brisk salute, then brushed the tip of his nose with his thumb as he brought his hand back down again.

"I saw that, Harlan."

"Rolly, I wouldn't of done it if I didn't think you'd notice."

"Go to work. G'wan."

With Harlan once again in the lead, and Cooter lugging a steel case of files and small hammers, the drilling team trudged deeper into the Shan-Rock.

CHAPTER 17

B en was beginning to think it was a shame he had sent Joseph to the city when he did. The way things were looking today, it might have been more sensible to have Joseph also talk to the family's law firm about representation here. If it came to that, Ben decided, he could wire Joseph at the hotel and ask him to attend to it.

But that was only in the event of last-resort measures. With any kind of luck, he should be able to persuade Hubbard and Dadley that their own best interests, and those of the railroad too, coincided with the things Ben Cartwright wanted to accomplish here.

If only they would listen to reason . . .

Ben decided to make another attempt at a calm and rational discussion. When he left the Canterbury he headed toward the bank building and Neal Hubbard's second-story offices.

Tom Keith was coming out of the bank just as Ben was about to mount the stairs to Hubbard's office.

"Hello, Tom. Missed you at coffee this morning."

The banker shrugged. "We thought we found a shortage in the cash accounts, and I had to stay to help clear that up. It turned out to be a simple transposition of numbers and not a shortage after all, but I couldn't leave until we knew for certain." He smiled ruefully. "As it happens, the error was my own. I'd curse and snarl if anyone else did that, of course, but since it was my own mistake, I decided to let the offender off with a few sharp comments and a slap on the wrist."

"Very sensible, I'm sure," Ben said dryly.

"Eminently," Keith agreed. "I take it that boy found you all right," he added.

"Boy?"

"Yesterday. The errand boy. You know."

"I'm afraid I don't know, Tom."

"Really? There was a boy. Yesterday afternoon, it was, shortly before the close of business. He came by looking for you. Had a note to deliver, I believe. At least he was carrying an envelope in his hand and had to refer to it to remember your name. I assume the envelope was the reason he needed to find you."

"Well, he never did."

"How odd. He didn't leave it at your hotel?"

"Not unless they neglected to pass it on to me."

"Mm, I think not. Not at the lodge. Some places in town I would believe it of, but not there. Bertie Bent—he hates to be called that, by the way, or even to have his real name known, so I don't recommend you use it face to face with him—is much too fussy to allow a mistake like that."

"You don't know who the boy is, do you?"

"Sorry, Ben. All small boys look pretty much the same."

Which only meant that Keith had no boys of his own, Ben thought. Not that that observation did anything to solve this matter of the missing note.

"And you didn't see where he went?"

The banker shook his head. "The only thing I could add is that the envelope wasn't one of those telegraph office forms. It was just a small white envelope with some writing but no postage on the outside. And not a full address either, just your name."

"I wonder . . ." Ben shook his head. There was no

sense speculating on what may or may not have been contained inside that envelope. The possibilities were simply too numerous to be worth the bother of guessing. "Thanks, Tom."

"Nice to see you, Ben."

"Good to see you too." The banker went off down the street, and Ben resumed his march on the offices of railroad partner Neal Hubbard.

"So," Ben said, shifting to a fresh position on the hard-backed chair he had been given, "I think you can see that I mean no harm to you or to Mr. Dadley. Far from it. And if the three of us can work together from here on, Mr. Hubbard, I think it will prove beneficial to you, to me, and to Johns Bend and the surrounding communities." Ben had been talking, calmly and pleasantly and with smiles, for the past five or ten minutes. "I hope we can start over anew and all pull together, as allies if not necessarily as friends."

"Now Mr. Cartwright, I must say that I am awfully glad you called here today. I have a much different feel of this situation now. And surely you can understand my position and Lucas's. I mean, our friend and trusted partner was hardly cold in his grave and there was this stranger standing in front of us demanding that we accept him like as if he was Les."

That wasn't precisely the way Ben remembered it happening, but he wasn't going to start another argument over a simple difference of perception. He kept his hands motionless in his lap and his mouth firmly closed. After all, Hubbard had given him the courtesy of hearing him out. It would be ungracious now, Ben thought, for him to do less.

"But I can see that we misjudged you, Mr. Cartwright. Especially so since I've spoken with some other gentlemen in the business community here. A number of them remember Les Shannon speaking of you, always in the highest of terms, they said. There are some who've heard of you otherwise as well. They say you are a fair-minded gentleman with a good head for business. Is it true that you grub-staked emigrants by the hundreds during the Sutter rush, Mr. Cartwright?"

"I don't know that hundreds would be accurate, Mr. Hubbard. Certainly I helped a number of men when they needed it. I couldn't in good conscience let people start across the mountains hungry and without food, not when I had plenty enough to share. But all of that was a long time ago and has nothing to do with here and now."

"Oh, but it does, Mr. Cartwright. Indeed it does. It tells Lucas and me what kind of gentleman you are. It tells us that we needn't fear having you replace Les in our partnership. So to that extent I would have to say that it does influence the here and the now of things."

"If you say so, Mr. Hubbard, although to me it is ancient history."

"Now you are being modest, Mr. Cartwright." Hubbard smiled.

"No, just more interested in tomorrow than in yesterday."

"Whatever you say, Mr. Cartwright, ha ha. Could I interest you in some tea? I haven't taken a moment to relax since I opened the office this morning, and if you wouldn't mind, I could certainly enjoy a pot of tea and some scones."

Ben smiled. "Scones? Good Lord, I haven't had any scones in years."

"You do know them, then?"

"Oh my, yes. There was an inn, a tiny wee little bit of a thing, just off the strand in Hamilton, Bermuda, that—"

"George Christie's Swan and Garter!" Hubbard said with excitement.

"You know it!" Ben exclaimed.

"Know it? I should say so. I have an uncle who's in trade in Hamilton. Albert Jones. If you know the Swan, you might know him."

"I'm afraid not, but it's been many, many years since I've been there."

"No matter. Think of it. Why, many's the time I've ordered scones at the Swan. Think of it."

Ben smiled, pleased to find a common meeting ground with this sometimes difficult businessman. Why, it was exactly this sort of thing that could sometimes take adversaries and turn them into the best of friends. Ben genuinely, truly, hoped that such might be the case with Neal Hubbard.

"Just think of that," Hubbard chattered gleefully. "You know the scones at the old Swan and Garter. That's wonderful. I take it you would join me in having something, then? Not that these compare with the Swan's, but they are the best you will find this side of Boston, I can promise you that."

Boston too, the gentleman knew? How remarkable, Ben thought. Why, it was beginning to seem they had more in common than either could have suspected. "I would be pleased to take tea and scones with you, Mr. Hubbard."

"Neal. Please call me Neal."

"If you'll call me Ben."

"Done and done, Ben."

"This is a great pleasure, Neal."

Smiling, Hubbard left the office to arrange for someone to fetch the tea and scones.

While Hubbard was away from the room, Ben fidgeted for a moment on the uncomfortable chair. A hard bottom and straight back ordinarily was not so unpleasant to him, and he wondered why. He stood and paced about a bit, careful to avoid approaching Hubbard's desk. It would have been entirely improper, to say nothing of being embarrassingly uncomfortable, for him to observe the papers Neal had laid out there, even if they were seen by accident. That was not the sort of thing Ben would countenance.

Instead he stood with his back to the desk. And after a moment frowned. Then began to chuckle.

No wonder the blasted chair was so deucedly miserable to sit in. Upon close inspection—and he only noticed it by a happenstance of angle of view—it seemed the front legs were fractionally shorter than the back ones. Anyone sitting on that slick wooden seat would be constantly pushed forward by the force of gravity. He would have to be constantly pushing himself backward just to maintain his seat and could never fully relax. But the amount of difference was so subtle that Ben hadn't noticed it when he was seated.

That was certainly a good way to keep one's interview brief and to put one's visitors at a disadvantage, Ben conceded. Clever.

Ben felt no animosity toward Neal because of it, though. After all, when he first walked in today, they were still at loggerheads. Now, thank goodness, the ice had been broken and things could proceed from here in a much more reasonable fashion.

There still was no sign of Neal returning, so Ben wandered to the side of the room and examined the titles on a bookshelf there. Many of them were duplicated in his own study.

He pulled his pipe and tobacco pouch out and idly began fiddling with them.

The bowl of the pipe was still full of dottle, cold now, from the last time he'd smoked it. He shoved the tobacco back into his pocket and brought out the flat-headed nail he used to clean the bowl and tamp tobacco. A poke or two quickly loosened the hard ash crust that held the dottle in place, and he crossed to Neal's desk so he could dump the burnt contents of his pipe in the waste bucket there. He bent low and tapped the upended pipe onto the rim of the bucket.

Black and gray dottle rained down onto the contents of the bucket. Because the waste seemed to consist mostly of paper, Ben was concerned lest a live spark remain in the leavings of his pipe. It would hardly do to test a budding friendship by burning the man's office to the ground. And, come to think of it, the town bank below. So he took some pains to assure himself there were no coals remaining.

There were none.

But when he straightened to full height, he was no longer smiling.

One of the bits of paper in that bucket was a torn envelope with a name scrawled in pencil on it. Mr. B. Cartwright, the name on that envelope read.

Could there be some innocent reason why Neal Hubbard would have an envelope, a torn one at that, with Ben Cartwright's name on it, thrown away in his wastebasket?

Possibly. But Ben couldn't think of any offhand.

Slowly, his thoughts very much elsewhere, he began refilling his pipe and tamping the tobacco into it.

"Five minutes," Hubbard said cheerily as he came sweeping back into the office. "Our tray of tea and scones will be up in five minutes, Ben. Sit down. Please." Smiling, Hubbard pointed once more to the deceptively, and deliberately, uncomfortable chair for his guest. "Make yourself comfortable."

"Thank you," Ben said politely. He sat, the stem of his pipe between clenched teeth, and wondered just how much of Neal Hubbard's facade could be believed.

CHAPTER 18

J oe's hands felt like he was holding tight to a fistful of bees that weren't stinging—yet—but were crawling around inside his clenched fist buzzing and grumbling to themselves.

At this point both his hands felt like they were vibrating even when he wasn't holding the dang drill.

The amazing thing was that Harlan was still able to swing the singlejack, just as steady and regular as a key-wound clock mechanism. Once he'd found his rhythm, Harlan acted like he could go on day and night and never falter.

But if he ever once did get so tired that he mis-hit the drill . . .

Steel rang on steel as the hardened face of the singlejack smashed into the long drill Joe was holding. The drill jumped and vibrated as the force of the hammer pulverized another tiny fraction of an inch of stone into gritty dust, and Joe's hands stung as he swiftly twisted the drill a quarter turn. He had to time his motions with Harlan's, the singlejack sweeping back and forward again without pause. It was Joe's responsibility to make sure the drill was in place in time for the hammer's strike, turned to a fresh position and holding tight against the face of the rock inside the slim hole they were pounding into the mountain.

Clang, turn, clang, turn, clang, turn. The work went endlessly on.

"Break," Joe called as once again the hammer hit, the drill vibrated in his grip, and Harlan swept the head of the singlejack back again.

"Yeah, you bet." Harlan sounded exhausted even if he didn't look it. But then, he wasn't even able to use an ordinary overhand swing of the hammer. Because the drilling they were doing was meant to follow the ore vein, they were working in close quarters. It is, after all, foolish to blast out any more rock than is necessary. Worse, the section of stope where they were working was angled upward so the ore would be easily cleared once it was blasted free. Harlan had to swing the heavy singlejack in a flat, sidearm sweep that was angled to meet the requirements of the particular hole he wanted to drill.

All Joe had to do was hold his drill steels firmly in place. And he was finding that difficult enough. He couldn't imagine how leaden Harlan's arms must feel by now. Yet if Harlan made the smallest mis-hit . . . Joe shuddered. That simply wasn't to be thought about.

Joe dragged the drill out of the hole—it was already a good two feet deep; another eight inches or so and they would start a new one—and handed it to Cooter, who laid another, freshly sharpened drill into Joe's palm.

"Let's slow down for a second, can't we?" Joe asked. "Cooter, hand me that water jug, please."

Cooter drank from the jug first, then gave it to Joe, and Joe handed it on to Harlan once he was done. The water was cool in Joe's throat as it cut through the dust and phlegm that choked him. There were times when it felt like the dust was being layered on with a trowel. There was no movement to the air underground, and the dust hung relentlessly, inescapably, in place. It was impossible to avoid breathing it in. The infrequent sips of water helped. Perhaps, he thought, it was no wonder that mining men were known as accomplished drinkers. "That's better. Thanks." He wiped his face with the back of one grimy wrist and turned his head to spit.

"You doing all right, Joe?"

"Sure. Fine."

"Once you get the hang of it, it goes easier."

"It's like that with anything, I expect."

"Yeah. A guy'd think so." Harlan picked up the singlejack and looked at Joe.

With a sigh Joe shoved the sharp drill bit into the slim hole in the rock until he felt a grinding contact with the stone at the other end of the steel. He hunched his shoulders and took a good grip on the drill.

"Ready?"

"Yeah."

Harlan began to swing again, quickly finding his rhythm.

Clang, turn, clang, turn, clang, turn.

Joe's hands stung and vibrated. Lordy.

He kept his eyes away from the drill in his hands. It was better that way. Otherwise he might think about what would happen if Harlan missed, if the face of the steel singlejack slipped off the butt of the drill and smashed into flesh and fragile bone instead.

That would be all the more awful now that they were so deep inside the hole. With the twister's hands so close to the rock they were drilling into, there would be no chance for him to snatch back away. The hammer would crush thumb, fingers, anything that was unfortunate enough to be caught between stone and steel. There were a great many hard-rock miners with parts of their hands missing who could attest to that.

It was something Joe would rather not think about, actually.

Clang, turn, clang, turn.

He looked instead at the work they had done already today. Neither Harlan not Cooter seemed much impressed by it, but Joe was. But then, both the other men seemed to know what they were doing down here.

Harlan started out with four holes placed close together in the middle of the white quartz ore body. Four holes placed in a box pattern about eight inches square, and each drilled hole angling in toward a center point more than two feet inside the rock wall.

Then four more holes were drilled in a vertical line on each side of those central four. Those were angled slightly toward the center also, but only a little. And now they were starting another line of holes outside of those. Harlan showed Joe where he intended to drill. The final, outside lines would be five holes each. Twenty-two holes, each placed just so, each angling inward by a greater or lesser degree, each positioned according to the discretion and the judgment of the driller. The drilling crew had their ten-hour shift in which to accomplish the job, then the powder monkeys would come in to put all that sweat to use.

The way Harlan explained it, all the holes would be filled with blasting powder that was packed snug, tamped in good and tight like Pa packed his pipe, or even tighter. Then fuses would be shoved in and the openings of each hole sealed. Wax would do for that. Some claimed hard soap was even better. Whichever method the powder monkey liked, he was responsible for choosing, placing, and cutting the fuses.

That part was critical, it seemed.

The idea was to blow the closely grouped center charges first. Those four had to blow at pretty much the same time but definitely in advance of all the other charges. Because of the way they were angled to nearly meet inside the mountain, the force of that first explosion would scoop a melon-sized plug of rock out of the mountain and make room for the outside charges to work. Otherwise, the explosions might shatter the rock but leave it in place. By using the initial explosion to create an open hole in the middle of the face, there was someplace for the rock dislodged by the main charges to go.

The center core charges went first, then the middle row, and the outside charges last by another fraction of a second. Done right, the charges would all blow so close together that the delays between them couldn't even be heard. But they had to blow in the proper sequence or the broken rock would still be attached to the stope wall and that day's work would be wasted.

"A driller," Harlan said, "he's the most important guy underground."

Joe didn't dispute with him, although powder monkeys, engineers, everybody made that same claim. When they were aboveground.

As far as Joe was concerned, well, right now, to him, there was no doubt at all that the driller, in particular driller Harlan Kane, was far and away the most important fellow underground. And would be for as long as Harlan was swinging that singlejack within a couple inches of his burning, tingling hands.

Clang, turn, clang, turn, clang, turn.

Lordy, but he would be glad when this day was over.

CHAPTER 19

Mr. Cartwright? Mr. B. Cartwright?"

"Here."

The lad came bounding through the tables in the hotel dining room and stopped with a lighthearted smile beside Mr. B. Cartwright. "Note for you, sir."

"Thank you, son." Ben accepted the envelope from the boy and gave him a nickel for his trouble. When the youngster turned away, though, Ben stopped him. "I don't suppose you're the boy who tried to deliver a note to me yesterday evening," he said.

"No, sir. Sorry."

"Never mind, then."

"Yes, sir." Once again the boy started away.

"Young man."

The kid stopped again. "Sir?"

"How many boys would you say there are in Johns Bend?"

"Gosh, mister, I don't know. A couple dozen maybe?"

"Would it be reasonable to assume you would be acquainted with all of them?"

"Sure, mister. The town ain't all that big."

Ben smiled. "That's what I was just thinking." He leaned back in his chair, not at all concerned now that his supper would be growing cold. "Someone tried to send me a note yesterday too, you see, but it wasn't delivered into my hand. I would like to know who received it for me."

"I already told you, mister, it wasn't me had that note yesterday."

"No, I understand that. But you know the lads in town, while I do not. And, um, it would be worth something to me to speak with that other boy."

"Yeah?"

"Fifty cents," Ben said. "For each of you."

The boy's eyes went so wide Ben was afraid the youngster might hurt himself. Fifty cents was a monumental fortune when a boy might run errands for an entire week and earn less. "You mean that?"

"I do indeed."

"I'll find him for you, mister. I promise." The kid started off then stopped again, this time on his own. "Say, mister."

"Yes?"

"You won't give nobody else this job, will you?"

Ben chuckled. "No, I won't. Not for, say, three days. Would that be fair?"

The boy grinned. "Mister, by that time there won't be no kid from here to Harptown that I haven't talked to."

"Good luck," Ben said. But by then he was speaking to empty space.

He took a look at the envelope—it was not at all similar to the one he'd seen earlier that day in Neal Hubbard's waste bucket, nor was the handwriting similar—and used his steak knife to slice the sealed flap open.

Ben:

There is a sporting event this evening at the F.O.A. hall commencing at nine or soon thereafter. Lucas and I would be honored to have you as our guest.

Your friend, Neal

Friend. Perhaps. Or not.

Still, the invitation had been extended. And in Dadley's name too. Ben had little choice but to accept it. He pulled out his watch and glanced at it, then compared the time he saw there with that on the hotel wall clock. Both agreed he had more than an hour in which to get ready for this unspecified sporting event. Whatever it turned out to be.

He leaned forward and once more gave his attention to his meal.

"F.O.A., that would be the Fraternal Order of Antelope."

Ben hadn't ever heard of that group before, but fraternal lodges sprang up like weeds in some of the isolated mining camps. Most withered, but there were some, even wildly improbable ones, that thrived.

"You go down three blocks," the clerk continued, "then left up the hill another two. It's the three-story brick building on the northwest corner. Has a carved wood antelope head mounted over the front door. I suppose you could miss it, but you'd have to work at it."

"Thanks." Ben followed the instructions and found that it would indeed have been difficult to miss the F.O.A. hall. Apart from the fake antelope over the door, the place was lighted as gay and brilliant as a circus tent, and there were men in suits and starched collars streaming in from all directions. There were no overalls or mud-covered boots to be seen. Apparently the Antelopes catered to the upper crust.

Ben joined the line of men moving into the lodge hall. There was a holidaylike air of excitement among them. He recognized a surprising number of the gentlemen. Tom Keith waved to him from across the ornate lobby. So did Victor Curtis. Henry Vickers and Dr. Willard Monroe were engaged in conversation off to one side. Ben looked for Craig Albritton in the hope the lawyer might be back in town, but if he was in the crowd, Ben couldn't find him.

"Sir." A tall, lean man wearing a cutaway and tails was blocking his way.

"Yes?"

"I don't believe you are a member here, sir. Would you give me the password, please."

"Sorry, but I'm afraid not." He brought out the note Hubbard had sent, glad now that he'd stuck it in his pocket instead of dropping it on the dressing table back at the hotel. "Would this do?"

The cadaverous guardian of the sacred portals—Ben had no idea what the exact title might be, but he was sure there would be one, and the fancier and more resounding, the better—bowed and apologized. "You would be Mr. Cartwright, I take it?"

"That's right."

"Follow me, please."

Ben trailed the exalted emissary of piffle-poof up a flight of stairs to a balcony that looked down onto a large, open room below.

A canvas platform had been erected in the center of the room, and ropes strung tight on corner posts surrounded the square mat.

"Fisticuffs?" Ben asked.

"Yes, of course," the gargoyle-in-training responded with a tone of mild annoyance that anyone could have been so uninformed as to not already know. "In here, sir." He stopped and opened the door to a private viewing box on the balcony level.

Ben stepped inside, and the annoyed one closed the door behind him.

The interior of the box was plush, fitted out with gilt and velvet. A black mesh curtain was draped over the open front of the box. The mesh was thin enough to see out through, but Ben suspected no one could look in from the other side. Certainly he could not see into similarly treated boxes opposite this one.

A pair of couches filled most of the available space. On the left, away from the door, there was a low table set with napkins, silver, tidbits of finger food, and an iced bucket with the neck of a champagne bottle protruding from it.

It was all really quite something.

Ben cleared his throat.

He'd been more or less avoiding staring at the only other occupant of the box. But that was impolite. To say nothing of being really quite impossible.

The lady was really quite lovely to look at.

And judging from her choice of attire for the evening, Ben suspected as well that the lady was no lady.

He cleared his throat a second time and gave thought to going back downstairs to pass the time with Tom Keith or Henry Vickers or . . . someone.

"You must be Benjamin," the woman said in a throaty, husky voice that reminded Ben of a cat's purr. She rose—levitated from the couch where she'd been seated—and glided toward him with all the sleek grace of a hunting feline.

Ben wondered if the mouse ever welcomed the approach of the cat.

Ben smiled and bowed. In almost the same motion he reached back to find the doorknob. Casually, as if he was doing it without thought, he pulled the door to the viewing box open and left it standing like that so that passersby in the hallway could if they wished look inside and see anything that might go on in the small room. "I am Ben Cartwright," he responded politely. "And you would be . . . ?"

"You may call me Morgana," the woman purred. "Don't you think, Benjamin, that it would be cozier in here if that door was shut?"

Ben looked at her. She was undeniably beautiful, but beneath that thin surface veneer she was considerably less attractive. "I think we'll leave it as it is," he told her.

The woman made a highly dramatic, pouty moue.

"Benny, you naughty boy, you. Really. Don't you want me?" Her brightly rouged lower lip curled and twisted in a fashion that he presumed she meant as a simulation of passion and sensuality. In truth it looked to him more like she had a gnat crawling about her mouth and was trying to dislodge it.

"Since you ask, madame, no, I do not want you. But I would be interested to know what purpose this is supposed to serve." There was no point in asking her who it was who paid her fees. He knew good and well it would have been either Neal Hubbard or Lucas Dadley. And between them it would hardly matter which had had this particular notion.

It took a moment for the fact to sink in that the gentleman wasn't being playful with her. This particular gentleman really and truly did not want her. Once she recognized that the impossible had indeed happened, the woman who called herself Morgana became quite red with sudden fury. "Hey! You can't ... what's the matter with you anyhow?"

Ben laughed and shook his head. "Don't worry about it. Have a glass of champagne. Have something to eat. Enjoy yourself." He turned and got the heck out of there.

Ten minutes later Neal Hubbard found him leaning over a section of open railing so he could watch the first of the pugilism contests being waged in the prize ring below.

"Ben. Someone said you were upstairs, but you weren't in the box. Lucas is already there. Won't you join us?"

"Thank you, Neal."

There was no sign of Morgana or of any other female in the box now, nor was there mention of her. It was like she never existed. Lucas Dadley, however, greeted Ben like an old chum, all cheery smiles and goodwill.

It was puzzling, Ben thought. Were both men in on the ploy—whatever it had been—or was Morgana Lucas's idea alone? Ben had the impression that Lucas Dadley's style was crude but direct. Subterfuge would likely be

Hubbard's game. But then in truth, Ben was not altogether sure what the game was supposed to have been anyway.

Blackmail? Possibly. A whisper, a note, a word to the little missus back home on the Ponderosa. That could well be what he or they had had in mind. And a man of Ben Cartwright's age and means would normally be assumed to have a wife. Neither Hubbard nor Dadley would be apt to know he was a widower. Certainly Ben himself was not close enough to either of them to have discussed his personal life with them. So blackmail was a distinct possibility, especially so since a man of his experience could hardly be expected to fall head over heels for some bawdy, blatant creature like Morgana. No, he thought, blackmail was far and away the most likely goal of their little game.

Now that he thought about it, it almost would have been worth the trouble to play along with the silliness just to see their expressions when they tried to spring a trap, only to have the jaws clamp tight on thin air. *Almost* worth the trouble, the fly in that ointment being that he would have had to spend time with Miss Morgana in order for the game to fall flat. Spending an evening with Morgana would have been more of a price than Ben was willing to pay for a simple laugh.

As it was, he settled for a glass of champagne and a light snack in the company of his new partners, while down below a succession of youngsters recruited from the mines pummeled and pounded on each other for the promised reward of a ten dollar per fight purse to the victors.

"Are you a devotee of the fight game, Ben?" Dadley asked at one point.

"I enjoy a contest as much as the next man, I suppose, but I can't claim any particular knowledge about it."

"Pity. I'm somethin' of an expert myself."

"What Lucas means to say," Hubbard put in, "is that he is quite the accomplished pugilist. There isn't a man twice his size or half his age who can stay ten rounds with him."

"Really?" Ben asked politely.

"Really. Lucas is the amateur champion of the district."

"I'm impressed."

"You look fit enough to go a few rounds yourself," Dadley said.

Ben smiled at him. "Thank you for the compliment, but I suspect boxing is a game best left to young men like the lads down there." He pointed down into the ring where a plucky red-haired boy with his nose mashed flat to his face was climbing gamely back onto his feet to once more toe the line and meet his opponent's charge. The rules were that a round ended when a man was knocked off his feet. From the time he went down he had one minute in which to regain his feet and toe the mark in the center of the ring, otherwise he was declared the loser. Matches between ringwise professionals could last upwards of a hundred rounds—some few had been known to go longer—but for the most part small-time affairs like this were concluded in a dozen rounds or less. Many of the fights were brief. All were bloody. This one had already lasted eight or nine rounds, and it was the red-haired boy who had been down each time, but each time he came stubbornly back to square off against the bruising Welshman he had drawn as his opponent.

"Bums like that mick kid there got no business fighting," Dadley observed. "He's so dumb he don't even know he's whipped. He oughta stay there next time he goes down, let us get a better pair to look at."

"Actually," Ben said, "I like the young man. He's light, but he's quick. And he's game. That's the biggest thing. The boy has heart. I believe heart will overcome muscle, in the ring or out of it."

Dadley snorted his disdain for such foolish sentiment. "That Llewellyn boy will put him away for keeps. It's only a matter o' time."

"I hate to disagree with you, but I really think the other lad will win out. Have you noticed how every round he rips a few body shots into the bigger man's ribs?

Llewellyn is slowing. I don't think he has enough to put the Irish boy out. I believe in the long run Llewellyn will lose, Lucas."

Dadley sat upright, a shrewdly calculating look about him. "You really believe that, huh?"

"Yes, I do."

"Five hun'erd says Tommy Llewellyn beats Danny O'Neal."

"Done," Ben told him.

In the ring below, the O'Neal boy reached for a towel handed in by a pal at ringside. He wiped some of the blood from his face, although it would have taken much more than a mere towel to clean him up at this point. His nose had been broken early in the fight, and now the entire lower half of his face was a scarlet mask. The broken nose did not seem to seriously interfere with his breathing, though, and blood coming from so low could not obscure his vision. Ben suspected the appearance was much worse than the fact.

Even though the timer, who was poised with a gong and hammer, ready to tap time if a fighter failed to toe the line, had not yet given the half-minute warning, O'Neal tossed the towel back to his friend, took a deep breath and went out to the center of the ring. He placed the toe of his left shoe carefully onto the center of the dark line, lifted his fists and sent an expectant look toward Tommy Llewellyn, who was being given a dipper of water by one of the men gathered in his corner.

Llewellyn looked at the timer, then at Danny. He seemed inclined to wait the full minute, but several of the men close to him leaned near and said something. Llewellyn nodded, gulped hurriedly from the dipper and tossed it back, splattering water into the crowd and drawing a round of laughter from it. Llewellyn swung his arms and flexed powerful shoulder muscles in a show for the crowd before he sniffed and came jauntily into the middle of the ring with O'Neal. Llewellyn placed his left toe next to O'Neal's and raised his fists.

"Time," the timekeeper shouted.

Llewellyn's right hand sprang forward at almost the same instant the first hint of sound came out of the timekeeper's mouth.

Danny O'Neal, who must have weighed a good thirty pounds less than the massively built Welshman, tucked his chin tight to his chest and ducked underneath Llewellyn's punch. O'Neal's fists pumped hard and fast, pistons forcefully driven, over Llewellyn's heart and lungs. He got in five, six, perhaps as many as seven blows before a slashing left hook landed over his right ear and he went flying. The round had lasted only a few seconds.

O'Neal hit the canvas on his left shoulder and went skidding across it. He bounced up almost immediately, a red abrasion showing where he'd scraped across the canvas. There was a trickle of blood streaming from his ear and down the side of his neck, but he appeared otherwise undamaged.

The Irish boy shook his head once and almost ran back to once more toe the center line.

Llewellyn had begun to head into his corner again but, seeing O'Neal's quick response, shrugged and also went back to the line. Llewellyn grinned and said something to Danny O'Neal that was too low for the crowd to overhear. The Irish boy flushed a dark red but said nothing in return.

Both carefully toed the mark.

"Time."

Danny O'Neal was still looking down to see to the placement of his toe on the line. Tommy Llewellyn took advantage of O'Neal's distraction and landed a haymaker flush on the smaller boy's mouth.

O'Neal, caught by surprise, was knocked sprawling, his head whipping back. He landed on his backside and rolled. The sound of it was loud in the huge and now strangely quiet lodge hall.

"That does it," Lucas Dadley chortled. "He won't get up from that one."

"Another hundred says he does," Ben gritted back at

the man, not really believing himself that O'Neal would make the mark again, but angered by the smug tone in Dadley's voice.

"Done," Dadley said.

Far below them, Danny O'Neal groaned and lay facedown on the canvas. The redhead stirred and tried to rise. He couldn't manage it. He lifted himself a few inches off the floor and then collapsed again.

"Thirty seconds," the timer said.

The crowd began to roar their accolades for Tommy Llewellyn.

"A hun'erd," Dadley prompted.

"Not yet," Ben told him. "He has half a minute."

"Yeah, he has half a minute, an' I have a extra hun'erd dollars."

"Not until time is up."

Danny O'Neal shook himself like a dog crawling out of a cold pond. He pushed his chest and upper torso off the canvas and, arms wobbly, brought his knees underneath him. He remained like that a moment longer, head hanging, resting on hands and knees. Then he took another long, deep breath and somehow found strength enough to come swaying to his feet. He blinked and shook his head. Blood flew in a wide, fanlike spray. He staggered two steps to his left, peered uncertainly down at the canvas, and with more determination than good sense, carefully placed the toe of his left shoe onto the mark.

Over in Tommy Llewellyn's corner the celebrations had already begun. Now Llewellyn gave O'Neal a look of mingled annoyance and disbelief. Someone in his corner said something, and Llewellyn laughed. But Ben noticed he did not look happy this time when he came back into the center of the ring and toed the line.

"Time."

Tommy Llewellyn threw another sweeping, roundhouse right hand. Danny O'Neal slid underneath it and hammered a tattoo of body blows into Llewellyn's belly and ribs.

Llewellyn chopped down at the side of O'Neal's neck,

a backhanded and highly illegal blow that staggered O'Neal but did not put him down. O'Neal reeled away, bounced off the ropes and stepped into Llewellyn as the Welshman came charging forward, intent on delivering a felling blow.

Instead O'Neal came inside, and this time as Llewellyn leaned forward in an attempt to protect his middle, the Irish boy lifted a hard uppercut onto the shelf of Llewellyn's jaw. The Welshman's knees turned rubbery and his eyes were unfocused.

Danny O'Neal stepped in again. Ripped a series of wicked lefts and rights into Llewellyn's midsection and backed away barely in time to escape a right hook that whistled viciously, but this time harmlessly, by his jaw.

O'Neal came in behind Llewellyn's missed punch, feinted another body attack and instead delivered a short, straight right to the side of Llewellyn's jaw.

Llewellyn stumbled backward and would have gone down, but O'Neal did not risk giving the bigger man time to recover. Before Llewellyn could fall, Danny O'Neal dashed forward. Even as the Welshman was dropping O'Neal pounded him with a right to the heart, a left to the head, another right to the head.

Llewellyn hit the canvas with a thud and fell spread-eagled with his arms and legs flung wide and his eyes rolling back in his head.

"Damn," Lucas Dadley mumbled.

Ben waited the full minute, until the timekeeper mouthed "time"—the crowd was so noisy by then it was impossible to hear anything any one man might say—before he turned to Dadley.

"Plenty of heart in that O'Neal kid," he observed.

Dadley scowled. But paid over the six hundred dollars he had lost to Danny O'Neal's stubborn stick-to-itiveness.

"Thank you, Lucas. Thank you kindly."

Tommy Llewellyn hadn't yet managed to get off the canvas, and they had to pick him up and carry him away so the next bout could be started.

CHAPTER 20

J oe sat with his back to the cold comfort of an ore cart,
his legs sprawled loose and awkward before him. After the cramped quarters at the ore face, it was a real
treat to be able to spread out and relax. The fact that he
was sitting on a filthy stone floor getting his britches just
as filthy as the floor was ... well, it didn't seem to matter
a whole heck of a lot at the moment.

His hands still stung and smarted as if Harlan were
still making the steel ring with his hammer blows. It was
funny the way he could keep on feeling something that
wasn't so. He sure hoped the sensation would go away
eventually. It would be pretty awful if a guy had to go the
rest of his life with his hands vibrating like that.

"You did all right today, Joe," Harlan said.

"Yeah, Joe. You're okay."

The compliment meant a lot to him. "Thanks, guys."
The praise made him feel much less worn-down and
leaden.

He looked around, marveling all over again at how
brightly lighted an unlighted drift could seem when a fellow was wearing a head lamp. Only a very few markers
and safety lamps were kept burning in the maze of drifts
underground, yet never once the whole day long had Joe

had any sense of being in darkness. That was because everywhere he looked, it was lighted.

It was funny that way. The reflector attached to his cap light threw a beam wide enough to cover nearly any normal angle of view, so whichever way he turned his head, there was light pointed there. Things seen very far away, outside the range of the cap light, might be dark. Or a fellow could get an idea of how dark it was if he held his head still and made a real effort to peer off to one side or the other. Then you realized that it was blacker than the blackest night when you were down inside a mine. But other than that, anywhere you looked you had plenty of light to see by. Shadows sometimes got long and jumpy when there were, say, three fellows looking at the same thing from different directions and so there were shadows running every which way at once. But except for that, a fellow could almost forget that it was dark down below and believe that everything was lighted up just as bright and natural as walking down the street on a sunny afternoon.

Joe spotted a candle stub and picked it up. It was an old thing, the wax brittle with age and dehydration. Someone had tried to carve a face into one side of it. Someone who wasn't much talented in that regard. What he'd done was more gouge than carve, and it was just barely possible to make out that it was a face he was trying to create. There were a good many such candle stubs tossed on the floor in this rock chamber where the drillers and cart handlers waited for transportation to the surface. Joe asked about them.

"Those old things? We used to have candles in our caps. You know. With reflectors like these here, but candles instead o' the carbide light. These lights are lots better. The candles, they don't last so long an' they blow out if you move around too quick or there's a puff of air, anything might put 'em out. These lamps, they're tons better. Cost more, o' course, but it's worth it. Believe me, you wouldn't've liked using candles."

"That's the dang truth," Cooter said. "The lamps are safer too. The guys working with the powder and the fuses are the ones to tell you 'bout that. Candles are scary when you got a open canister o' powder not more'n a foot or so away from a candle flame."

"I'd think so." Joe took another look at the misshapen face on the candle stub and tossed the thing away. His arm bumped the side of the ore cart he was leaning against and a small piece of quartz was dislodged from the rim. It fell onto the point of his shoulder and made him jump even though the bit of ore wasn't heavy enough to really hurt. Cooter and Harlan saw it happen and got a laugh out of it. Joe made as if to chunk it at them, but stopped short of actually throwing it. Both his shift partners obligingly ducked as if in great fear. Working with these fellows, Joe thought, wasn't all that bad.

He leaned back against the cart again and took a closer look at the ore piece. He'd seen plenty of the stuff still on the wall today, but this was the first good look he'd gotten at the object of all their hard work.

Not that mineral ores are so exciting to look at. Joe knew that from growing up close to the Comstock, where the finest silver ores in the world looked pretty much like any old trash rock. The minerals trapped inside ore bodies are so tiny and minute they mostly can't be seen by the naked eye, or even with a jeweler's glass. The ores themselves don't look like anything special, and for that matter aren't worth much until they are processed. Even a genuine expert can't look at a bit of ore and judge it without a proper assay. Joe knew that. Still and all, this was what he and Harlan and Cooter had sweated over the whole day long. It was only natural for him to want to look it over.

Oddly enough, this gold ore wasn't at all like the silver ores he'd seen back home. The particular vein they were following now was quartz in shadings ranging from white to dark pink. The bit in his hand was a milky white piece. The quartz was translucent and sort of pretty. Joe held it up close to his eye and examined it. There were bits of stuff trapped inside the quartz, little tiny bits like a sprinkling of pepper in a half-cooked egg, but these bits of pepper were a dark yellow. Sort of a . . . gold color.

"Hey, is this really . . . ?"

Harlan and Cooter laughed at him again.

"O' course it is. What'd you think?"

"I dunno. I guess I never thought I'd be able to see it in the rock like this. That's all."

"Well, you can't all the time. But some of it's pretty good stuff. Sometimes you'll get into pockets of it—not all the time, but here an' there—with ribbon gold. That looks like little gold worms or scraps of ribbon down inside the stone. But that's high-grade stuff. You don't see it real often."

"Sometimes you do," Cooter confirmed. "Why, I've seen some that's near free gold. Chunks of it. Long, five-sided chunks of the stuff, shaped almost like crystals, but gold."

"And I heard tell about one chamber," Harlan said, "it wasn't here, but some town up north o' here, where they found, like, one of them round nodes or nodules or whatever you call 'em. But this thing was big. Ten feet across. An' when they busted it open, it was all lined with gold inside, almost solid with it. They took it out with pickaxes and didn't even have to crush it or anything. It was practically pure just the way it come outta the mountain."

"Aw, you don't believe that," Cooter said.

"I do too," Harlan swore, crossing his heart with the tip of his thumb to demonstrate the depths of his conviction on the subject. "I got a buddy that worked in that mine. He told it to me for true."

"Well, I never seen anything like that."

"Never said I seen it neither, just that it's so."

Joe waved aside their bickering and went back to his examination of the quartz that came from the Shan-Rock mine.

"Bucket's down," the foreman called to them, leaning

inside the portal that led from the main drift into the side chamber where they were waiting. "Next eight men can go up now."

That meant the powder monkeys and their assistants were nearly done setting charges into the holes the drillers had made. Until they were close to done, the bucket continued to transport ore to the surface, but as the powder men came closer to finishing, they had to start taking the crews up. The charges were set and fuses cut while there were still men below ground, but they wouldn't shoot the charges until the level was cleared of workers. The last bucket up would take the foreman and lead powder man. They would be the ones to touch off the slow-burn fuses and leave. Normally they would be halfway to the surface before the shift's charges blew. Then there would be another hour and a half or so before the next shift came down to start clearing the ore blown free by those shots and to drill holes for the next sequence. It seemed a well-ordered and efficient operation, the way it had been explained to Joe. Not that he ever expected to be underground to see those last few actions before the shift ended and the charges were blown, but he found it all mighty interesting.

He stood, tossed the piece of ore back into the cart where he'd gotten it, and brushed off the seat of his pants. "Are we ready?"

"After you, Bo."

"No, Bo, after you."

"But, Bo, I insist."

Chuckling, the three of them ducked to clear the low passageway into the main drift and went to take their places in the big steel bucket.

The lead driller signaled with the bell cord, and a moment later the steam donkey far overhead began to whisk men and bucket alike to the surface.

Once there, they stepped across a gap that would have meant a fearful fall if anyone took a misstep. Joe felt his stomach lurch in protest as he moved from the bucket onto solid footing, but the other men seemed to take the whole thing—quite literally—in stride. Certainly they were casual enough about it. Looking down, Joe decided, was a bad idea and a mistake he wouldn't repeat.

"This way, Bo," Harlan said, beckoning for Joe to follow. Cooter ambled along behind.

The men exited the lift shed through a narrow door and down a set of enclosed stairs leading away from the working part of the mine buildings. The staircase ended in a small, windowless shed where Superintendent Burke was waiting. There were no chairs or stools in the room, but a long, sturdy table was placed in the center of the floor, and there were pegs on the walls.

"All right, boys, one at a time. Who's first?" Burke asked.

"I'll go," Harlan said.

"It figures you'd want to be the first one to the feed trough, Bo. I know your kind, don't I?"

"You sure do, Fitz. You know me through an' through." Harlan grinned and dropped his lunch pail onto the table with a clang. The superintendent opened the pail and fingered through the contents, then pushed it aside. Meanwhile everyone else was setting their pails onto the table too. Joe, mildly confused, followed suit.

"Turn 'em," Burke said.

Harlan emptied his pockets—not that there was so very much to take out of them—onto the table beside his lunch bucket, and then, one by one, pulled out the pockets in his clothes until every single pocket had been turned inside out.

"What—"

"Checking to make sure nobody's high-grading," Cooter explained in a whisper. "That's stealing ore."

Joe knew what high-grading was, all right. It was just that such a thing had never occurred to him. Obviously the same could not be said of Fitzhugh Burke.

"You're next, Bo," Burke said, pointing to a man from another crew.

Harlan patiently returned his pockets to their proper state and reclaimed his things from the table.

"Does this happen every day?" Joe asked.

"This? Hell, this is nothing. We should be so lucky an' have it like this every day. When we're in real good ore, ribbon ore like we told you about before—that stuff's real valuable, I mean a guy could bust some up if he was a mind to and carry a hundred dollars away inside the heels of his shoes—anyway, when we're in a run of really good ore, they make us strip off all our clothes, shoes, all that." He shrugged. "Some places they issue two sets of clothes, one for guys to wear aboveground and other clothes that never leaves the mine. At least they aren't that crazy here. And it ain't real often that Mr. Burke bothers with all that other stuff anyway. Mostly it's like this. Don't worry, it don't take as long as you might think. And you'll get used to it."

"If you say so," Joe told him, not at all sure that it was the truth. He supposed it was necessary and all that. But it certainly didn't say much about the bosses trusting the workers. Somehow the idea of being searched before he could leave the job made him feel sleazy and like they were accusing him of being a thief.

For sure they were as good as telling him that they suspected he would steal from them if they gave him the chance. That wasn't fair, dang it. It wasn't right. And it made him feel demeaned and put-upon.

With things being like this, it was no wonder there would be hard feelings at times between the owners of mines and the miners who worked them. Joe had observed those hostilities virtually all his life without ever fully understanding how the feelings could come to be. Now it was clearer in his mind. It was something he wanted to remember in case he was in charge of men sometime.

He shuffled forward and, while Superintendent Burke rummaged through the leavings of his lunch, began emptying his pockets and turning them inside out.

CHAPTER 21

The article about Ben Cartwright and his new acquisitions in Johns Bend was wildly enthusiastic if not particularly accurate. What he lacked in information, Henry Vickers made up for by way of imagination. Still, Ben had to concede that the nearly full-page newspaper article was more than adequately flattering. It fair made him blush. It certainly made him wish all the things Vickers said about him were true.

One thing, though, true or not, once the *Intelligencer* article made its appearance, the service and the smiles at the Bent Lodge took a turn for the better. Not that they had been bad before, merely indifferent. Now even the prissy desk clerk was becoming practically obsequious in his dealings with the wealthy and industrious—how could Ben deny either of those appellations when they were both so prominently proclaimed in the newspaper story—Mr. Cartwright, leading citizen and most influential entrepreneur of Virginia City, Nevada, and surroundings.

Ben read the article with some amusement and tucked it away to show to Adam, Hoss, and Joseph later. He suspected they would get an even bigger kick out of it than he did. Richest family between San Francisco and New York indeed. That was a laugh if ever there was one.

But no harm done. Ben put the article away and forgot about it.

"Is there anything I can get for you, Mr. Cartwright? Anything at all?"

"Nothing, thanks." Ben folded his napkin and laid it beside the plate. In seconds the soiled napery and tableware were whisked away and a cigar was laid before him. Ben didn't enjoy cigars at any time of day. The thought of one with breakfast was particularly unappealing. He rose, having to do it in a hurry in order to escape unwanted assistance, and made his way outside.

The day was bright and fair, the sunshine warm on his face and the air temperature cool but rising. The sky overhead was a clear and brilliant blue. All in all it looked like a fine day ahead.

"Sir? Mr. Cartwright, sir?"

He turned. For a moment he could not recall who this small boy was who was speaking to him. Then he did. The boy in the lead was the one who'd brought him that note yesterday evening inviting him to the fights. The second lad Ben was sure he had never seen before.

"Yes?"

"You remember what you said, mister?"

"Of course," I promised you a reward if you found the boy who carried that other note for me earlier."

"Yes, sir. Fifty cents. Each," the spokesman for the pair of three-foot-tall businessmen said.

"That's right."

"You meant it?"

"I did."

"Well, this is him," the boy said, pointing to his companion. "This is Bobby. He's the one."

"Is that so, Bobby?"

"Uh-huh."

"Tell me about it."

The boy shrugged. "Mr. Albritton, he gave me the note. Said I should find you an' give it to you. He paid me a nickel. Mr. Dadley, he heard me calling for you. He said he'd be seein' you and I should give him the note to carry to you. He gave me a dime."

"And you gave the note to him?"

"Sure. But it was all right, wasn't it? I mean, he said he was gonna see you and he'd give you the note. That was okay, wasn't it?"

"That was fine."

That was also interesting. Lucas Dadley took the note, which wound up—or at least the envelope did—in Neal Hubbard's waste bucket. Well, there weren't exactly any surprises in the information. But Ben was pleased enough to have it. At least now he knew for sure. Except, that is, about the contents of the note. For that he would have to inquire of Craig Albritton.

"Thank you, son. Both of you." Ben dug into his pockets and came out with a pair of silver dollars instead of the promised fifty-cent pieces. Neither boy objected to the change of plan.

Ben watched them scamper off with their newfound wealth, then turned in the direction of Albritton's office. It was possible, he supposed, that the lawyer might have returned by now.

In fact he had not. The office remained closed. Under the circumstances, Ben decided there was no point in trying the lawyer's home. Instead he walked on to the Canterbury Café. Much as Ben loved the vast Ponderosa and the life he and the boys had there, he had to concede there were some benefits to living in town too. Ben Cartwright was a man who cherished his friends and who thoroughly enjoyed a good conversation. Or a spirited argument conducted with humor and goodwill. He was learning here that a gathering of gentlemen to share talk and coffee was a habit that could become highly addictive.

"Good morning, gents. May I join you?"

"That depends. Are you willing to take your chances in the game, Ben?"

"Oh, I hear our friend Mr. Cartwright is a first-class gambling man, Tom."

"Is that right, Henry?"

"Mm, the way I hear it, Ben won a tidy sum from Lucas Dadley last night."

"Now how would you have heard a thing like that?" Ben asked Henry Vickers.

"We newspapermen have our ways." Vickers laughed. "Besides, Lucas closed the bar at the Antelopes' lodge last night. Everyone who wanted a nightcap had to hear a blow-by-blow account of how that good-for-nothing Welshman let down the side."

"I hope Tommy Llewellyn doesn't work for Lucas, because if he does, then I suppose he doesn't," Victor Curtis said with a grin. "So, um, to speak."

"Lucas was certainly angry enough to fire the poor clod last night, that's for sure," Dr. Monroe added.

"That's a shame," Ben said. "I hope the young man worked—for that matter still does—elsewhere."

"Did you stick it to him bad last night, Ben?" Willard Monroe asked.

"Tommy Llewellyn?"

"Of course not. Lucas."

Ben shrugged. "We played for stakes he set. I have to assume he was prepared to lose."

"Lucas? He only prepares to win."

"Speaking of winning . . ." Tom Keith said. He pulled out a coin and slapped it down onto the table, covering it with the palm of his hand.

The others did likewise, and Ben imitated them. Within moments every man at the table had a coin hidden beneath his hand on the table edge. There were five at the table: Henry Vickers, Tom Keith, Willard Monroe, Victor Curtis, and Ben.

"You're the last arrival, Ben, so you're the odd man."

"What does that mean?"

"It means you wait," Henry said. "Victor?" he asked, looking at the lawyer seated directly across the table from him. "Odd or even?"

"Odd."

Both men lifted their hands. Curtis groaned and rolled his eyes. Both coins were tails. Henry Vickers smugly retrieved his coin and returned it to his pocket. His coffee and roll would be paid for by someone else this day.

Monroe and Keith matched, the doctor calling even and winning.

"Your turn, Ben. You have your choice. You can go against Tom or Victor, either one."

"Very well. Tom, you're closer. Would you mind?"

"Only if I lose, Ben, only if I lose." The banker winked and laughed.

Each man put his coin down and covered it.

"Odd or even, Ben?"

"Even."

"Sorry," Keith said, sounding not the slightest bit sorry.

"Now what?"

"Now you and Victor play it off. The loser this time buys coffee and rolls for everybody."

"Unless I lose, in which case Lucas Dadley pays," Ben joked.

"Now I want to win more than ever," Curtis said.

"Shall I forfeit?" Ben offered.

"What, and have them on my aching back for the next two weeks? Never," the lawyer protested.

"Ready?"

"You're odd man, Ben. You call it."

"Very well. Odd it is." Ben lifted his hand, displaying a head.

Curtis peeked solemnly at his coin. And barked out a short, happy bleat of pleasure. Only then did he lift his hand to disclose another head. Even it was.

"Thank-you notes may be addressed to Mr. Dadley at . . . where does he work, anyway?"

"The Madrid."

"That's a rather large operation, as I recall," Ben said. "Any man with property that valuable can afford to lose the few dollars he put up last night."

"Oh, Lucas doesn't own the Madrid."

"No?"

"Heavens no. It's a publicly held corporation. Headquarters in New York, I think. Lucas is general manager for them, that's all."

"I had the impression . . ." Ben began, then paused. "Now that I think about it, no one ever did say anything about what he did. I merely assumed something other than the truth."

"Easy to do, Ben," Victor Curtis said. "Like assuming two coins are odd when in truth they're even." He smiled. "Not that I would ever mention it."

"Of course not, Victor," Tom Keith said. "That would be impolite."

"And I would never commit such a breach as to be impolite," Curtis said happily, his mood for the day positively sunny now that someone else was buying the coffee and sweet rolls.

"So tell us, Ben," Henry Vickers put in, "have you seen my article about you?"

"Indeed I have, Henry," Ben said, scrambling in an effort to think of something that would be polite yet fall short of outright falsehood, "and I would have to say that nothing remotely like it has ever been written about me before. Not even in the San Francisco papers." Well, that was certainly truthful enough.

Henry Vickers beamed and preened under what he perceived to be praise for his journalistic endeavors. Ben nodded and smiled and reached for the platter of sweet rolls. He might as well help himself to all he wanted, he thought. After all, he was buying them. Or Lucas Dadley was, however one wanted to look at it.

After the morning break, Ben accompanied Tom Keith back to the bank. Since he was going to be in Johns Bend long enough to see Chloe Shannon through her problems, he might as well open a bank account here. He used the bulk of Lucas Dadley's gambling losses as seed money in the account, and added much of the cash he'd been carrying in a money belt. Money belts are convenient and reasonably secure, but they are also deucedly uncomfortable, and Ben was happy to be rid of both the weight and the bulk. He felt like he'd just shed ten pounds once the belt was empty and its contents on deposit with the Miners and Merchants Bank.

"Thanks, Tom. I feel better now," Ben said, slapping his belly.

"Thank *you,* Ben. Believe me, I appreciate the business. I, um, don't suppose there is any chance you would consider bringing the railroad business back here, is there?"

"That's something I must ask Hubbard about. It doesn't make any sense to me for a business to place its assets where they'll benefit some other community."

"You can say that, Ben, where I cannot. After all, I do have a vested interest in the question. But the amounts involved are considerable. And I am certainly willing to discuss comparative interest rates. I can't promise to beat whatever the San Francisco banks are paying, but I would very much like an opportunity to compete for the business."

"I'll try to remember to talk with the shareholders about that, Tom."

"Then that's twice I must thank you this morning, Ben." Keith chuckled, and snapped his fingers as if just that moment remembering something. "No, make that three times. I have you to thank for the coffee and rolls, eh?"

"Now you're rubbing it in, Tom."

The banker grinned. "Of course. That's half the fun."

Ben smiled and picked up his brand new account book.

"Mr. Keith," a diffident clerk said in a voice barely above a whisper.

"Yes, Charles?"

"This is Mr. Cartwright, is it not?"

"That's right."

"Did you remember to ask him for those signature cards, Mr. Keith?"

"No, I didn't. Thank you, Charles."

"What's this?"

"We need you to fill out authorization cards showing us who is allowed to sign drafts or make withdrawals against your other accounts here, Ben. I meant to ask you to come by and do that, and then it went and slipped my mind, even with you right here in the building. I should be ashamed of myself."

Ben glanced down at the thin pile of paperwork he'd been given after opening his new account. He was almost certain that one of those forms had to do with whose signatures would allow access to the funds. As always, he included each of the boys on the personal account.

"Not on that one, Ben."

"I don't follow you, Tom. This is the only account I have here."

"Oh, far from it, Ben. Goodness, you have payroll accounts, operating funds, investment accounts, escrow accounts ... Charles, how many different accounts would you say are included with Mr. Shannon's old properties?"

"I should think more than a dozen, Mr. Keith."

"You'd best pull all those records, Charles, and get the paperwork in good order so Mr. Cartwright can update the authorization cards on each of them."

"Yes, sir, right away."

The banker looked at Ben and spread his hands in apology. "This could take half an hour or so, Ben. I'm sorry. I should have thought of it ahead of time and gotten everything ready for you."

"That's no problem, Tom. I'll tell you what. I said I would discuss the railroad banking situation with Mr. Hubbard. Why don't I just go upstairs and do that now while your clerk is seeing to all the paperwork."

"I hate to inconvenience you like that."

"No inconvenience at all, Tom, I assure you. I had no

other plans for the moment, and I'm only a few stair steps away. Now would be a perfectly good time to attend to that."

"I do appreciate it, Ben. Regardless of the outcome, I'm grateful to you for considering me."

"Nonsense. No gratitude necessary for a little thing like that. I'll go up now and take my time about it. Tell Charles he needn't rush."

"Thanks."

Ben stuffed the new bankbook and paperwork into a pocket and went outside so he could take the staircase to the suite of offices overhead.

Neal Hubbard was at his desk and seemed pleased to see his visitor.

"Good morning, Ben, good morning. Can I get you some coffee, perhaps something stronger for an eye opener?"

"Nothing, thanks. I just finished coffee and sweet rolls."

"At the Canterbury? That's a group of fine gentlemen who gather there. Wish I had time to join them."

It hadn't occurred to Ben before to wonder why neither Neal Hubbard nor Lucas Dadley was ever among the businessmen and community leaders who met daily at the Canterbury. Now he did so, but had no answers. He reminded himself to ask Tom Keith or one of the others sometime. Naturally, though, it was not the sort of question one might raise with Neal Hubbard himself, lest the answer prove an embarrassment.

"I agree," Ben said. "There are some mighty fine folks here in Johns Bend. I am quite thoroughly impressed."

"May I count myself among the class of people you mean there, Ben, ha ha? Thank you, I'm sure. No, don't take that chair. This one is much more comfortable."

And so it would almost have to be, Ben thought, recalling the discovery he'd made earlier about that maddeningly miserable chair in front of Hubbard's desk. Surely it was significant of something—he only wished he knew what—that the man was steering him away from that chair to a proper one with all its legs the same length.

"Are you sure I can't get you something, Ben?"

"I'm quite comfortable now, thank you."

"Before I forget, I thought the article about you in the current *Intelligencer* to be very commendably written. I've taken the liberty of asking Mrs. Phillips—she operates a ladies ware shop in town, does millinery work and sewing and the like on the side—I've asked her to a make a silk ribbon mat to surround a clipping of the article and frame it under glass. Thought it might make a nice remembrance for your wife."

"That was very considerate of you, Neal."

"My pleasure, Ben. After all, we are partners, are we not?"

"Yes, I would say that we are," Ben conceded with a smile.

"Of course. And anything for a partner. Or a friend." Hubbard was smiling now too.

Ben couldn't help but question whether he might have misjudged Neal Hubbard in the past. The man could be quite charming and just plain likable. Perhaps eventually he would feel close enough to Hubbard to want to explain about his personal life, about the losses he had suffered when first Elizabeth and then Inger and finally Marie came into his life and then were taken from him again, leaving their sons behind as the legacy of their love and their lives. Perhaps eventually. But not now.

"Something else I wanted to talk to you about today, Ben." Hubbard cleared his throat and looked away. "This, um, is a trifle awkward to bring up."

"Yes?"

"About last night."

"I thoroughly enjoyed the matches, Neal. Thank you for inviting me."

"Yes, well, I'm glad you did. Both Lucas and I are. But there is one thing . . . we only meant to do a kindness for a new friend, don't you see? Never intended any affront or, um, unpleasantness."

"The woman, you mean," Ben suggested.

"Exactly. Yes, thank you. I didn't, that is to say we didn't—"

"No harm was done, Neal, and no offense need be taken."

"That's good of you, Ben, because certainly none was ever intended. I mean, well, in business . . . you know how it is. And some men . . . that is to say—"

"I do understand, Neal. I just don't happen to be one of those men."

"So I realize now, Ben. And I truly did not intend to insult or demean you. I realize now you are a man of higher character than that. I apologize."

"Fine, Neal. We needn't speak of it any further."

"Good. Excellent. Thank you, Ben. Truly."

It seemed to Ben that the man was genuinely relieved to find that he held no ill will concerning the blatant offer of Morgana's favors in that very private viewing box.

Ben found himself feeling bad now for the suspicions he'd had about Hubbard and Dadley last night. Blackmail was what he'd thought then. But now, well . . .

It was true, sad but nonetheless true, that a good many businessmen equate success with the abuses of their money and their power. All too many seemed to feel that the greater their success, the less they need concern themselves with common decency and honor and prudence. All too many tended to place themselves above the restraints imposed by society upon its ordinary peoples, for they, after all, viewed themselves as extraordinary.

Hubbard's assumption that he would be someone of that ilk was likely more a matter of the man's past experience than any reflection of his opinion about him as an individual. Or at least Ben was willing to believe that of Hubbard now.

"I hope you have a little time this morning, Neal,"

Ben said. "There are some things I'd like to discuss with you."

"Of course. Anything. Absolutely anything at all." Hubbard's smile was warm and open.

"For one thing, the railroad's financial accounts. How they stand and, for that matter, where they are located. I understand they've been moved from the Miners and Merchants, and of course I'm sure you had a good reason. But I must admit that I believe in supporting local business whenever possible. Tom Keith seems a fine gentleman and his bank entirely reliable."

"I couldn't agree with you more, Ben," Hubbard told him, "but I suspect you will concur with the decision all the stockholders made when it came to the transfer of our working capital away from Miners and Merchants."

"All the stockholders?" Ben questioned.

"I would have to check the minutes to be sure about that, but I believe we were all present at that meeting." He stopped, frowned. "No, now wait a minute." Hubbard shook his head. "Dang it, Ben, I lied to you. It wasn't all of us. Craig Albritton is a shareholder, and I don't believe he was able to attend that meeting. I believe his five percent share was unrepresented in that vote, now that I think back on it."

Ben felt a wash of relief. He already knew that Albritton had been unaware of the change. But could Neal have been aware of that? Unlikely.

Perhaps it was small of him to have posed that test for his new partner. But no matter. Neal passed with flying colors. No claim of unanimous consent was falsely made here. Excellent.

"As for why, the reason are twofold. One, most of our purchasing is necessarily being done out of San Francisco. It only makes sense to have our money in hand where it will most often be required. That, however, is a very minor consideration. You and I both know that Tom Keith's bank is entirely respected. A draft on the Miners and Merchants would be honored virtually anywhere that

we would be apt to conduct business. The decision really
rested on the interest rates to be earned on our deposits.
Tom pays one and three-quarters on normal deposits, up to
a maximum yield of two or a tick over that on preferred
accounts. Which I would have to assume we could have
earned, as eventually I'm sure we would have become his
major depositor. Still, two and a bit is a long way from the
three percent we receive with our current holding company."

"Pardon me?"

Three percent was exceptional. In fact, three percent
was virtually unheard of. Why, banks rarely earned three
percent when they put deposits back out in the form of
loans. And for a bank to pay three percent to its deposi-
tors . . . Ben had never heard of such a thing. Two and a
half was the very most he'd ever heard quoted, and then
there had been warnings that the investments were high-
risk ventures and the interest yield could not be guaran-
teed. But three percent!

"Neal, you know I have to ask you where in the
world a man can make that kind of return on his money."

Hubbard's smile remained comfortably in place. "It's
a private bank, Ben. Mason and Lytle. Perhaps you've
heard of it?"

"No, never."

"Very private, very quiet. They take on only a very
few select clients. If you like, I can put you in touch with
them. You might want to open a personal account in addition to our corporate accounts with them. I'm sure that
could be arranged."

"That's very kind of you, Neal. Certainly I would like
the opportunity to meet with them." He did not add that he
would also learn much more about Mason and Lytle than
any simple conversation like this could disclose. Before he
ever sat down to talk with the gentlemen—if ever he did—
the family's factor, Alton DeShong, would long since have
investigated the reputation and reliability of the firm, inside and out. "Thank you very much."

Hubbard waved the thanks aside. "Think nothing of it, Ben."

"And I take it there will be no objection to my looking over the books and corporate records?"

"No objection whatsoever, Ben. In fact, I'll be pleased to receive your views. I know Lucas will also."

"I have to say, Neal, that I am most pleased with our discussion today. Most pleased."

"I'm glad to hear you say that, Ben. I promise you that you are no happier about this than I. If someone had to replace Lester, poor man, I am glad it turned out to be you."

"Do you think I could start going over those books now?"

"I wish you could, Ben."

"Pardon me?"

"The books. You are more than welcome to examine them, of course. Like I said, I personally am looking forward to receiving your suggestions after you do. But the actual records are kept in a fireproof vault, Ben."

"Is there some problem with that?"

"No problem. Except that the vault happens to be at Mason and Lytle."

"The minute book and financial records are all in San Francisco?"

"Yes, that's right. For safekeeping." He waved his hand, an extended finger sweeping in a wide arc. "This whole town is made of wood, Ben. It's all combustible. Why, Harptown burned to the ground not two years ago. They lost more than eighty percent of the buildings in the town. Eighty percent. And there was a fire in Devonwold the year before that. That one was almost as bad. No, I wouldn't consider keeping anything so valuable as those records here in Johns Bend, Ben. That would be much too dangerous."

Ben frowned.

"We do keep an unofficial log, of course," Hubbard added, his smile diminished. "You are more than welcome to see that and everything else we have, here or in San Francisco or both, whatever you wish."

That was better. At least there were *some* records he could use to begin getting an understanding of the railroad venture that Les Shannon had been so heavily involved with.

"Tell you what, Ben. It's almost lunchtime. Why don't we walk up to the lodge. You won't find any finer meal than what they serve at the F.O.A. My treat. Then afterward we'll come back here and I'll point out to you the drawers where all the railroad's records are kept. You're entirely free to go through them yourself. In fact, I have other business to attend to. I'll just show you where everything is and leave you alone to poke and prod without anyone hanging over your shoulder to see what you're into. That way no one can claim that I've held anything back from you. Does that sound fair?"

"Entirely fair," Ben admitted. He did not add, although it was certainly true, that this was far and away above any expectation he could have had when he walked into the office a little while earlier.

He was still disappointed that the official records and account books were maintained elsewhere. But under the circumstances, he had to count himself well-pleased with Neal's attitude of openness and cooperation. Very well-pleased indeed.

"The only thing I might object to," Ben said, "is your claim that lunch be your treat. You were kind enough to extend your hospitality last night. This time really should be mine."

"We can argue about that over brandy afterward," Hubbard said cheerfully, rising and reaching for his hat. "And with luck, Ben, that will be the only sort of argument our partnership need ever have."

"Now that, Neal, we can certainly agree on."

The two businessmen left the office, leaving Hubbard's secretary in charge.

CHAPTER 22

This sure is one busy operation," Joe said admiringly as he and Harlan and Cooter walked through the snow shed that connected the boardinghouse with the lower end of the Shan-Rock's buildings. Not that there was need for protection from snow at this time of year, but Joe could easily imagine what the conditions would be like in winter. Then the tunnel created by the wooden shed would be cold and airless, lighted by lanterns hung on the now empty hooks spaced at regular intervals along the plank walls. Then the roof of the shed might be buried under a dozen or more feet of snow, and networks of tunnels would be the only way men could move about. "They keep going all year 'round?"

"Sure. Two shifts, year in an' year out. The Shan-Rock, she never fails," Harlan said.

"Pretty old, is it?"

Harlan hooked a thumb over his shoulder in the direction of Cooter, who was bringing up the rear. "Ask him. He's been here ... what, Cooter? Five years? More?"

"More. Closer to nine, I think. Long time, anyhow."

"You'd think a mine would play out in that long a time," Joe suggested.

"That's something a guy never knows about. You follow the veins wherever they lead till they pinch out, however long that takes. Why, there's some mines still digging all the way since the 'forty-niners came into this country."

"This'un isn't that old, is it?" Joe asked.

Again Harlan looked to Cooter for the definitive answer. "Naw, not that old. But it's gotta be fifteen, sixteen years. Maybe even longer."

"That's a long time."

Harlan shrugged. "There's still a vein to follow. That's all you and me got to care about."

"Good thing too," Joe said. They reached the end of the snow shed. Without asking the others, Joe took the outside staircase that climbed along the side walls of the series of buildings that, along with the maze of diggings underground, comprised the workings of the Shan-Rock mining operation. It was a fine day, and Joe was enjoying the sunlight and fresh air aboveground. He wanted to be able to breathe deep for as long as possible, and Joe savored and enjoyed it while he still could.

Had the weather been foul, though, or had it been winter and necessary to use the snow shed, they could have remained indoors while they made the long walk up the mountainside to the lift house.

The uninitiated tend to think of a mine as being a hole in the ground from which ore bodies are removed. And to some extent that is true. But as this experience was reinforcing to Joe, the underground chambers were only a part of the mining process. The aboveground workings consisted of a series of buildings constructed one below another down the side of the mountain. As always in the search for efficiency in the mining process, the buildings were laid out in such a way that gravity—free and effective—was the principal motive force for the ore once it was brought to the surface.

Harlan, Joe, and Cooter labored all day to help break ore free of the mountain's interior. Once it was shattered and loose, the ore was carried to the huge bucket that dragged up and down the main shaft. Hauling the bucket to the surface was the one and only major expense of lifting the ore. From that point on the ore was encouraged to "fall" the rest of the way through its processing.

From the bucket at the top of the lift, the ore was dumped into a chute. The chute fed out of the hoist station and down into the next building, where it was sorted. Waste rock was tossed aside. Large chunks of ore were broken into smaller pieces, and the pieces already small enough to handle were sent into the next downward-flowing chute. In a chain of stair-step operations from that point, the ore was pulverized by the steam-driven "feet" of a small stamp mill, treated with chemicals to "float" the valuable metals away from the unwanted rock to skim off the desirable materials, treated with other chemicals intended to keep the metal while floating rock away, and finally the more or less concentrated ore was deposited in a gooey, muddy mess at the bottommost part of the process.

The mud obtained in this way did not look particularly valuable, even after the ore was concentrated as much as was possible at the mine site. The concentrates still had to be refined and the myriad impurities driven off before the material could be separated into its individual components of gold, silver, lead, and other base metals. When it left the Shan-Rock, the ore concentrates looked very much like water-logged charcoal with shiny, sparkling bits embedded inside. It was only afterward, in a process that required great expenditures of energy, that the refining took place and recognizable gold could be produced. The railroad would provide cheap access to those processes, making the mining operation much more cost-effective and producing greater profit. The railroad would also make it possible to bring in grinding equipment much more effective than the crude and inefficient stamp mill, which wasted more metal than it recovered from the ores. As it was now, the processing costs were far and away the most expensive part of the operation, and the stamp mill the most wasteful. The introduction of rail freight in and out of Johns Bend would pay benefits in both those areas.

To Joe, the physical processes of mining were still

new enough to be fascinating, now that he was beginning to take an interest in the subject. To Harlan and Cooter, the whole thing was all quite boring, but they willingly answered Joe's questions.

Adam had tried to explain most of it to Joe before, but at the time, Joe hadn't been much interested in his solemn older brother's pontifications. Now he wished he'd paid closer attention. Still, he was learning from experience, which he considered the best way anyhow.

They reached the changing room, and Joe took an oilcloth jacket off the rack provided for the workers. He selected a carbide lamp and checked to see if it was filled and functioning well, then put it on and made sure the lunch pail provided at the company boardinghouse hadn't gone astray.

"Did you fellas come here to work or are you gonna lay about an' cool coffee today?" Joe teased, finding himself ready before the others.

"Gimme a minute," Harlan said. "I'm thinking."

Cooter grunted something under his breath and picked up his satchel of dressing tools.

The threesome got into line with the other crews slowly winding their way to the hoist bucket and the long ride deep beneath the earth's surface, ready to start a new day's work.

CHAPTER 23

It was late afternoon when Ben finally emerged from Neal Hubbard's offices and trudged slowly downstairs to the sidewalk. He was so deep in thought that he almost knocked Tom Keith sprawling into the street. The banker was on his way home for the evening and had been moving at a brisk walk when he and Ben collided at the corner.

"Whoa, are you all right there, Tom?"

"Fine, you?"

"I'm terribly sorry, Tom, it was all my fault."

"I should have watched where I was going."

"No, really, it was my fault."

"Well, let's not argue about it."

"Could I buy you a brandy, Tom? As a peace offering?"

"That isn't necessary, Ben."

"Necessity has nothing to do with it. Would you join me in a brandy?"

The banker pulled a bulbous, pear-shaped watch from his pocket and checked the time. "Dora has some dinner thing scheduled tonight, so I dasn't be late. But I think I have time for a short one, if you like."

"I would appreciate it, Tom."

The two men dodged a trio of small, very heavily

built wagons carrying mineral concentrates, greeted a dozen or more other pedestrians, detoured wide around a loud and dusty dogfight, and eventually arrived at a store-front doorway with a brass placard overhead that read F. K. SMEALE. The outward appearance gave no clue to what lay within. It could have been an apartment or a haberdashery. "Have you been here before, Ben?" Keith asked, and Ben shook his head. The banker winked at him and turned the knob to enter without knocking. The business proved to be a small, very nicely appointed saloon that had an upper crust clientele and a wine list that ran to eight pages.

The gentlemen who frequented it could stand at the bar or choose among half a dozen groupings of soft, plush upholstered chairs. There were no gaming tables, but read-ing lamps were emplaced close by each seating area, and there was a rack of newspapers and periodicals for the guests to peruse.

"If Mr. Smeale ever tires of Johns Bend," Ben said, "I could find a welcome for him in Virginia City."

"Did you hear that, Fred?"

"Sorry, Tom, what was that?"

"We have another one wanting to kidnap you and move you off. Virginia City this time."

The bartender, a thin, bald man in his sixties or there-abouts, smiled.

"Fred, this is Mr. Cartwright."

"Oh, yes. The gentlemen in the *Intelligencer*. A plea-sure, Mr. Cartwright." Smeale extended his hand. "I had heard of you before the article, but it was interesting read-ing. Consider yourself welcome here any time you wish."

"Thank you, Mr. Smeale." Ben had the impression that the personal invitation from the owner was an initia-tion of sorts into a club that did not formally exist.

"How may I serve you this evening, gentlemen?"

"Have you a decent brandy, Mr. Smeale?" Ben asked with a smile and a wink.

"Oh, I might be able to find something satisfactory."

Smeale nodded pleasantly and went to rummage among his bottles.

"He'll be back directly with something too grand for my poor old palate," Keith said. "Where would you like to sit, Ben?"

"Over there, I think." He pointed to a grouping of chairs well removed from the few other customers in the place.

The armchairs were even more comfortable than they looked. Ben sighed and glanced around the dark-beamed, dimly lighted room. The walls were decorated with hunt scenes and coats of arms rather than the usual tobacco advertisements and buxom nudes. Ben found Smeale's to be quite comfortable.

The proprietor reappeared bearing a dust-crusted bottle and a pair of snifters on a tray along with a candle. He made what amounted to a theatrical presentation of the brandy, carefully decanting each serving and then slowly warming it over the flame before serving it. By the time he was done, Ben almost felt obligated to applaud the performance.

"Excellent," Ben declared after going through the obligatory sniffing and savoring. In truth, he found this to be a nice brandy. Period. But then he did not pretend to know brandies any better than Tom Keith did.

"Shall I leave the bottle, gentlemen?"

"Please."

"If you need anything else . . ." Smeale backed away the first few paces, then turned and went back to his bar.

The banker lifted his snifter in a brief salute, then downed the contents in a gulp. Apparently he knew as little about brandy as Ben did, and appreciated it even less.

"Have another," Ben suggested.

"Thanks. One more, then I have to go. Can't be late tonight, remember."

"Quickly then, Tom, let me ask you something."

"Of course, Ben."

"Have you ever heard of a bank—a private bank, I believe—called Mason and Lytle?"

Keith pondered the question for a moment, then shook his head. "No, I don't believe so. Certainly they aren't anywhere around here."

"This would be a private investment bank in San Francisco," Ben prompted.

"No, I'm sure I've never heard that name. Is it important?"

"I don't know. It's where the railroad accounts are being kept."

Keith shook his head again. "I'm sure I haven't heard of them before. Kind of strange that I wouldn't have, too, because I try to keep up with such things. I mean, I belong to both the major professional organizations for banking in California, and we do tend to talk among ourselves. I would have thought I'd have heard of any bank as close as San Francisco."

"Are you familiar with Porter and Gates, Tom?"

"Certainly. Tip-top reputation, Porter and Gates. They specialize in maritime affairs, I believe."

Ben nodded. This small-town banker in tiny Johns Bend did know his business. Porter and Gates was a private investment bank dealing, as Keith said, in ships and shipping. Ben had had occasion to work with them once or twice in the past or he certainly would not have heard of them. He decided to try one more test of the local banker's knowledge, if not an entirely fair test. "What about Condon and Moat, Tom?"

Keith frowned for a moment, then shook his head. "No. Sorry. I've never heard of them."

Ben smiled. That was good, because he'd just invented the good firm of Condon and Moat for the purpose of finding out if Tom Keith would admit to not knowing yet another—or so he would believe—California bank.

"Do you know Marcus Simeon?"

"Heavens, Ben, everyone in banking knows Marcus. Not only in California either. I doubt there is a banker in

New York State who hasn't at least heard of the genius in the wheelchair. And likely most have met him. Marcus Simeon is one of the leading bankers in the country, Ben."

"I didn't know that."

"Oh my, yes."

Marcus was one of Ben's friends from very long ago. If Tom Keith couldn't help with information about Mason and Lytle, Ben thought now, surely Marcus would be able to. Between Alton DeShong and Marcus, some knowledge had to be available.

"There isn't telegraph service in Johns Bend, is there?" Ben asked.

"Not yet. That's one of the things we were hoping the railroad would bring."

No matter, Ben decided. One way or another he would have to get a message off to Marcus. He wanted to discover what, if anything, Marcus knew about this Mason and Lytle firm.

"Thank you for the drink," the banker said, interrupting Ben's thoughts. Keith tossed down the last of his brandy and stood. "I don't mean to rush, Ben, but Dora's expecting me."

"Of course. Thanks for taking the time to join me here, Tom. Have a pleasant evening."

"I'm sure we will. G'night now."

Tom Keith departed, and Ben was alone in the odd but charming little saloon. Alone with a most excellent brandy and some fairly disquieting thoughts. How very strange that Tom would not have heard of Mason and Lytle.

Soon, Ben thought. Soon he would have to get his request off to Marcus.

With a sigh, Ben gave up pretending to read. The truth was, he had read this same page three times now and still had no idea what it was all about. He laid the book aside and reached over to lift the globe on the bedside lamp. It took two tries before he could blow the flame out.

The hotel room plunged into darkness, and Ben lay back on the plump feather pillow.

It was late, but he was not sleepy.

He wished ... He smiled to himself in the night. There were a great many things he wished, actually. He wished he hadn't sent Joseph to San Francisco. Better yet, he wished Adam were here to discuss all this with. Or Alton DeShong. Or Marcus Simeon. Or ... well, that was a *very* long list, and there was no point in trying to name all the names that could be placed on it.

The point, he knew, was his difficulty in trying to determine what the truth was here. And then, if that much could be accomplished, what he should do about it.

What he wanted was someone to talk it over with, but there was no one in Johns Bend whom he could unburden himself to. Under ordinary circumstances he might have gone to Chloe to talk. But these circumstances were hardly ordinary, and anyway, Chloe had more than enough to worry about without Ben Cartwright adding to her burdens. Craig Albritton, perhaps, except that Albritton remained away. Tom Keith ... except that the banker really was not a party to any of it and, the rest of the truth, Ben did not know Keith well enough to determine if he might have personal interests that would taint his judgment, one way or the other. Henry Vickers? Hardly. A very nice man, of course, but one doesn't go to a newspaperman when one's object is to speculate about the reputation and reliability of a local businessman.

For the time being, really, he was very much on his own here. He wouldn't mind that, really, except that he *really* did not know how to determine the truth.

Ben sighed again and stared sightlessly toward the ceiling, lacing his hands behind the nape of his neck and wondering if it might be in order to ask for a bit of divine inspiration. A hint would be enough.

None was forthcoming, so once again—he'd been doing little else this whole long evening—he sorted through the few facts he had in a futile attempt to build a solid structure from a few flimsy matchsticks of fact.

Fact One: Neal Hubbard, and presumably therefore Lucas Dadley as well, had made a complete turnaround in their outlook and attitude toward him. Once Ben made it clear he intended them no harm, all the closed doors were flung wide open. This afternoon Ben had been given un-limited and unstinting access to the High Sierra Short Line records. Such as they were.

Which brought up Fact Two: the sketchy records kept in town were virtually worthless. More a diary than a ledger, the book noted the receipt of assessments from the stockholders and offered cryptic, quite indecipherable notations regarding expenditures.

Among the many examples that so thoroughly frus-trated Ben was one that read "Stock 45,000." Stock. Won-derful. What *kind* of stock. Livestock? Railroad rolling stock? Stock shares? And the figure: 45,000. Equally won-derful. Did that mean the corporation spent $45,000 on this unknown stock? Or that 45,000 of something were purchased for an unrecorded dollar amount? Or . . . or something else entirely?

"Stock 45,000." Thank you very much.

Neal had been as good as his word. He'd unlocked the appropriate filing cabinet, showed Ben the area he needed to examine, and then said good-bye, taking his leave at that point, not to be seen again. Had Neal been there, or Lucas, perhaps sense could have been made of that notation. As it was . . .

As closely as Ben could tell—and he was not at all sure that it was at all close, but by his very best guess—the High Sierra Short Line so far had been dabbling here and inquiring there but in reality accomplishing very little.

Apparently, money had been paid out to engineers and to consultants, but as yet no real work had begun on the line. No rolling stock had been purchased, although de-posits might—or might not—have been placed with man-ufacturers. No rails, ties, spikes, scrapers, mules, or crushed rock had yet been purchased and stockpiled. But contracts for them may—or may not—have been worked out, ready for implementation. Rights of way had not yet been purchased. But discussions toward that end may have been held.

The problem, really, was that even after going over Neal's records, he had little more information now than he'd had to begin with.

And what he did have was . . . confusing.

So little had been accomplished. And at such a high cost.

If he was reading the notes correctly, the railroad's cash resources were nearly exhausted. Yet nothing worthwhile seemed to have been accomplished.

Proceeds from the pledged holdings—Les Shannon's Caroline, Mobeetie, Whist, Tosh, and Shan-Rock; Neal Hubbard's Vorstok No. 5, Highboy, and Bright Wing mines; and Lucas Dadley's Ace's High property—were not enough to keep pace with the rate of expenditure. Worse, when Ben compared the early records against more current entries, it was glaringly apparent that those contributions were in decline. The mines in the Johns Bend district seemed to be losing production rapidly. It was a dilemma, a matter of the dog chasing its own tail harder and faster, faster and harder. The mines needed the railroad if they were to achieve the greater recovery rates from their ores and rebuild profit levels. And the railroad needed greater profit levels from the mines if it was ever to be built.

All in all, Ben thought, this was not an attractive picture. Had he been walking into it cold and looking at it as a purely impersonal business venture, there was no question but that he would politely refuse any offer that he buy in.

But as an owner—well, sort of one—with the livelihood of a good friend's widow at stake, that was a rather more ticklish call to make.

Fact: the High Sierra Short Line Railroad seemed a near-dead and fast-dying business proposition.

Fact: Chloe Shannon needed the High Sierra Short Line Railroad to succeed if she were to enjoy financial security.

Making the situation worst of all was that Ben still was not entirely convinced that Neal Hubbard and Lucas Dadley were being straightforward with him.

It was a terrible thing to admit after the men had proven to be so agreeable and cooperative after a bad beginning, but niggling, nagging little doubts persisted. If the full records had been here to be examined, or if the banking were undertaken with someone of known repute, or if—barring all else—Ben simply had a good *feeling* about the partnership . . .

"Damn and double damn," he grumbled under his breath.

Probably, Ben conceded, his best course here would be to recommend dissolution of the High Sierra corporation. Get back what little he could for Chloe—if anything—and advise her to plan on the flagging and perhaps soon disappearing production from Les's old mines to support her through her old age.

And if that was the best he could come up with, dammit, then he had to regard himself as a mighty poor friend when Les's time of greatest need arrived.

Thinking about that, fretting but seeing no clear path, Ben tossed and turned on the rumpled hotel bed. After a time he gave up on trying to sleep. He got up and, not bothering to dress, found his pipe and tobacco. He carried them to the open window and pulled a chair close to it so he could get the benefit of the chill night air. He filled and lighted the pipe and sat there, a slight breeze ruffling his hair and lifting the pale, aromatic smoke away from him.

He was still there, the pipe cold now and laid aside, but his position otherwise unchanged, when the first roseate blush of dawn brought shape and color to the street below.

If only he knew what to do now. If only.

CHAPTER 24

J oe folded the brown, grease-spotted paper back and peered at the contents of his packet with undisguised loathing. "Again!" he grumbled.

"Might as well get used to it. It'll near always be the same," Harlan said.

"Except Saturdays," Cooter put in. "We don't never have it on Saturdays. I dunno why."

Good enough reason to wish for a week of Saturdays, Joe thought.

The sandwich in his lunch, distributed by the boardinghouse to each of the men as they filed out in the mornings, consisted of two thick, dry slabs of crumbling bread, as inch-thick chunk of sharp cheese almost as dry and crumbly as the bread, and a barely discernible smear of unsalted butter to glue the whole, horrid mess together.

It wasn't that Joe had anything against cheese. But this stuff was sharp enough to whittle with. And dry. Lordy, but it was dry. A sandwich like this, he figured, ought to be served with a bucket of water for dunking in.

"If you don't want that," Cooter said, "I'll take it."

"I can't say that I want the dang thing, but I don't wanta go hungry either," Joe told him. Cooter looked disappointed. The tool dresser was already halfway through his sandwich.

Joe took a tentative bite of the offensive stuff and brushed the resulting crumbs off his shirt. The choices were clear: eat the lousy thing or stay hungry until supper.

"What else did you get, Joe? I got me some pound cake. See?" Harlan held up his hunk of dessert as if it were a trophy. Which in a manner of speaking it probably was. Joe liked pound cake. He set the dull sandwich down and pulled his own dessert package out of the pail. Whatever the stuff was, it was wrapped carefully enough. There was newspaper wrapped around it four layers thick before he got to the wet and soggy brown paper that held the ... he peeled a corner back with care, then grinned ... wedge of dried apple pie. The pie oozed white, thickened juices so syrupy-sweet that not all the sugar could dissolve in it, and tiny crystals of the stuff flowed and floated along with the melted butter and baked juices. Oh, now this was more like it.

"Want to trade, Joe?"

"Not on your life, Bo."

Harlan looked disappointed. So did Cooter, and Cooter hadn't yet opened his dessert.

"Cooter."

"Yeah, Joe?"

"I'll swap you the rest of my sandwich for your dessert."

"You don't know what I got here."

"You don't either. You wanta swap or not?"

Cooter thought it over for a moment, then grinned. "Sure, why not?"

Joe could have provided him with some answers to that question but decided against it. There was no point in messing up a trade that was going so nicely.

They made the exchange, and Joe unwrapped this second half of his lunch. Another piece of pound cake. That was all right. He liked pound cake just fine.

He ate the pound cake first, saving the pie for last. Joe did dearly love pies. He hadn't yet tasted one he didn't like and kind of suspected he never would.

"That looks awful good," Harlan suggested.

"Yup, 'tis." Joe winked at him and used a thumb knuckle to capture a trickle of juicy syrup that was running down his chin. He salvaged it and sucked the sweet, luscious stuff off his knuckle and, for Harlan's benefit, let out a loud, contented sigh.

"Dang you, Joe."

"Now tell me you'd've done different if you'd been the one to grab this pail."

"That'd be different."

"Yeah, you betcha. The difference is that it woulda been you not sharing with me. This way it's me not sharing with you."

"That's a pretty serious difference, all right," Harlan said cheerfully.

Cooter, well into his second sandwich, sat there dribbling small crumbs of bread and cheese. He seemed perfectly content just the way things now were.

Joe needed both hands to get around his slab of pie with a bare minimum spillage. When he was done, he was only mildly sticky with leaked juices. The boardinghouse hadn't thought to provide the, um, gentlemen with any napery for their comfort. Such a serious oversight, Joe thought. He really should admonish them. In the meantime . . .

There was still the wad of newspaper that had been wrapped around his pie. That was relatively unsoiled and should serve nicely enough as a napkin, even if the ink did smear a little. No one down here was apt to care. He pulled it out and went to wipe his hands on it, then stopped. A word set amid the gray mass of type caught his attention.

Cartwright. It said it right there. And again there. Absently, Joe wiped his hands on his pants legs, something he had been trying to avoid but now forgot entirely, and spread the newspaper open.

There was an article on the page about Pa. How odd to be sitting more than a thousand feet underground, and carrying a false name at that, and have your own father's history put onto a page of newsprint right under your nose.

Well, a purported history anyway. It wasn't especially close to the truth in most areas. Still, it seemed Pa was getting along right famously with the local folk. What he'd read of the newspaper story so far made Pa sound like the Thomas Jefferson of the West. Or if not Jefferson, then an Alexander Hamilton at the very least.

Why, reading that article was enough to make Bo Burns wish he'd been born a Cartwright.

On a whim Joe said as much to his companions.

"Who?"

"The fella in this article here. Have you read it?"

"Naw, not me. I don't read much."

Cooter looked at Harlan and chuckled. " 'Course you don't read much, Harlan. You can't. Not no more'n I can."

"I can too."

"You can like hell. I never seen you read one thing, and I've known you off an' on for, what, two years? Three?"

"What difference does it make if you've known me since I quit wearing dresses? What you just said proves you don't really know me for nothing, Mr. Lee Roy Barcoot, 'cause I can too read. I can read good."

"Then how's come I never seen you?"

"Well, I would hope you got better things to do than set around and watch to see am I reading stuff."

"This isn't worth getting hot over," Joe said.

"The hell it ain't. Here, gimme that." Harlan leaned over and grabbed the newspaper away from Joe. He glared down at the sheet as if it somehow offended him, tilted his head first one way and then the other, squinted and scowled.

"You want Joe to read it to you, Harlan?" Cooter suggested.

"Shut up, Lee Roy, or I'll do some readin' to you. Except it won't be off no paper that I take my message."

Cooter laughed, unintimidated by Harlan's threats.

"Listen here now," Harlan said after several minutes of silent study and, no doubt, agonized preparation for his recital. "What this says is, um ... where do I wanta start? Okay, here. What this says is, 'Cart ... riggit's faith an' con-con-confidence in this d-district should be inter-interpreted as a' ... I mean, 'an ... an in-inspi-inspiration to all. Mr. Cartriggit,' " it took this second iteration before Joe recognized Harlan's mispronunciation as being his own name, " 'proves his con-confidence by way of the inv ... estment of capital des ... despite reported l-losses in the ap-ap-ap' ... Joe, what's this word here?"

"Applicable."

"Yeah, I see that now. Thanks." Harlan glared at Cooter briefly, then dipped his eyes back to the newsprint. " 'Applicable mining p-properties an' spec' ..." He pointed to the word and held it over to Joe.

"Speculative."

"Right. 'Specu'tive railroad shares.' So there, dammit. Can I read or can't I?"

"Better'n me by a long shot," Cooter said in amiable concession. "I can make out my name, but that's about the size of 't."

"Don't you never again say that I can't read, Lee Roy Barcoot," Harlan warned.

"I said you could read okay. What more d'you want?"

Harlan climbed down off his high horse and relaxed. He gave Cooter an aw-shucks smile and said, "Reckon I want an egg in m' beer. Anything wrong with that?"

"It's fine by me," Cooter agreed.

"All right, then."

"I'm sorry if I went an' made you mad, Harlan."

"Well, I'm sorry if I got my back up."

"Yeah, well, you read just fine. Anything I need read, I know I can come t' you."

"Except we'd both be better off to get Joe t' do the reading 'round here." Harlan handed the sheet of news-print back to Joe, who wanted to finish reading it and see what else the paper had to say about Pa and his doings here.

Before he could get back to it, though, Rolly came around blowing his whistle and calling everybody back to work. Joe hurriedly stuffed his trash into his lunch pail, then folded the damp, syrup-spotted newspaper and shoved it into a pocket. He could finish reading it later.

"How you doing, Joe?"

Joe worked his hands, forming them into fists and then extending his fingers, doing that over and over several times. "Not so bad, Harlan."

"Tingles, don't it? All pins an' needles?"

"Sure does."

"They say a guy gets over that after a while, gets so it don't hardly feel that way at all."

"Is that so?"

"No, but they say it anyway." Harlan grinned. "A guy has t' have hope, don't he?"

"Will you two quit jawing? If Mr. Burke sees you two coffee coolers malingering like this, he'll dock all of our pay, not just yours."

"Just you keep up with your end, Cooter. Me and Joe, we'll drill holes from here to Harptown if we can find us a man t' keep our drills sharp enough for the job. Ain't that right, Joe?"

"Don't be dragging me into the middle of your bickering," Joe said.

"Smart, I tell you," Harlan said happily. "My partner here is plenty smart."

The three of them trudged back to the stope face, where they still had seven holes to drill before the end of the shift.

CHAPTER 25

S orry I didn't get back to you last night, Neal, but it was late when I got in. Too late to bother you then, I thought." A note had been waiting for him when he returned to the hotel the previous evening, but he simply hadn't felt like responding to it at the time.

"That's no problem, Ben. Was it, Lucas?"

"No, no problem at all," Dadley agreed solemnly.

The three were assembled in Neal Hubbard's office. Ben had come over first thing at the start of business hours. The tone of Hubbard's note asking to meet with him implied a measure of reasonable dispatch if not outright urgency.

"I assume there was something in particular you wanted to discuss," Ben prompted.

"Very much so. Lucas and I have been examining our mutual situation from every possible angle, and we feel we have no choice but to levy another assessment on ourselves, Ben. We just don't see any other path. The railroad must have capital to survive."

That was an interesting turnabout after these same two gentlemen's response of only a few days ago when Ben had suggested exactly that. But then, of course their previous refusal had to do with emotion, not logic, Ben thought. Now that they had accepted him as a stockholder and partner, they obviously were reconsidering his suggestion that more money was needed. And, Ben suspected, after the glowing sentences in Henry Vickers's newspaper article, Hubbard and Dadley no doubt now believed that an infusion of additional cash was conveniently available. Ben decided against mentioning the rather heated refusals of their first meeting.

"We need a stockholders meeting and formal vote before an assessment can be made," Dadley said.

"What about Craig Albritton?" Ben asked.

"As far as I know, Craig remains unavailable. For the record, we will have a notice of the meeting delivered to his office. But with only a five percent share in his name, his presence certainly is not necessary. We can move along without him."

"Yes, I suppose so."

"Would you be agreeable to convening a shareholders meeting now, Ben?"

"Is that legal?"

"If we three agree to it, it certainly is. In fact, if any two of us present in this room agree to it, there would be a majority approval."

"I have no objection," Ben said.

"Excellent. Thank you. I'll ask my secretary to send the notice to Albritton's office, then he can step in here and take notes for the official minutes of the board." Hubbard left, brisk and businesslike. He was back within moments, and his secretary was not far behind. "Gentlemen, I hereby declare this meeting of the board of the High Sierra Short Line Railroad to be opened. A majority of voting shares are represented. Mr. Secretary, please make note of the participants and the stock ownership of each so that the record will show that we have a quorum on hand."

"Yes, sir."

"I move we waive reading of the minutes of the last meeting," Dadley said, "and move on to new business."

"Do I hear a second to that motion?" Hubbard was looking at Ben.

"Second the motion."

"All in favor? Fine Any opposed? No. Mr. Secretary, please record a unanimous vote of those present in favor of the motion."

"Yes, sir."

"New business?"

"I move we initiate an assessment against shares," Dadley said, "at the rate of one thousand dollars per share of common stock, assessments to be paid to the chairman of the corporation and deposited in corporate accounts no later than, um, one week from today?"

Hubbard nodded. "Do I hear a second to the motion?"

"I hope we will discuss it before a decision is made," Ben said.

"Of course, but we have nothing to discuss until there is a motion on the floor."

Technically, of course, he was correct, Ben acknowledged. "I second Mr. Dadley's motion as to the assessment."

"Thank you. Are we ready to call a vote?"

"No, we are not, Neal. I thought I just said that."

"Of course, Ben. Sorry. What is it you want to say?" He smiled. "After all, I believe I recall you suggesting very much this same thing a few days ago."

"Yes, but . . . we're talking about raising a hundred thousand dollars here."

"Ninety-five, actually. Craig is in this as deep as his circumstances allow. I doubt he could come up with another five thousand. As soon as the motion passes, Ben, we intend to vote an exemption in Craig's favor allowing him to make his contribution in kind, by way of legal services, rather than in cash. Not that that matters, particularly, but I wanted you to know. Frankly, Ben, anything else would be unfair. It would force Craig out, and we don't want to do that."

"Force him out?"

"Oh, yes. That is clearly stated in our bylaws. Any

stockholder of record who cannot or for whatever reason does not fulfill his obligations, will forfeit the voting rights as to his shares and forfeit dividends or other financial disbursements until the amount of arrears can be recovered by the corporation."

"I see."

"It is all right there in the bylaws."

"I don't believe I've ever seen the bylaws."

"Remind me, Ben. I'll see that you get a copy before you leave today."

"Thank you, Neal."

"Was there any other discussion you wanted, Ben, or shall I call for the vote?"

"Well, I would like to know what this money will be used for, Neal."

"Specifically?"

"Yes, specifically."

"Lucas, I believe that would lie within your, um, area of expertise."

Dadley harrumphed and cleared his throat. "Of the ninety-five thousand dollars to be raised," he said, "we propose to allocate twenty thousand to the hiring of surveyors to stake out the right of way. Thirty-two thousand will provide a contract with Wickes Brothers to begin grading and roadbed preparation. Twenty-two thousand will be needed for the purchase of hardware. You know, rails, spikes, and so on. Ten thousand is owed on our next installment payment toward the purchase of rolling stock. That leaves six thousand. That won't go very far toward hiring and maintaining construction crews, but we will just have to make do. I'm sure we can manage somehow."

"You have this worked out already."

"Yes, very much so."

It occurred to Ben that they more than had it worked out. They had it assured. Having decided what they wanted to do, Neal Hubbard and Lucas Dadley held enough voting power between them to approve their plan regardless of anything Ben Cartwright might say or want to do.

Furthermore, they had the voting power to do it by way of a motion that Ben himself had already seconded.

Neat. Tidy. Ben rather admired how nicely they'd worked it out between them. And in truth, there was little he could find to fault in their program. Everything Lucas Dadley said they wanted to do certainly needed doing, and then some. No point in creating friction where none need exist, Ben thought.

"Mr. Chairman, I call for a vote on the motion now before us," Ben said.

"Very well. Mr. Cartwright?"

"Aye."

"Mr. Dadley?"

"Aye."

"Mr. Secretary, you will record the vote as being unanimous. An assessment of one thousand dollars per share of common stock is hereby ordered, monies to be payable one week from today." Hubbard smiled. "Do I hear a motion regarding shareholder Albritton and the matter in which his assessment obligation may be fulfilled?"

"I would like to make a motion toward that end," Ben said.

A few minutes more and the required business of the stockholders in the High Sierra Short Line Railroad had been completed.

"Excellent, gentlemen. Simply excellent. Thank you," Hubbard said, rubbing his hands together. "Oh, yes. Barry, before Mr. Cartwright leaves this morning, do remember to give him a copy of the corporation bylaws, will you?"

"Yes, sir, I'll be glad to."

"Ben, thank you so much for coming over here today. Speaking for myself, I must say that if we had to be deprived of Les's companionship on this board, I cannot think of anyone more agreeable and congenial with which to replace him."

"I second that motion," Dadley offered. "Glad to have you with us, Ben."

"My pleasure, I'm sure," Ben said.

"I don't mean to rush you, Ben, but I have several appointments I'd already scheduled for this morning. Otherwise it would be my pleasure to visit with you more."

"Oh, that's quite all right, Neal. There are things I should be doing too." Ben retrieved his hat, shook hands with both Hubbard and Lucas Dadley. "Good day, gentlemen."

"Good day, now."

Ben went out into the outer office. True to his word, Hubbard's secretary had a holographic copy of the corporation's bylaws waiting for him to pick up. "Would you like a copy of the minutes of this meeting too, Mr. Cartwright?"

"Oh, I shouldn't think that would be necessary. I suspect I can remember what was said. Thank you, though."

"Very well, sir. If you change your mind, just let me know. Mr. Hubbard stressed to me that you are to be given every cooperation, sir. Anything you need, anything at all, you let me know."

"I shall, thanks."

"Very well, sir. Good day, then."

Ben went outside and paused on the landing to check his watch before going down to the street level. He was pleased to discover that he was still in time to make it over to the Canterbury Café for coffee and sweet rolls with that friendly crowd if he stepped right along and didn't dawdle about it.

As he strode purposefully down the sidewalk, something occurred to him that brought a wry smile to his lips.

Here it was, still early enough to meet with the coffee crowd, and he'd already spent $35,000 today. At this rate it would take very little effort at all and he could beggar himself before dusk.

*　　*　　*

"Why, Ben. How very nice to see you. Please come in."

"Thank you, Chloe." Ben removed his hat and wiped his feet on the mat before he accepted the invitation.

"Have a seat in the parlor, Ben. I won't be a minute."

"All right."

"Try that old blue armchair. I think you'll find it comfortable, and there is an ashtray beside it."

"Thank you, Chloe." The chair had been Les's. Ben suspected Chloe might be deliberately testing her own responses to the idea of someone else being in the situations and using the things that once belonged to Les. Little things like that could be very painful, as Ben remembered all too well from his own past losses, but it was necessary to explore and to examine them if one hoped to heal and once again to live. It was not what he himself would have preferred, but he sat in the chair that had been his friend's.

By the time he filled and lighted his pipe, Chloe, true to her word, was back. She returned to the parlor bearing a tray of crustless finger sandwiches and bite-sized sweetmeats. "Would you like tea or coffee with this, Ben?"

"Tea would be nice, thank you."

She trotted off into the back of the house again. This time when she returned, she was carrying a tea service for two.

"I certainly didn't mean to put you to all this trouble," Ben apologized. "I only wanted to stop by and see how you are."

"Much better, thanks to you," she said as she removed a thick, quilted cozy from the teapot and poured for both of them. "Sugar, milk, or both?"

"Both, thanks." He held up a finger to indicate she'd tipped enough thick cream into the tea, then did the same again a moment afterward to tell her two sugars were sufficient. Chloe stirred the mixture briskly and set it beside Ben before doctoring her own brew heavy with sweetener but light on the cream. Finally she placed the food tray at Ben's elbow and took a seat on the sofa nearby.

"Now tell me, dear friend Benjamin. Will the railroad be built, or have I burdened you with a lame goose?"

"Actually, Chloe, I'm beginning to think the railroad will indeed be built, and if it is, then I'm certain it will have all the impact Les believed it would."

"I would feel badly, you know, if you suffered a loss out of your concern for me, Ben."

"Thank you, Chloe, but I don't believe that will happen. Neal and Lucas have become positively chummy since they decided I'm not out to 'get' them somehow. We had a meeting only this morning to talk about raising capital so we can go ahead with the construction plans."

"Well, I hope you had better luck with them than my Les ever did. It used to worry him no end how they ever expected to come up with their fair share. It was hard enough for us, and we had some very good properties supporting us."

"Come to think of it, Chloe, just what is it that Neal Hubbard does? Other than think up plans for railroads and so on?"

"Oh, he's into this and he's into that, but I think most of it is bluster and big talk. He owns small shares of a number of things and sits on too many boards to keep track of, which gives people the impression that he's more powerful than he really is, but I can't think of any one property or business that he owns outright."

"No? I thought he owned, oh, three or four mining properties here. Something called the Highboy, I think? And the Bright Wing? And there was some other foreign-sounding name too. I forget what that one was."

"There isn't any Highboy mine in the Johns Bend district, Ben, I can tell you that. Nor one called the Bright Wing either. Perhaps somewhere else?"

"Perhaps," Ben agreed. "What about Lucas Dadley, then? I understand he is general manager of one of the local mines, but that he also owns something called the Ace or—no, that wasn't it—Ace's High, that was the name. He owns the Ace's High mine."

"There again, Ben, I can't tell you that he does or doesn't, but there is no Ace's High in this district. Not that I ever heard of, and Lester used to talk to me at the dinner table about any and every little thing he'd heard or discussed or thought while he was working that day. I don't pretend to be an expert on the mines in Johns Bend, but at least I've heard all their names over and over through the years. I am quite certain those properties you mentioned are not local."

"Odd," Ben mused. He tried one of the sandwiches, a light and delicate flavor with cream cheese that had something else mixed in with it, some fresh, garden flavor that he couldn't quite identify but which, fortunately, he liked. He ate that one and reached for another. "Lucas Dadley does work for one of the local mines, though, doesn't he?"

"Oh, yes. He manages the Madrid mining property for Mr. Evan Eubank. Evan is from the Philadelphia Eubanks, you know. He and Les were quite good friends. Evan had dinner with us several different times when he visited here."

"Eubank. The name sounds familiar. I think he has property in the Comstock district too."

"Oh, I would think so. Evan is one of the leading members of a consortium of financiers from New York, Philadelphia, Baltimore, I don't know where all else. They pool their investment capital and buy up properties of proven value wherever they find them, then hire people to manage the properties on site for them. Evan and Lester got on so well that Evan invited Les to participate with them at one point. But of course we didn't have the sort of capital Evan and his cronies do. Amounts that were pin money to them were riches to us." She sighed and took a sip of her tea. "Do you know, Ben, sometimes I think the reason Les was so keen about making our fortune with this railroad idea was so he could become wealthy enough to play with the grown-ups like Evan and his eastern friends. Les didn't care about the money itself so much as he did the thrill of success. Taking little and making much of it. And of course it would have been a real benefit to the district too. That was important to him. But it wasn't just the money. It really wasn't."

"I certainly knew Les Shannon well enough to know that, Chloe," Ben agreed. Returning to his original point, something he was much more interested in than he would expect Chloe to be, he added, "Was Lucas Dadley already employed at the Madrid when Eubank and the consortium came on the scene, or did they bring him in from somewhere else?"

"Oh, they brought him in. I have no idea where he came from. Evan's group hired him, though, and brought him here to manage the mine for them. I'm quite sure of that."

"And Lester liked him?"

"I do not recall saying that, Ben."

"Les didn't care for him, then?"

"Personally, well, no. Professionally, Les accepted Evan's judgment of Lucas: rough, sometimes cold, but effective. Evan once said—over dinner right here in this house, it was—Evan once said that if all the miners walked out in the middle of a shift, Lucas Dadley would find a way to complete the shift using just the burros and canaries. He is a man who will get the job done, whatever it is. But I think even Evan found Mr. Dadley a difficult person to really like."

Ben grunted and reached for another of those sandwiches. The anemic-looking little things tasted better than they had any right to. He was beginning to suspect they could become addictive.

"May I freshen that tea for you, Ben?"

"Thank you."

It occurred to Ben that he was spending an inordinate amount of time asking about things that really should be of no particular concern to him.

Yet they were. Undeniably they very much were.

There was ... something ... something he couldn't

quite pin down. Something nagging in the back of his mind, which would neither come to the surface where he could examine it nor go away and leave him be. Something that he suspected he should be able to identify but could not.

"You say Les was concerned about the other partners' ability to raise investment capital, Chloe?"

"Oh my, yes. Very much so. After all, of the three principals, we were the only really strong leg. When they first began the venture, Les had thought Neal was probably the best off of the three. Then later he changed his opinion about that. He never told me what made him believe otherwise. I think he didn't want me to worry about the possibility of the railroad failing and us losing everything we'd put into it by then. But I'm certain that at some point close to the end there he had become ... well, to be perfectly honest about it, Ben, he had become rather disenchanted with Mr. Hubbard and with Mr. Dadley. Mr. Hubbard the more so, I think, because Lester had put so much faith in Mr. Hubbard's support for the project. In fact, I think it was the day before the ... the accident, at one point he grumbled that the whole project was dependent upon us and us alone. Do you know, Ben, I think that may well have contributed to his accident. I think he may have been down in the Shan-Rock that night searching for ... something ... some new vein, some new reason for hope that the production values would rise again and make it possible for us to carry the railroad construction costs by ourselves. I don't know that, of course. But I believe it."

"He didn't normally go down in the mines himself, surely," Ben said.

"Gracious sakes, no. Les was much too busy aboveground to be able to spend much time in the diggings himself. Not that he wasn't still capable of it, mind you. Lester dug the exploration shaft with his own two hands, you know. There never would have been a Shan-Rock or any of the others if Les hadn't been willing to swing a pick or drill a hole in hard rock."

Ben smiled. "I remember those days very well, Chloe."

"Of course you do, Ben. You among all our friends would remember that. Why, in those days you were the only person who really and truly believed in Les and his dreams. Others sometimes said they did, but you backed what you said with your cash. If it hadn't been for the help you gave him then—"

"You say you don't really know why Les was underground the day he had the . . . accident?"

"No. He never told me he was going into the Shan-Rock. Not that he necessarily would, of course. But it seemed a strange time for him to do it. You know."

"Sorry, but I don't know what you mean."

"Oh, going down at a time when he was the only one below. That seems so unlike him. I would have thought at the very least he would have taken Mr. Burke with him."

"I still don't follow you," Ben said.

"It was a Saturday night when it happened, Ben. We give Sundays off, of course. All the mines in the district do. Our men work ten-hour days, six days per week. Les went down after the Saturday-evening crew had come up. They wouldn't be going down again until Sunday night, you see, so the mine was empty. The last powder shots of the day had been fired, and everything was shut down. When he left here, Lester told me he was going to the boxing matches at the Antelope lodge. They have fights there every so often. Les used to enjoy them. And in fact he did go that night. Several people mentioned seeing him there. At some time that evening, though, he took it into his mind to go down into the Shan-Rock, for what reason I suppose we never really will know for certain. The result . . ." Chloe gave Ben a look of bleak emptiness and turned her head away.

After a moment she looked back at him with forced, and patently false, cheerfulness. "Enough of that," she said in a bright, brittle voice. "The wake is over and done with, and it's all left to the worms now."

"Chloe—"

"It's all right, Ben. I'm all right. Really I am." Her eyes sparkled with unshed tears that she refused to let spill. She bounded to her feet. "Dear me, I do keep forgetting things. Excuse me one second, please."

"Of course."

Chloe hurried away, reaching to dab at her eyes as she rounded the turn into the foyer beyond the parlor door. Her voice floated behind her. "There is something that belonged to Les. I know he would like for you to have it, Ben. It meant so much to him, and I know he would like for it to be yours now."

Ben heard a distant slamming of drawers in another room, then silence. After another moment Chloe's voice reached him once more. "Drat. It isn't in this room at all. Wait a second, please. I have to go upstairs."

He heard footsteps on the stairs, and a few minutes later she came back down holding a small box.

"Here, Ben. It would please Les—it would please me—if you were to take this." She opened the box. An ugly bit of gray rock the size and approximate shape of a lima bean lay on a green velvet pad. A streak of cream-yellow ran through the center of the rock. A tiny harnesslike contraption made of jewelry grade gold had been fashioned to hold the rock and allow it to be suspended from a watch fob or tie clasp or whatever.

Ben smiled, certain of what this had to be. "From Les's initial finding?"

"That's right. This bit was the surface showing that brought us the Shan-Rock. He kept it all this time, and it was very special to him. I know he would think it right and proper if you were to have it now."

"Thank you, Chloe. I'll cherish it." Ben accepted the gift, carefully closed the box again and slipped it into his pocket. The tiny ore sample had meant much to Les once. Now it meant at least that much again to Chloe. Ben felt honored that she would want to entrust it into his care. That was, he felt, an indicator of more than was actually said.

She smiled, the tears welling full in her eyes again, and tried to maintain control with inconsequential chatter. "Dear me," she said, "so silly of me. I went rumbling about in Lester's office, going through his file drawers and everything. Why, I knew good and well that wasn't where he kept things like this. Never had been. I must be getting old, Ben, to go looking into all the wrong places like that. And when I knew better too."

"We all do that sort of thing from time to time, Chloe. Why just—" He stopped, frozen in place as one mental cog suddenly meshed with another.

"Ben. Are you all right, Ben? You look pale. Are you sure you're all right?"

"I just ... thought of something."

"You look like you've seen a ghost."

"No, but I think I've seen a lie."

"Pardon me?"

"Oh, not you, Chloe." His eyes changed, their focus returning to reality after several moments during which they'd been elsewhere. He smiled and gripped Chloe by the shoulders. "Thank you, Chloe. Thank you *so* much."

"Ben?"

"You did it, Chloe. Thank you. You showed me what it is that's been nagging at me all morning. You broke the logjam and made it all clear to me now."

"But I didn't—"

"Oh, but you did. Thank you. Would you excuse me now? I hate to run, but I have some thinking to do. Business. I hope you'll understand."

"Yes, of course. Come back any time, Ben. Any time at all."

But Ben was no longer really listening. He picked up his hat and left the house, moving slowly and as if in a daze while he thought back, trying to recall and recapture sequences of events and compare them, as it were, side by side. He was so bemused at the moment that he failed to tip his hat or even so much as acknowledge a pair of ladies he passed on the sidewalk.

CHAPTER 26

Joe pulled the length of heavy steel out of the hole and set it aside. Harlan, every bit as anxious as Joe was to get this last hole in, picked up the stick they used to gauge the depth of the newly drilled hole.

"Good enough," Harlan declared. Joe thought they were maybe a fraction of an inch short, but for a quarter inch or so he certainly wasn't going to squawk. "That does it for t'day," the driller said.

"That's it?" Joe asked.

"That's it."

Cooter hadn't bothered waiting for any confirmation. He was already packing his kit before Harlan even began measuring the depth.

Joe wasn't carrying a watch, but he guessed they were done well ahead of the shift-end whistle. If the lift wasn't busy carrying ore, they would be able to go up ahead, but men took second priority when there was ore to be removed, so they might or might not have a wait before they could grab a ride to the top. Either way, not working would be a marked improvement over working.

At the moment Joe's hands stung and tingled, his back ached, his arms and shoulder muscles burned, and he had the beginnings of a sore throat. He was commencing to think that starting young horses to harness or saddle and keeping watch over a bunch of stupid cattle wasn't quite so onerous a burden as he used to believe.

He picked up the forty or fifty pounds of drill bits they'd been working with today.

"You fellas ready?" Harlan asked.

"Whenever you are," Joe said.

Cooter merely nodded.

"Then let's go." They carefully picked their way down the sloping, rock-littered floor of the ever expanding stope and passed by the foreman on their way out. "You can send the monkeys in, Rolly. This here hardworkin' crew is drilled out an' gone home."

"Getting pretty quick to finish here lately, aren't you," the foreman observed.

"Hey, we're an A-number-one, first-class drilling crew, we are," Harlan told him.

"If that's so, maybe I ought to move you boys over onto the big face."

"Fine by me, Rolly. It's bonus money in our pockets if you do."

"What was that all about?" Joe asked once they were beyond Rolly's hearing.

"Oh, there's one big, tall vein that takes more shooting than where we been working. Gotta drill six holes more for every shoot over there. But it ain't as hard as it sounds, because you got more room to work in too. Don't have t' bend and cramp yourself so much, so it goes pretty slick. Point is, whoever drills that face gets an extra fifty cents a day. It's good bonus money."

"What about the crew that's working there now?"

Harlan gave him an odd look. "What about them? If we can do it better, Rolly will give it to us. Maybe they're slowing down or shorting the holes or something. How the hell would I know?"

"You don't have to get testy about it."

"I ain't."

"All right, then." They continued walking at a slow, tired pace through the drifts, their way lighted by the cap lights. "Have you ever worked the big face before?" Joe asked.

"As a twister. I never drilled on it."

"Cooter?"

"Oh, sure. Till Rolly or Burke or somebody'd get mad at me. Then I'd be back to working with stiffs like you guys."

Joe wasn't really sure if Cooter was kidding or not. Probably he was. Probably.

They came to the sealed-off passageway they passed twice each day, and this time Joe remembered to ask, "What's in there that it's walled off like that?"

"That's the start of a stope, except they don't use it no more," Harlan said. "Poison gas, I heard."

"Poison gas, hell," Cooter put in. "Whoever heard of gases in this formation? Nobody, that's who. No need to even keep canaries in this hole."

"If it isn't gas, then why did they close it off?" Harlan asked.

"That's where the old man blew hisself up," Cooter explained.

"Old man?" Joe asked. He wasn't supposed to know anything about that.

"Mr. Shannon," Cooter said. "His name was Shannon. Not a bad fella for a big shot. Friendly. He always acted nice when he came around. Never lording it over people the way some do."

"You say he blew himself up?"

"That's right. Nitroglycerin. Not that I'd know where he got the stuff. He wouldn't allow anything but giant powder for working with, and I never heard of any nitro in this here or any other of his mines. But they say he had some down here that time an' that he dropped it or whatever. It don't take much to make a real serious mistake with that nitro. Can't abide it, myself. Scares me. That's one o' the reasons I like working in Mr. Shannon's properties. No nitro. Except this one time that killed him."

Cooter shook his head. "It's terrible what nitro can do to a man."

"You seen it?" Harlan asked. They'd stopped for a breather and were all leaning against the wall not far from the sealed-off passageway where Lester Shannon died those weeks earlier.

"I seen it," Cooter said. "I was working on the shift that come down an' found the mess. It was awful, let me tell you. Worst I ever seen."

"Will they just leave that stope closed off?" Joe asked, relieved that Cooter did not insist on giving details about the scene behind that wall.

"Sure they will," Harlan said. "Say, a man died in there, didn't he? And he wasn't no working bum neither, he was the owner of the place. You can bet they'll leave that one closed off."

"You can bet they won't," Cooter said.

"No?"

"No way. I told you I was working in that stope, didn't I? Well, it was a Sunday night when we come down to go back to work and found what was left of Mr. Shannon. Saturday evening just before we went off shift the holes my driller was making was hitting into one helluva ore body."

"Aw, how would you know a thing like that?" Harlan scoffed. "You couldn't see into the other end of those holes."

"I'll tell you how. An' I didn't need to see inside no hole in the rock neither. I'm the guy as dresses those bit faces, and I'm telling you that he was hitting into some stuff that was close to being free gold. Closest thing to it I ever seen that wasn't placer gold. No way t' know if it's ribbon or crystal or what after the bits got done pounding and mashing on it, but I can tell you that I was having to clean flakes off the heads o' them drill bits before I could sharpen 'em. Now mind, I never seen what it looked like after they blew them shots. Next time I came down we, all of us, was awful busy with Mr. Shannon's accident an' everything. But I can tell you for certain sure that we was just then hitting into one helluva ore body. Best that's been seen in years, I'd wager. Mayhap the best there's ever been found in this whole damn district. And I'm here t' tell the both of you boys, with that kinda strike behind that wall there, they're gonna go back in an' dig it. It's one thing to honor the dead. That's a right an' proper thing to do. But it sure as hell won't keep anybody from digging ore with that much pay in it. There's never been a mining man born yet who'd let something like that stand between him and a really good ore strike."

"You saw this yourself, Cooter?" Joe asked.

"I told you what I seen. I saw the flakes collected on them drill bits where you'd only expect to see rock dust. I saw right good and well that the driller on that crew had broke clean into the rich pay, so the powder shoot had to uncover it. No way it couldn't help but break out since the drilling had reached it. I seen that. As for the other, well, if you wanta look for yourself, Bo, all you got to do is bust a hole in that wall and see for yourself. Straight in from that door and to your right. It ain't forty feet from the entrance. If you don't believe me, then the hell with—"

"Hey, I believe you. Okay? No need to get your back up, Cooter, I believe you."

"We both do," Harlan said quickly.

"Well, all right, then," Cooter said, mollified.

"You know," Joe mused aloud, "I bet you're right about something else too Cooter."

"What's that?"

"I bet you're right that they'll go back in and work that stope sooner or later, even if Mr. Shannon did die inside there."

"You two can stand and gab your lives away if you want," Harlan said, "but I don't wanta die of boredom just yet. I say we drag this scrap steel outta here and see can we get a lift to the top."

"You sound like a man with a hot date."

"I am. It's just that the lucky girl don't know it yet," Harlan told him.

"Then I expect we'd best hurry. It'd be a crying shame for you to break some poor girl's heart tonight, and her not knowing it." Joe laughed and set off at a swift pace to lead the rest of the way to the lift shaft.

CHAPTER 27

B en caught Dave Ossamer just as he was about to lock up for the evening. "Do you have a minute that we could talk, Marshal?"

"A minute or an hour, Mr. Cartwright. Since my wife died, I'm in no hurry to rush home."

"I know the feeling, Marshal. I'm a widower myself."

"I'm sorry to hear that, Mr. Cartwright. Reckon we both know how lonesome that can get."

"I'm afraid so, Marshal. But, please, call me Ben."

"If you'll make it Dave, Mi—I mean, Ben." Ossamer grinned and pushed the office door open for Ben to enter, then trailed along behind. "I dumped what drinking water I had left this afternoon," he said. "It gets kinda stale sitting overnight. But I have some goat's milk yet. Would you like a glass of that?"

"No, thanks, I'm quite comfortable." Ben reached for his pipe, then remembered that Marshal Ossamer did not allow smoking in his jail. Ben left the pipe in his pocket, leaned back and crossed his legs.

"Word has it that you're a nice man, Ben, but I'd expect you to be a busy man too. Too busy to come here socializing, is what I'd guess."

"True, Dave. I've, uh, been thinking about that situation we discussed earlier. Have you reached any conclusions?"

"You mean about Les Shannon's death being on the odd side of things?"

Ben nodded.

"You wouldn't believe how much sleep I've lost over that already, Ben. And likely to lose more. Why, I keep pulling and twisting and turning at what little I know, tugging at it like it was saltwater taffy, but no matter how I prod it, I can't ever make the facts fit into any shape that tells me anything. All I had to begin with is the same thing I got now: a gut-deep hunch that what little I know isn't half what there is to know. And the unimportant half at that."

"You still don't think Les died by accident?"

"I still don't think the man I knew would have taken nitroglycerin into that mine with him. I mean . . . think about it. What reason would he have? Even if you're willing to believe he would change his ways and take to using the stuff, why would he go and do it without telling anybody?"

Ben shook his head. He couldn't understand it either. "The thing that bothers me, Dave, is why would he do it when they say he did. Why on a Saturday night when the mine was empty?"

"Fitz Burke says it's because he didn't want anybody else hurt if anything was to go wrong. Which it did."

"But a Saturday night? Why not between shifts on a normal working day so there would be people close by to know if there was trouble?"

"Burke says that might've been because he didn't want anyone else to know. Didn't want anyone insisting that they go down with him." Ossamer gave Ben a close look and then leaned forward. "I'll tell you the question that's driving me nuts, Ben. Assuming all this other stuff is just the way everybody says it was . . . how the hell did Les get down to the bottom of that shaft?"

Ben shrugged. "Why, naturally he . . . Oh! Wait a minute. I see what you mean."

"That's right. If the mine was closed down for the weekend . . . *who the hell was operating the lift so that Les could get down to the working level of the Shan-Rock, with or without a bottle of nitro in his pocket?*"

It was a question to which Ben had no answer. And one Ben hadn't thought of himself. Ossamer was right, though. That did make for a very pretty puzzle. "I am beginning to think, Dave, that you and I should have a long, serious discussion. There are some things—guesswork only, mind—that you may be able to help me with."

"Believe me, Ben, if it will help me get to the bottom of this business of Les's death, I'd be pleased to do anything short of breaking the law. No, I'll tell you the whole truth, an' that is, I'd be willing to do anything short of breaking a *serious* law. There's some I have to admit I regard as being more serious than others, and some that I expect I'd be willing to bend hell out of if not break outright. Most anything to set this matter to rest, even if it's only in my own mind. Until now, Ben, it's been gnawing on me but I haven't come up with any ideas strong enough to let me try an' do anything constructive in the way of an investigation. Couldn't be anything formal, so to speak. If you have something I can hang on to, anything at all, I'd be real interested t' hear it. So you go right ahead, Ben. You speak up and I'll see what I think of whatever it is you have to say here."

"Fair enough, Dave."

Ben laced his hands over his knee and thought for a moment, trying to put his thoughts in order. It was all pure speculation, of course, with nothing concrete to back him up. Just guesswork and suspicion and—like Dave Ossamer said himself—some gut-deep hunches.

Still, it was all he had, and he might as well either lay it out for the town marshal to examine or else forget it and try to make himself believe that everything was as it seemed.

Finally Ben leaned forward, wishing he could have the comfort of a smoke to help soothe his jangled nerves, and began in a calm and carefully controlled voice to speak. He went on that way for quite a considerable time.

"You're crazy as hell. You know that, don't you?" Harlan complained.

"So what's wrong with that?" Joe asked with a grin.

"You'll get yourself fired."

Joe shrugged. "I've had worse things happen."

"Dang you, I been getting kinda used to having you for my twister. You do all right."

"Why, thank you, Harlan. It's nice of you to say that." Joe's grin flashed again. He leaned down and plucked Harlan's freshly brushed derby off the foot of his cot and tossed it into Harlan's lap. "Don't forget your war bonnet. Anything that fancy is sure to take the eye of some passing filly."

"Dang it, Joe, get serious."

"I am. Now don't worry about it. I mean, all I did was ask you a simple question. You gave me an answer. You ain't responsible for anything else that happens. Go on down to town now and enjoy yourself. I'll be just fine. Okay?"

"No, it isn't okay. If you think you got to do it, well, I'm just fool enough to go an' do it too."

"You? You got no reason to go down there."

"Neither d'you, Joe. None that you've told to me, anyhow."

"I'm not trying to hide nothing from you, Harlan. I just don't wanta get you in any trouble with me."

"Fine. But I'm going with you, an' that's that."

"You might get yourself fired."

Harlan laughed. "There's worse things has happened to me than that."

"All right, then, let's go."

They walked through the empty snow shed to the stamp mill and climbed the chain of staircases to the lift house. The changing room was empty. It would be an hour or more until the next shift came on. Harlan selected a pair of cap lamps, checked to make sure they were full of fuel, and lighted them. The pressurized carbide burst into flame with a soft pop and quickly settled to a slow sizzle.

There was no sign of the lift operator from their shift. Joe did not know the man who was there checking the fire box for the donkey engine's steam boiler, but Harlan knew him. Sometimes it seemed like Harlan knew everybody in or around Johns Bend. He claimed to have worked with at least half of them and partied with the rest.

"H'lo, Angus."

"What t' 'el 're you doin' here, 'arlan?"

"Angus, this is my twister. His name's Bo, and he's gonna help me look for something I lost down in the hole this afternoon."

"What'd you lose, 'arlan?"

"What I lost ain't none o' your nevermind, Angus."

"You're high-gradin', ain't you? You're wantin' t' go down an' high-grade somethin' you tucked away while you was workin'. That's it, 'arlan. Ain't that it?"

"Angus, you got more imagination in you than a little girl with pigtails and a cornshuck dolly. We ain't high-grading, dammit, we want to find something I lost. Something personal. Now are you gonna let us down or ain't you?"

"I'll let you down, 'arlan, but you got to make me a promise. Anything you high-grade, I get a third of it. You got to promise."

"Okay, Angus, if we decide to steal anything while we're down there, I'll give you a share."

"A third, 'arlan."

"A fifth. Two-fifths for Bo, two-fifths for me, an' one-fifth for you."

Angus beamed his approval of the arrangement and pointed to the bucket that hung at the top of a thousand-foot-plus drop into the mountain.

Harlan and Joe climbed into the bucket—funny, but

the step was much less frightening to Joe now than it had been the first few times he'd made this trip—and Angus gave them a nod and a conspiratorial wink as he tripped the lever that sent the cable spool free-wheeling swiftly down and down.

Harlan laughed. "It's a good thing Angus isn't as good a thief as he'd like to be or this mine would go broke."

"Why'd you offer him a share when we aren't stealing anything?" Joe asked.

"Because stealing is something he'll believe. Breaking into a tomb isn't."

"I told you before, dang it, we aren't breaking into any tomb. Mr. Shannon is buried in the cemetery just like anybody else. We're just gonna go into that stope there and . . . look around." Joe grinned. "Kinda."

"I still say you're crazy."

"That's all right. I have company, don't I?"

Harlan laughed, then grabbed the nearest bucket chain for support as far overhead Angus began applying the brakes to the cable drum.

"I dunno, Ben. This feels kind of spooky."

"Do you want to wait somewhere else, Dave?"

"I can't do that, Ben. I'm the only one who's authorized to execute that search warrant. You know that."

"You could deputize me," Ben suggested. "That would make it legal, I think."

"We're on thin enough ice without adding any more complications, thank you."

The search warrant was duly signed by the county judge, but there was serious question whether it would stand close examination if it were ever challenged in a court of law. For one thing, Judge Martin Peavy had been knee-walking drunk when he signed the document. For another, Marshal Dave Ossamer had helped coerce him into that condition, pouring a succession of drinks for the bleary-eyed little jurist before producing the search war-

rant affidavits and, with no explanation at all, placing pen
and papers into the judge's hands.

Still, however obtained, the warrant was signed and
therefore enforceable. Which was all they were trying to
do now. If, that is, they could get through this darn ...
locked ... door.

"There," Ben said with some satisfaction as he felt a
tumbler inside the lock give in to the pressure he was ex-
erting on it by way of a very recently obtained crochet
hook.

"You got it?"

"I think so. Wait. Yes!" The knob turned easily under
Ben's hand this time, and the door swung open. He
stepped inside, Dave Ossamer close behind him. Ben had
to admit that he felt considerably better now that they were
indoors. Standing there on the outside staircase landing
had made him feel like the sliver of moon overhead had
become bright as stage lights, so that everyone for blocks
around was sure to see the two shadowy figures lurking
outside Neal Hubbard's office in the middle of the night.

"Better close the door, Dave."

"I'll get the window blinds too. We're gonna need
some light to see by. No sense in making this any worse
than it has to be."

"I'll help you."

It took the two of them several minutes to close,
check, and recheck the door and windows until they were
finally satisfied that the place was as light-tight as they
were ever going to get it.

"You know, Dave, I don't know how professional
burglars do it. I think I'd have a heart attack before I could
ever get a single job done." They had a legal right to be
there, of course. The search warrant, after all, was enforceable on the premises, not the person, so it was entirely legal for Ben and Dave Ossamer to enter the office
unannounced. Which for some reason did not make Ben
feel the least bit better about it down in the pit of his stomach. He winced with every tap or rattle of noise. In a way,

he almost wished they'd gone ahead and looked Hubbard up to inform him the warrant was being served; almost, but not really. This way there was no chance that anything could be surreptitiously hidden before they might find it. And this way too there was no chance Hubbard could quickly challenge the warrant and render it invalid. This very likely would be the one and only shot they would have at this idea, and nervous or no, Ben did not want to risk wrecking it at this late hour. Better to take a firm grip on his nerves . . . and be awfully quiet while he was doing so.

"You and me both," Ossamer agreed. He sounded quite as nervous as Ben felt. Apparently neither one of them was cut out for a life of villainy, if neither could comfortably sneak about when doing so was perfectly lawful.

"Did you think to bring a candle or anything?"

"No, didn't you?"

It took them several more minutes of groping in the dark and bumping into things before Marshal Ossamer located a wall lamp and managed to noisily disengage it from its mount. "You got a match, Ben?"

"Yes. Over here."

There was some more banging and thrashing and finally Dave Ossamer materialized under Ben's nose.

"I hope Tom doesn't keep a watchman in the bank overnight," Ben mumbled.

"He doesn't. Good thing too. If there was a night guard downstairs, we'd wake him out of a sound sleep, sure enough."

Ben struck a match and lighted the lamp. Ossamer immediately turned the wick as low as it would go without extinguishing itself. The dim glow that resulted was enough, if barely, to illuminate a ghostly circle ten feet or so around the lamp. Gargantuan shadows leaped and curled with every movement either man made, adding to the sense of guilty intrusion Ben was feeling. Spooky, Dave had called it, and spooky it was.

"Where?" Dave asked.

"Somewhere in this room. The secretary was out here

at his own desk or close to it. He didn't have to take anything out of the files in Neal's office."

"I hope this shows what you say it will, Ben."

"I hope so too. Of course, even if it does, it won't give us all the answers. But it should be a start."

"If I can't make a murder charge stick, I suppose fraud would do," the marshal said.

"If they did what you think they did, then I want more than that."

"So do I, Ben, but after a while you learn to settle for what's possible, never mind what's right."

"Lucky for me, I've never had to learn that lesson."

"Look, Ben, could we talk about this later, please? I'd like to find what we need and get the heck outta here, if it's all the same to you."

"Hold that light closer, will you?" Ben pulled a drawer open at random. The only approach he could think of from this point would be to just start looking and keep at it until something turned up.

He started pulling records out of Neal Hubbard's secretary's files and holding them up to the light, one by one by one.

CHAPTER 28

Y ou!"

Ben looked up from his sweet rolls and coffee—paid for by Dr. Willard Monroe this time—and nodded a noncommittal hello to the rather unhappy-looking pair of gentleman who were standing nearby.

"You," Neal Hubbard repeated in the same accusatory tone of voice.

Lucas Dadley was more to the point in his greeting. "You son of a bitch."

"Y'know, Lucas, you really should be careful what you say. There are some who would take exception to that particular turn of phrase," Ben said mildly. "I must admit that I am among them."

"Is that a threat?"

"You could take it that way."

"You son of a bitch," Dadley snarled for the second time.

"Gentlemen," Henry Vickers said, his interest quickening, "am I to take it that there is dissension within the, ahem, partnership?"

"Shut up, you imbecile," Dadley told the newspaper editor. "And don't you dare print a word about this or I'll sue for everything you ever hoped to own."

Neal Hubbard was not willing to be sidetracked from the main issue. "How dare you. How *dare* you?" He looked close to an apoplectic seizure. "My private property . . . breaking and entering . . . as soon as I can find the marshal, Cartwright, I'll have you behind bars. I swear I will."

Ben laughed. "If you want the marshal, Neal, you can find him at the courthouse. He's talking with the judge and prosecutor now about what charges to bring. For fraud, misrepresentation, theft, murder—I really don't know what-all the possibilities might be. And as for last night, gentlemen, you should know that no crime was perpetrated. A legal search warrant was served. Certain property was confiscated and is now in the hands of the authorities." Ben gave them both a smug look.

"I don't suppose you would elaborate on this," Vickers said hopefully.

"Wouldn't mind at all, Henry," Ben told him. "These two gentlemen here have been conducting a scam. Upon Lester Shannon most of all, but upon you, the businessmen of this community, really against everyone here. Raising false hopes about the construction of a railroad when all they really wanted to do was to raise money for work that would never be performed. Money that went into their own pockets."

"But surely—"

"Oh, you can believe it, Henry. Last night Dave Ossamer executed a search warrant. He found corporation records and bank statements in Neal's office that proves what I say.

"It was really a very simple plan they had. They looked the town over and came up with Les Shannon as the one man who had the two requisite attributes necessary to become their pigeon: he had money, and he had integrity. Worse, Les believed others were as honest as he. That made him perfect for their plan.

"They created their railroad corporation with themselves holding sixty percent of the voting shares. That meant the two of them could vote anything they wished. And vote they did. They collected cash from Les both to capitalize the initial stock offering and as ongoing assessments against operating and construction costs. They collected cash from Les, as I say, but without his knowledge they also voted that their own contributions be made in kind. Neal contributed his services as chairman and Lucas as treasurer of the corporation. They valued those services in excess of ninety thousand dollars. Each. Les, of course, had to make his contributions in the form of cash. I peached to that idea when they suggested Craig Albritton— who is an innocent in all of this, the wool was pulled over his eyes too—be allowed to fulfill an assessment in kind rather than cash. That was when, thanks to your newspaper article, Henry, they were trying to skin me for a quick thirty-five thousand-dollar cash assessment. Obviously they expected to get away with it. And might have except that Neal telegraphed the lie when we met yesterday morning."

"I don't know what you're talking about," Hubbard blustered. "I did no such—"

"But you did, Neal. Or your secretary did for you. Do you remember the other day when you were pretending to be so open and honest and pleasant with me? You showed me where all the railroad files were kept and allowed me to go through them as much as I wished. I might have gone on believing everything you said except yesterday when you offered me a copy of the bylaws, your secretary didn't go to that drawer in your office. He got the information you wanted me to have, but he got it from somewhere out in the working part of the office—in the second file cabinet, bottom drawer, if you'd like to know. That was where Marshal Ossamer found the railroad minute books and bank statements when he served that warrant last night."

Ben looked at Henry Vickers and smiled. "These two weren't half as bright as they thought they were either. Probably they didn't trust anyone they couldn't keep an eye on. That seems to be a problem among thieves. They can't even trust each other. So they took the money they were stealing from Les Shannon and deposited it into their personal accounts in the Miners and Mechants Bank. Can you believe anyone could be that stupid? These two were. They even invented a nonexistent bank in San Francisco to explain why I couldn't inspect the records. Well, they'd have been better off if there had been such a bank. This morning Marshal Ossamer took another search warrant to the Miners and Merchants. You notice that Tom isn't here? He's busy making an abstract of the bank records involved. There is a direct correlation between Les's withdrawals and the deposits these two made into their own accounts. Minus a share that must gave gone to someone we haven't yet identified. But Tom is working on that now too. Probably the bank deposits will point a finger at the other member of their little group."

"I'll be damned," Vickers said. "Do you know if—" The newspaperman never had a chance to finish his question.

With a roar of unpent rage, Lucas Dadley hurled himself at Ben Cartwright.

Dadley's fist lashed out, catching Ben on the temple and spilling him, chair and all, into Willard Monroe's lap.

"I'll kill you, you son of a bitch, I swear I will!"

The left side of Ben's face was numbed by the force of Dadley's blow, but he was far from being incapacitated.

And although Lucas Dadley was the amateur boxing champion of the Johns Bend mining district, Ben Cartwright had experienced more than a little rough and tumble as a young sailor in half the seaports of the western hemisphere.

Dadley bored in behind that first punch, trying to take full advantage of surprise while he yet had it. He closed in on top of Ben and began digging short, hard body shots into Ben's unprotected side and back.

Ben could not rise to defend himself. Not with

Dadley's weight pressing down on him and keeping him pinned against a startled Willard Monroe.

Instead Ben wriggled forward a few inches to achieve room enough for leverage. Then he speared Dadley in the nose with the point of his elbow.

Dadley cried out, apparently stunned by the pain and quick spurt of blood, and his attack abated long enough for Ben to shove Willard hard to the side and slide out from between him and Lucas Dadley. Ben stood, balancing light on the balls of his feet, and waited for Dadley to make the next move.

Dadley shook his head, splattering bright blood from his nose onto the tablecloth and the patrons seated nearby. It distressed Ben to see the platter of sweet rolls had been fouled too. That seemed rather senselessly wasteful, but too late to worry about. Dadley glared at Ben and, head down, charged.

Ben almost laughed. He had no intention of falling for that one. A man is not likely to become amateur pugilistic champion of anywhere if he fights as foolishly as Dadley wanted him to believe now. Ben danced backward, sidestepping the right feint and, more importantly, the very expert left hook that Dadley tried to land.

Ben darted back away from the blow, then followed the missed punch in to deliver a rapid left-left-right tattoo onto Dadley's already broken nose.

The pain of that combination had to be extreme, but Dadley appeared to not so much as notice it. Instead he adopted a classic prizefighter's stance, giving up his pretense of ineptitude, and began bobbing and boxing in front of Ben.

Dadley was thick-bodied and heavily muscled. He was also a good many years younger than Ben and probably had the advantage in strength and stamina. Ben could count on reach and his own experience. If he had taken time to examine that, he might well have been discouraged by the necessary conclusions, so probably it was just as well that there was no time for contemplation. He ducked and darted just outside Lucas Dadley's reach, flicking jabs onto the bridge of Dadley's broken nose whenever he could find an opening, or barring that, deliberately battering Dadley's forehead.

Dadley seemed mildly annoyed but not at all concerned by the constant peppering of his brow. The younger man's pugnacious stance, with his fists high and chin tucked low, left no opening for his opponent to deliver body blows. About all that could be reached would be his forearms or forehead, and he seemed unconcerned about either of those.

For his part, Ben continued to punch and move, punch and move. If he tried to stand toe to toe with a bull-strong boxer like Lucas Dadley, he would soon be done for, and he knew it. So he kept on. Punch and move. Punch and move. Dadley's forehead was quickly bruised and swollen. So were Ben Cartwright's knuckles. He punched and moved, punched and moved.

"Dammit," Dadley spat, trying to bore in close.

Ben snapped a left jab low on Dadley's forehead and quickly retreated, leaving Dadley's hard right hook to find nothing but air.

"Stand and fight, you."

Another left to the forehead. Battered flesh finally could take no more of the pounding. The skin split along the inside of Dadley's right eyebrow, and blood began to flow into the man's eye. One more sharp jab, and a split opened over the other eye. Dadley was near blinded by the blood and had to know he was in trouble now. Ben pedaled backward.

His heel caught on something and he tripped.

There was a roar of disapproval from the crowd of men who were ringed tight around the combatants, and Ben was dimly aware of the flurry of movement as the onlookers grabbed Neal Hubbard by the arms and pulled him away to keep him from tripping Ben again.

By that time, though, his object had been gained. Dadley ran in behind his partner's distraction. A right hand landed on the shelf of Ben's jaw, staggering him and nearly blinding him with the awesome force of the blow.

Ben spun away, righted himself by clutching someone's shoulder and ducked low as he turned back to meet the rush he was sure would follow.

He caught Dadley coming in. Ben came in underneath Dadley's punches and buried first a right, then a left, then another right deep into the pit of Dadley's belly. He heard Dadley gasp, and the Johns Bend champion gave ground, his legs suddenly rubbery. There might have been a time when he could have taken punches to the midsection, but that time was not now. Easy living had taken that away from him sometime during the recent years.

A series of weak blows rained down on the top of Ben's head and heavy pads of muscle on his shoulders, but he stayed low and moved forward as Dadley tried to back away.

The breadbasket was where Dadley was weakest. Ben followed, timing himself to Dadley's movement, and when Dadley tried to take a stance, Ben pressed in, bracing himself and delivering a right into the man's boiler room. The punch was aimed at a point that would have been frowned upon under the rules of tournament fisticuffs, and it was delivered with every available ounce of Ben Cartwright's weight behind it.

Lucas Dadley went pale. He gasped and clutched both hands to his belly as if trying to hold himself together.

Ben straightened, took time to measure the spot he wanted, and ended the fight with a right cross to the jaw. Lucas Dadley's eyes rolled back until only the whites showed, and he dropped to the floor like a poleaxed shoat, his knees thudding hard onto the boards and his torso going down face forward like a massive tree being felled by an expert lumberjack.

"Well, I'll be damn," someone said.

Ben looked at his hands. His right hand was swelling already, and the skin over his knuckles was split open and oozing blood. This was going to sting for days to come. Somehow he didn't very much mind that.

"Dang it, Pa, can't I turn my back for a few days without you getting into trouble?"

"Joseph, whatever are you doing here?"

"Pa, this is my friend Harlan Kane. Him and me made a discovery last night, Pa. A mining discovery. Then this morning we got fired for it. I think it's something you oughta know about."

"Then by all means, son, you catch me up on your news and I'll tell you mine."

Ben stepped wide around the fallen Lucas Dadley and gave Neal Hubbard a baleful look. "Shall we continue this at the marshal's office, Neal, or do you want to wait for someone to come and get you?"

"I haven't done anything like ... well, not nearly so bad as you claim, Cartwright. And that's the truth, whether you like it or not."

"Let's go talk it over with Dave Ossamer and see what he says. Joseph, come along, son. And say, whatever happened to your new suit? If I didn't know better, I'd take one look at you and think you were working in the mines or something."

Joe and his friend Harlan began to laugh.

CHAPTER 29

B en sat with his hand in a basin of cool water. Lucas
Dadley, considerably the worse for wear, sullenly
sat as far away from Ben Cartwright as he could
get, holding a cold compress to his forehead. Both his eyes
were blackened, and his clothing was stiff with dried
blood. He had not said anything since Marshal Ossamer
dragged him along to the office under the threat of arrest
if Dadley did not choose to come voluntarily. Neal Hubbard, for some reason, seemed positively eager to come
along and tell his side of things.

"Look, Dave, I'm not saying anything about these
other charges. You can talk to my lawyer about that. But
as for Les Shannon being murdered, you have to understand that he died in an accident. That's all it was. A mining accident. It happens, Dave. You know that. Why, no
way would I have killed Les. For one thing, I'm not a
killer. Not that I expect you to take my word for it, but
I'm not. The other thing, though, is that I wouldn't have
considered killing the goose that was laying all those fat,
golden eggs for me. Les was my pigeon, Dave. I mean . . .
I'm not admitting to anything that man said, Dave. I want
you to understand that. But if any of that stuff was true,
why, no way would I want to lose Les Shannon as a
source of income. You know?"

"What about him?" Ossamer asked, pointed to Dadley.

"He wouldn't have had any more reason to kill Les than I would," Hubbard insisted.

"Or him?" The marshal indicated the third conspirator, who had been identified by way of the bank records at Miners and Merchants. Every time Les Shannon made a contribution to the railroad, shortly thereafter deposits had been made by Neal Hubbard, by Lucas Dadley, and, in much lesser amounts, by Fitzhugh Burke.

"None," Hubbard stated.

"Don't be so sure about that," Joe spoke up. "The way I understand it, these jaspers wanted to take everything Mr. Shannon had. They wanted all of it, isn't that right?"

Ben nodded. "The way those bylaws are written, it could very well have worked out like that. They could have imposed assessments on top of assessments until he was no longer able to pay. Then they legally could have forced him out of the corporation. The wording in the bylaws is clear on that point. The remaining partners would have ended up with everything."

"Would it have mattered if Mr. Shannon thought he was giving up property that wasn't worth anything anyway?"

"Of course it would. No one is liable to fight very hard for something that is of no value."

"Well, you know how we been told all along that the production levels of the Shan-Rock and those other mines was dropping? Pa, that wasn't so at all. I've been talking with the fellows in the Shannon mines, and there hasn't been a lick of change in the values coming out of any one o' those mines—not that anybody working in them can remember, not for years and years. Fitz Burke there reported losses to Mr. Shannon, but there weren't any. Every one of those mines is still paying out as good as ever. And I'll tell you something else." Joe pulled a piece of rock from his pocket and laid it onto Marshal Ossamer's desk. The marshal picked it up, took one look and whistled. The rock was a pale, translucent white quartz that was larded heavily with ribbon gold so thick and rich it could have been picked out with tweezers.

"That's some piece of ore, son."

"It came out of the Shan-Rock, Marshal. Out of the stope where Mr. Shannon was killed. Me and Harlan—"

"Harlan and I," Ben corrected without thinking.

Joe gave him an exasperated look but nodded. "Yes, sir. Harlan and I went down there last night and opened up that area. The tool dresser on our crew said they'd been drilling into a big find in that room the afternoon before Mr. Shannon died. So we went to see what was what. We found the vein, all right, just like Cooter said. That ore should assay well over a thousand dollars a ton, I bet. Harlan thinks more. No one knows how deep that vein will run, but the surface showing is awful good. What's more, somebody went in there and tried to cover it up. There was loose rock piled to try and hide the showing, and dust thrown over what couldn't be covered any other way. And to top that off, it wasn't no—sorry, Pa—it wasn't any nitroglycerin accident that killed Mr. Shannon neither. I don't know what kind of residue that nitro stuff leaves behind when it blows, but I can sure tell you by now what kind of black, greasy gunk giant powder leaves after you shoot it. And it's powder residue that's on the floor where Mr. Shannon's body was found."

"I've worked with nitro in other places," Harlan put in. "It leaves a lot cleaner mark behind it; pale gray, and in some places almost white. You can see the direction the charges take, everything. It's real distinctive stuff, nitro. An' that wasn't it that me an' Joe found where Mr. Shannon was killed. This was blasting powder just like we use all the time down there. You can go see for yourselfs if you don't believe me an' Joe." He gave Ben a nervous look and corrected himself, "I mean, I an' Joe."

"Mr. Shannon must have gotten wise somehow," Joe said. "Maybe he heard someone talking about the likelihood of that new find. The men liked Mr. Shannon. Someone could have mentioned it to him. I'd bet he went down to see, and Mr. Burke knew about that ... same way Burke found out Harlan and I went down there last night and fired us for it afterward ... and knew he had to do something or his plans with Mr. Dadley would be ruined. They had to kill Mr. Shannon or lose their chance to steal the mine off him."

Neal Hubbard bolted to his feet. "Those bastards were trying to cheat me. Their own partner, damn them. They killed Shannon and would have cheated me out of my share. They never let on to me that those mines were still strong. Hell, I thought the production was down, right along with Shannon. All I had in mind was to shake Les down with the railroad scheme. The idea was to involve Les in the railroad, collect the stockholder assessments from him, and then declare the corporation bankrupt later on so we could pull it off with no one the wiser. We were going to create another corporation to buy the railroad's assets for a pittance in the bankruptcy dissolution. Les never would have had to know we were involved with the corporation that bid in on the railroad assets. He was supposed to think we were burned just as bad as he was. That was my idea. I admit that. And it would have worked too, except for Les dying when he did. But falsifying mine production reports or causing harm to our pigeon, that was no part of what I had in mind. Why, I expected—I mean still do expect, of course—to go right on in this community. That is ..." Hubbard looked quite thoroughly miserable now. "These two lied to Les and to me too, damn them. They lied to their own partner. And if, as you say, they had something to do with Les Shannon's death, well, I can't countenance anything like that. And I won't stand on any gallows next to them either. I'll tell you everything I know, I promise. But don't try to tar me with that brush. All I intended, all I had anything to do with, was the railroad. I played no part in anything more."

"Neal, shut your mouth," Dadley snarled, willing to speak for the first time since the session began.

"No, Lucas, I won't shut up. You murdered Shannon, didn't you? You and that lying SOB Burke. The two of you tried to cheat me. After all I did for you!"

"After what you done for us? Don't make me laugh. You prissy high-hat, you. We did all the work, and you took most of the money. We were entitled to more. It should have been share and share alike, but no, you wanted the biggest share. Well, you got it, damn you. You deserved to get shafted just as much as that rich bastard Shannon did."

"Tell me something, Lucas," Ben said.

"Why should I?"

"I'm curious about something, that's all. Just a minor little thing that can't hurt you, but ... what was in that note from Craig Albritton that you intercepted?"

Dadley spat on the floor. There was blood mixed in with his sputum. "That's what I wanted to know too. Turned out it was only that idiot lawyer telling you he was going outta town for a few days. Why?"

Ben smiled a little. "It was a small enough thing, it's true, but I noticed the envelope in Hubbard's wastebasket. That little detail went a long way toward convincing me that you two were up to no good. In a manner of speaking, you could say that it created the train of thought that led to you three being here right now."

Dadley scowled and spun around to turn his back to Ben, his shoulders hunched and his jaw tucked tight to his chest. Ben suspected they would get nothing more from Mr. Dadley for a while. Until, probably, the man decided it was in his own self-interest to point a finger at someone else. None of these people was what Ben would consider a reliable sort.

Ben motioned to Dave Ossamer. The marshal leaned close, and Ben whispered, "I think you have enough to place some charges by now, Dave. Why don't you lock them up separately, somewhere far enough apart that they won't be able to talk among themselves. I'll bet if you play one against the other, you can have them all chirping loud and fast before supper. They sound ready to spill each other's deeds in the hope you'll overlook their own."

Ossamer chuckled and nodded. In a loud voice he said, "Let's break this up, gents. I'm placing you under arrest. You, Neal, and you, Lucas, and you, Fitz. You're all under arrest."

"On what charges, may I ask?"

"You may, Mr. Hubbard, and I'll give your lawyer a nice, long list whenever he presents himself. In the meantime, I want you—no, I think I want you in that cell there, Lucas. And you, Fitz, in that one down there. Neal, I'm gonna take you over to the county an' ask them to lock you up. Ben, is there anything you want to ask them?"

Ben gave each of the conspirators a long, accusing look. "No, Dave, there's nothing I might say that the court can't say better. The court and the hangman." He thought Hubbard went particularly pale at that suggestion. It seemed almost certain that Hubbard would spill everything he knew or ever suspected rather than risk facing a noose and gallows along with the others. And, oddly, Ben believed Neal Hubbard when he said it was the other two who were responsbile for Les Shannon's murder. Damn them.

"Joseph, walk with me, son. We need to go talk with Chloe. She is entitled to the truth. Come to think of it, we need to sign her property back to her now. When I bought it, I made sure there was a separate agreement stipulating she can buy it all back without suffering any loss. I think now it should be safe to return her holdings to her. I don't know how much of the amount Hubbard and Dadley stole from her can ever be recovered, but if that new find in the Shan-Rock is as good as it looks, she will be just fine now."

"Y'know, Pa," Joe said as they headed down the street, "maybe you and her should look into going ahead with the plans for that railroad. I mean, Mr. Shannon sure thought it was a good investment, and he was a smart man. For that matter, Adam thinks it's good, and you know how careful Adam is."

"As a matter of fact, that's something I want to discuss with Chloe first—after all, she holds a thirty-five percent share in the corporation. The railroad plan was a better one than Hubbard and Dadley seemed to have realized. Odd, isn't it, that if they had gone about this same plan honestly, they would have become wealthier than their confidence scheme ever could have made them? Instead they tried the dishonest way and wind up with nothing. Well, we'll talk about the railroad with Chloe and some of the other businessmen in Johns Bend too. I've met several gentleman of excellent character here who might well want to go into a genuine railroad construction partnership. And we probably could be talked into participating, eh?"

"We won't be staying here too awful long, though, will we, Pa? I'm getting kinda homesick for my own bed an' Hop Sing's cooking." He rubbed his stomach and said, "That boardinghouse can't hold a candle to what we got at home, Pa."

"Another day or two, then we can start home. I . . . Joseph, I have to say that I'm proud of the way you handled yourself here. Not that I approve of deception, but you never lied to me. You just went ahead and did something that you thought needed doing. I'm proud of you for that."

"Thanks, Pa."

Ben put his hand on Joseph's shoulder and squeezed it. "You're growing up, Joseph. More than I sometimes realize. When we get home, I'll try to . . . darn it, son, at least give me the courtesy of letting me meet this young lady of yours before you go getting yourself engaged."

"Sir?"

"You know. Miss Samantha Whittacker? And the diamond rings Blauhaus was selling? I promise you, Joseph, that I will make an honest effort to be . . . open-minded and accommodating. For your sake. You are my son and I love you. I certainly owe you an open mind on this subject."

Joe laughed. "Pa, that's real nice o' you, but by now I'd guess Sam and her pa's wagon show oughta be to Sacramento at the least and moving on."

"But I thought—"

"Pa, did you get this from Hoss? Of course you did. Me and Sam—excuse me, Sam and I—was just flirting, Pa. It wasn't anything serious. As for the ring, I never wanted no dang ring. Jimmy Poole was looking at one in Mr. Cuddahey's store. For Jane Louise, Pa. Remember?"

Ben did remember something about those two making plans together.

"For gosh sakes, Pa, Jimmy has been one of my best friends for as long as I can recall. Of course I went with him when he was looking at rings. But I never wanted one myself. Is that what Hoss said?"

"No, someone else." It had been Armand Blauhaus who made the erroneous assumption, actually. And he had gone right along with it, Ben recalled, thinking Joseph didn't trust him to discuss—

"Why, Pa, I wouldn't think o' doing something like that without talking it over with you first. I'd've thought you knew that." Joe grinned. "Besides, Pa, I'm not ready to settle down. Won't be for a long time, I'd bet. Why, there's s' many flowers to sniff and s' much nectar to gather ... especially for a fellow as handsome as me. I mean, I do cut quite the figure among the ladies, Pa. You got to admit that. Don't you?"

Ben squeezed Joseph's shoulder again. Sharply this time.

"Ouch!"

"You'd best quit, son, before you start believing all that about yourself. Besides, that's Mrs. Shannon's house there. Now mind your manners. And remember to wipe your feet. Come to think of it, dirty as those clothes are, you'd best be careful where you sit."

"Aw, Pa. C'mon. What do you think I am, a baby or something?"

Ben stopped. He smiled. "You always will be my baby, Joseph. But you're right. You are growing up now. Keep reminding me of that, will you?"

"Yes, sir, that I will."

"Good. Now let's go break all the news to Chloe. And Joseph . . ."

"Yes, sir?"

"If we're lucky, she might have some milk and cookies she can set out for you."

"Pa!"

Chuckling, the two made their way onto the porch of the home Lester Shannon built.

BONANZA

The Cartwright saga continues!

If you enjoyed *The High-Steel Hazard*
by Stephen Calder, be sure to look for the
next novel in his BONANZA series,
JOURNEY OF THE HORSE
available in Summer 1993 wherever Bantam
titles are sold.

Turn the page for an exciting preview of
the next stirring adventure of Ben,
Adam, Hoss, and Little Joe.

On the Chinatown street, the girl clung to Hoss as a baby would to its mother. All around him Celestials stared, some nodding with knowing smiles. Hoss glared back at them, standing frozen for a moment, wondering where best to turn for help. He must borrow more of Hop Sing's money, for food, a room, and maybe medicine. He could not keep her in the opium den. He considered his options, but he had few. He ignored a shout over the clamor of the Chinese.

A white woman approached him from across the street, her purse swinging in her hand. She yelled again and Hoss realized she was talking to him. "Where'd you get that child?" she shouted, brandishing her purse like a weapon.

"What?" Hoss said, his eyes focusing on an enraged woman in her thirties. "In there," Hoss said, motioning with his head toward the auction house.

"You bought her?" Her green eyes flared in anger.

"Yes, ma'am," Hoss replied, "I plan to take her—"

Before he could finish, the woman swung her purse, aiming for his head but striking his shoulder. She drew back and swung again, striking his back as Hoss spun around to protect the girl. "You, you, you animal," she sputtered. "How dare you buy this child. You're as bad as the heathens. You vulgar oaf, give me that girl so I can protect her from your filth."

Hoss dodged her blows as Hop Sing stepped between them, fending the woman off and shouting English among bursts of Chinese. "Hop Sing buy sick girl for Mr. Hoss."

"What?" the woman yelled, her purse slicing through the air for Hop Sing, who danced around her blows, muttering Asian epithets.

"You vile men!" she shouted.

"Stop it, ma'am," Hoss called out. "You don't understand."

The woman paused, hands on her hips, purse in her hand. "I don't understand," she said softly, then exploded, "so explain it to me." She attacked again with a swirling purse. "You smell like an opium fiend."

"Dad-blame-it, ma'am!" Hoss dodged the purse and shoved the girl toward Hop Sing. "Take her," he shouted as the woman pummeled him with the purse. Hoss yelled at one sharp blow and spun around to confront his attacker.

She feinted for his knees then swung the purse over her head, aiming for his. The purse sliced through the air, her legs solidly braced for the direct blow she expected to land.

Hoss ducked, but the purse struck his hat and knocked it aflutter like a wounded quail.

Her faulty aim and the unexpected miss surprised her, and she half spun around to maintain her balance. Hoss charged, grabbing her under her arms and hoisting her into the air. She screeched and blindly swung the purse at him. With his great strength, Hoss held her aloft, shaking her roughly until her brown hair tumbled in curls from the bun where it had been neatly pinned.

"Let me down," she cried out. "Let me down, you animal."

Hoss rattled her some more. "Dad-blame-it," he shouted back. "Think you can be quiet long enough to listen?"

"No," she shouted back, "not as long as you buy little girls."

"Dad-blame-it, woman, you don't know what I planned to do with that poor girl. Who are you, anyway?"

"None of your business until you put me down," she said icily.

Hoss shook her again, rougher this time, until the hand with the purse went limp.

"Aldina Cuthbert," she replied wearily.

"Ma'am," Hoss said, "you think you can listen for a moment instead of jumping to so many confusions?"

"I'll try," she replied, "if you'll just let me down."

Hoss eased her to the walk as she muttered her displeasure at this forced compromise.

She pulled hairpins out of her collapsed brown hair, waving them at Hoss, as if to tell him she was not defenseless even if he were more powerful than her. Then she ran her fingers through her long hair which cascaded below her shoulders. Holding the hairpins unladylike in her teeth, she tucked her shirtwaist into her green skirt, which was gathered in back.

Hoss studied her, taking in her green eyes, aristocratic nose, high, slightly rouged cheekbones and full lips. When she wasn't swinging her purse, she had an attractive bent to her. She was obviously one of those headstrong women who could match any man in intellect, but had never learned to channel her emotions. Slender and elegant, she stood just over five feet, six inches tall.

"Now, what are you doing in Chinatown?" Hoss asked.

"That's what I'd like to know from you," she said sarcastically.

Hoss felt his fingers wad into a fist on his right hand, and he pounded his left palm with it, trying to get her attention. He wasn't debating her all day over this. "Now what is it you're doing in Chinatown?"

"I come here every auction day to save these poor

girls. You know what they do to these children? You must, seeing how you bought one."

"Ma'am," Hoss answered, "me and Hop Sing are in Chinatown looking for his niece. This was a sickly girl in the auction, the last one sold. We bought—I mean, I bought her, to see if I could find her medical attention."

Aldina Cuthbert looked stunned for a moment, as if she didn't know whether or not to believe him. Hoss shrugged.

"Bless you, sir," Aldina Cuthbert apologized, "and forgive me, please. I see so many of these girls abused, I get zealous defending them." She stooped over and picked up Hoss's hat, dusting it off, pushing out the dent from her purse, and offering it to him.

Taking his hat, Hoss pulled it over his head, then suggested they get away from the auction house. Hop Sing sidled up to Hoss, gave him the young girl and picked up Aldina's purse.

Aldina Cuthbert hooked the strap of her purse over her wrist and stepped to Hoss. "I'll carry her," she said, taking the young girl into her arms and rocking her gently. "Poor baby," she cooed at the girl, "you feel hot, fevered."

As they walked away from Chinatown, Hoss introduced himself and explained how he had come to San Francisco to help Hop Sing find his kidnapped niece before she was sold into slavery and a life of prostitution. He explained they were likely too late to save her virtue, but perhaps they could find her and spirit her out of San Francisco in time to save her life.

"Hoss Cartwright." Aldina Cuthbert kept repeating the name. "Hoss Cartwright, where have I heard that name before?"

Hoss shrugged. "I'm not from around these parts. You ever been to Virginia City?"

"Hoss Cartwright," Aldina mused for a moment, alternately glancing between Hoss and the young girl in her arms. "Oh," she tittered, "now I remember. The paper. One of the papers told of a man named 'Horse' going to the Palace Hotel and ripping the guest register in half when they wouldn't give him free lodging. They said you had the strength to match a name like 'Horse.' "

"It's Hoss," he corrected.

"You know the papers." Aldina slipped her hand out from under the sick child, poking it in Hoss's direction. "I'd like to shake your hand, someone standing up for these people that way. Their culture's different, they need some education on things, like how they treat their young girls, but they're still people."

Hoss took her hand and shook it gently so as not to wake the girl now sleeping in her arms. "You're a perplexing woman, first attacking me and now congratulating me. It beats all."

Aldina Cuthbert directed Hoss and Hop Sing down Dupont and then along a side street toward a block of modest residences clinging to the slopes of a steep hill. As she started up the hill, she grew winded from the load. Hoss took the child from her, marveling that she had carried the girl as far as she had without complaint. Hoss studied her slender frame, attributing it to a spiritual determination or dedication more than physical strength. That was the case with most crusaders, he thought. After witnessing the auction today, he figured San Francisco needed more women like her. A hundred women who put their mind to something can accomplish it quicker than a thousand men, Hoss figured.

At the top of the hill Aldina stopped at a narrow clapboard house clad in a coat of fresh white paint and trimmed with green gingerbread. It was a small, but neatly kept house with bay windows stacked one atop the other on the first and second floor. Aldina turned through the opening in the wrought-iron fence and strode up the steps to her home. Opening the door, she motioned for Hoss to enter. "Place her on the sofa," she commanded Hoss, then allowed Hop Sing to pass before she went in.

Gently, Hoss lowered the slave girl to the plush maroon cushions of the high-backed sofa. Aldina rushed into a back room, and by the clatter of pots and pans, Hoss knew she was in the kitchen.

Hoss followed her to the stove. "You need wood, ma'am?"

Nodding, she pointed to the back door. "By the stoop, you'll find all you need."

Hoss went outside, grabbed an armload and returned to the kitchen, filling the wood box, save for a couple medium-sized pieces he shoved atop the coals glowing in the stove. The coals took to licking the wood, and shortly the stove grew hot to the touch.

Aldina placed a kettle of water atop it and scurried about the kitchen as it boiled. Then she prepared a cup of warm tea and carried it into the parlor. Kneeling on the floor by the girl, Aldina lifted her head and slid the cup beneath her nose. The girl's eyes fluttered at the aroma and a smile washed the frown from her face. Her lips parted and she drank the tea greedily. "That's a good sign," Aldina said to Hoss.

When the girl finished, Aldina retreated to the kitchen to find Hop Sing studying the stove. "Hop Sing good cook. Ask Mr. Hoss," he said. "Hop Sing fix meal."

Aldina smiled. "Thank you, Hop Sing. There's rice in the cabinet and tins of tomatoes and peaches too. I think rice and soda crackers would be good for our little angel."

Hop Sing grinned widely, held his hands together and bowed toward Aldina. "Hop Sing work."

Aldina prepared another cup of tea and returned to the girl, lifting her head and sliding a cushion beneath it. She helped the girl drink the tea and then stroked her head and cheek. "Tea and food should help, Mr. Cartwright."

"Just Hoss, ma'am."

A frown clouded Aldina's attractive face as she nodded at Hoss. "How much did she cost, Hoss?"

Realizing he was still wearing his hat, Hoss jerked it off and rolled the brim between his fingers. "She being sickly, cost us sixty-three dollars."

"Damn," Aldina said, jerking her hand to her lips as

her face reddened with embarrassment. "Pardon my crude language, Hoss."

"No bother, ma'am, it was an experience I'm not proud of. At least I could save the little one there." Hoss thought he saw the glistening of tears in Aldina's eyes. He sat down.

Aldina looked down at the sofa and gently stroked the girl's face. "They keep them in cages, girls her age and younger. They are forced to sleep with men, Oriental and white, for four or five years. By then, they may still have their youth, but they are no longer children. Their looks are gone and likely they are diseased. Their owners turn them out on the street or keep them in back rooms until they die."

"Dad-blame-it, can't something be done?" Hoss asked, leaning forward in his chair. "We treat livestock better."

"Nobody cares, except me and a few others. Police won't do anything about it. The Chinese accept it. Most people don't believe it." Aldina's fingers caressed the child's face, soothing her sleep.

"Can you take her and keep her, ma'am?"

"Oh, yes, Hoss, that was my intention. She'll be the forty-seventh I've taken in. I'll find a school or boarding-house or, at worst, an orphanage. But the girl you're after, tell me more."

"Best I know," Hoss explained, "she's Hop Sing's niece, named Mai Ah Toy. Kidnapped and sold last week at the auction house to a Dr. Lin Wo Pai."

Aldina scowled, the sudden change in her expression catching Hoss off guard. "Doctor," she said, fairly spitting the word across the room, "he's a snake oil salesman, a medicine man. It would be enough if his wicked ways had only taken in his own kind, but many fashionable San Franciscans go to him for his heathen cures. They make him rich, and he either gambles the money away or buys young girls for his personal use."

"You know him, then you can show us his place."

"Sometimes it takes weeks to get an appointment, the rich demand so much of his time," Aldina said. "Every ailment, he says, is attributable to liver problems, and he concocts bizarre potions to pass as cures. But the rich are gullible. What he does to innocent girls like this one is despicable."

Hoss kept rolling the brim of his hat between his fingers. "I'd like to get my hands on the one who bought Hop Sing's niece."

Aldina frowned and bit her lip. "The Celestials, they know not to harm whites, and they don't unless their graft is threatened. I can agitate because they don't take women seriously. But you, you must be careful, you and Hop Sing. They will kill you if you disrupt their despicable activities."

"But I gotta try."

"You've got to be careful as well," she said, sniffing at the aroma coming from the kitchen. "Smells good, Hop Sing," she called, then turned to Hoss. "Can I ask you a question?"

"Yes, ma'am," he shrugged.

"Do you smoke opium? It's a vile habit, you know, and your clothes smell like they are saturated with opium smoke."

Hoss stood up and tossed his hat on a table. "No, ma'am. I got away from home with no money and can't buy a decent room."

Aldina cocked her head as if he were lying. Her green eyes narrowed. "Then why'd you seek a room at the Palace if you were broke?"

"My father stays there, has a standing agreement with them. When they wouldn't let Hop Sing in, I tore the register and left, no place else to turn. Hop Sing took me to stay with his cousin in an opium den. Worst two nights sleep of my life."

The smile returned to Aldina's face. "Then you and Hop Sing should stay here the night, much safer than in Chinatown once word gets around who you are looking for. I've a spare room upstairs. You and Hop Sing both can stay."

"Obliged, ma'am."

Hop Sing came to the kitchen door. "Hop Sing need dishes help, then meal ready."

Aldina carried the girl to the table, having Hoss bring a pillow she could sit on, then motioning for him to take a place beside her. Aldina retrieved dishes and eating utensils as Hop Sing placed a pot of rice and a bowl of tomatoes on the table. She added a tin of soda crackers and provided cups of tea all around, then pointed for Hop Sing to take a seat. She disappeared in the parlor a moment and returned with a bible in her hands.

"I always read a scripture when I have guests," she explained. "From the seventh chapter of Proverbs, I read today." Then she started: " 'The merciful man doeth good to his own soul; but he that is cruel troubleth his own flesh. The wicked worketh a deceitful work; but to him that soweth righteousness shall be a sure reward.' " She closed the bible and went instantly into a prayer. "Thank you, Lord, for this meal and these righteous men as they save your noble creatures such as this girl you have blessed this house with. Watch over and protect us all. Amen."

"Amen," said Hoss.

Aldina served the girl's plate, giving her abundant rice and crackers and a small serving of tomatoes. "We don't even know your name, child."

Hoss pointed at Hop Sing, "Ask her her name."

Nodding, Hop Sing spoke quickly in Chinese.

Meekly, the girl answered. "Hin May." She stared at her plate, looking up from Hop Sing then back.

Aldina realized the problem, picked up the spoon by the plate and inserted it in Hin May's fragile hand. Gently, Aldina showed her how to work the spoon. Gradually Hin May grasped the principle, though her execution was not without spilled rice. Nonetheless, she was able to eat under Aldina's careful gaze. "This is good," Aldina said, as much about Hin May's appetite as Hop Sing's cooking.

By early afternoon they had finished their meal and Aldina had bathed Hin May and put her to bed. Hop Sing cleaned the kitchen, drawing praise from Aldina when she returned downstairs.

"You two should get your belongings and come here to stay, where it'll be safer and you won't smell like an opium den. And Hoss, when you get back, you can bathe and I'll want to wash your clothes."

Hoss lifted his hand to argue, but she motioned she would have none of it. When Hop Sing was done, he took off his apron and said he was ready. Taking his hat from the table in the parlor, Hoss and Hop Sing marched out of the house and back toward Chinatown. Hoss had a better bearing of Chinatown's layout this time and thought he could find his way to the opium den, but Hop Sing kept taking unexpected turns, confusing him.

Finally, they reached an alley that looked familiar, and Hop Sing turned down the garbage-strewn path that led from the street toward the narrow passageway in back. At the door, a big black dog was licking at the threshold. Hop Sing and Hoss held back to give the dog room to escape. "Get," Hoss yelled, throwing a stone at the dog. The stone banged off the door and the dog darted from the passageway.

Hoss and Hop Sing slipped to the door, a new and troubling odor bothering Hoss's nose. Hop Sing called in Chinese to be admitted. No answer. He called again. The peephole stayed closed, and the door remained shut. Hoss leaned over Hop Sing and pounded on the door, which swung open from the impact. There was the smell of opium escaping and then the smell of something much more sinister. Death. Hoss pushed the door open, gasping at what he saw.

There on the floor in pools of blood were Hop Sing's cousin and two of his customers, their bodies hacked to pieces. Hoss thought of the hatchet men, wondering if they had come for him and took their anger out on the others.

Hop Sing spoke quickly in Chinese. Hoss lowered his head, not interested in seeing any more of the gruesome sight than was necessary. His eyes focused on a puddle of blood at the threshold.

Hop Sing caught his breath, then stepped inside, tiptoeing around the bodies, he moved back into the corner for his bundled possessions. He retreated quickly, then ran past Hoss out into the alley. Hoss pulled the door shut and followed.

They emerged onto the crowded street and moved swiftly and wordlessly away from the alley, away from Chinatown. Only on the outskirts of Chinatown did they slow, but even then they had nothing to say. Their eyes had seen too much for there to be anything to discuss.

Finally reaching Aldina's, they entered without knocking, startling Aldina, who was sitting on the sofa reading the bible.

"Hop Sing's cousin, two others murdered," Hoss blurted out.

Aldina sighed and dropped her head. "They're telling you to give up. You'll be next, if you keep seeking the girl."

RECEIVE A FREE LOUIS L'AMOUR
WALL CALENDAR JUST FOR PREVIEWING
THE LOUIS L'AMOUR COLLECTION!

Experience the rugged adventure of the American Frontier portrayed in rich, authentic detail with THE LOUIS L'AMOUR COLLECTION. These riveting Collector's Editions by America's bestselling Western writer, Louis L'Amour, can be **delivered to your home about once a month.** And you can **preview each volume for 15 days RISK-FREE** before deciding whether or not to accept each book. If you do not want the book, simply return it and owe nothing.

These magnificent Home Library Collector's Editions are bound in rich Sierra brown simulated leather—**manufactured to last generations!** And just for previewing the first volume, you will receive a **FREE Louis L'Amour Wall Calendar** featuring 13 full-color Western paintings.

This **exclusive offer** cannot be found in bookstores anywhere! **Receive your first preview Collector's Edition by filling out and returning the coupon** below.